Shaun Meeks is the author of the Dillon the Monster Dick series (*The Gate at Lake Drive, Earthbound and Down*, and *Altered Gates*), as well as *Shutdown, Down on the Farm*, and upcoming release, Maymon. He has published over 50 short stories, the most recent appearing in *Midian Unmade, Zippered Flesh 3, The Best of the Horror Zine, Dark Moon Digest, Rogue Nation*, and *Fresh Fear*. His short stories have been collected in *From Nightmares, Dreams, Dark Reaches, Brother's Ilk (with James Meeks), At the Gates of Madness*, and the upcoming *Blood on the Ground: Six Shots of Southern Discomfort*. This year Shaun is working on the fifth novel in the Dillon series, two standalone novels (*The Place Where the Shadows Live*, and *The Desolate*) Shaun currently lives in Toronto, Ontario with his partner, and their micro-yeti, Lily, where they are always planning the next adventure. To find out more or to contact Shaun, please visit www.shaunmeeks.com, www.facebook.com/shaunmeeks, or www.twitter.com/ShaunMeeks

T0054286

Shaun Meeks' Dillon the Monster Dick series published by IFWG Publishing International

The Gate at Lake Drive (Book 1, 2015)
Earthbound and Down (Book 2, 2017)
Altered Gate (Book 3, 2019)
Heads, You Lose (Book 4, 2022)
A Touch of Death (Book 5, 2024)

Book 5:
Dillon the Monster Dick series

A Touch of Death

by
Shaun Meeks

A Touch of Death

All Rights Reserved

ISBN-13: 978-1-922856-64-7

Copyright ©2024 Shaun Meeks

V1.0

Printed in Palatino Linotype and Arno Pro.

IFWG Publishing International
Gold Coast

www.ifwgpublishing.com

Acknowledgements

I can't believe this is book five of the Dillon the Monster Dick series. Originally, I had this character in a short story where I figured he would appear once, and that would be it. Now we're on book five, and I'm currently writing books six and seven at the same time. It's been a fun, and wild ride. A lot of my other work is very dark, and tends to end poorly for everyone involved, but I love these characters so much partially because they are so different than the ones I've written in the past. They let me add a little humor and hope, which is something we all need more of I think.

Whenever I start to write a book, I tend to sink into my own little world, but that doesn't mean I don't get any help during the process or after. In my years working with Toronto Police Services, I've been shown a lot of how the system works, and some of the nuances of what happens during investigations. I obviously can't share the names of those officers, but I thank them for the knowledge they've passed on.

I have to give a huge amount of thanks to Steve Santiago who once again came through with an amazing cover for this book. Since the first in the Dillon series, Steve has been capturing the feel of these books in a way I never thought was possible. It's as though he was able to snatch the vision from my head. They add so much to these books.

I also can't thank Noel Osualdini and Stephen McCracken enough for the edits they did on this. As someone who has struggled with dyslexia my whole life, sending my work off has always been a hard thing. I've been so self conscious about the mistakes, and just hoped the stories themselves made sense. The things they picked up on and helped me rework really do make all the difference, and improve the quality of the story. I can't thank them enough for all the hard work they put into this.

Gerry Huntman and the team at IFWG Publishing are such a great group to work with. The fact that they have set me up with an amazing artist, and a group of editors that have improved my craft, and continue to publish this series is a dream come true. Since I was in the fourth grade and wrote my first—and terrible—horror story, I had dreamed about seeing my books in print, sitting on my book shelf. Gerry and his team have made that possible, and I'm indebted to them.

How do I write something like this without thanking my amazing and wonderful wife? Not only was she the original inspiration for Rouge, being a former burlesque queen herself, but her sense of humor, and how fast I fell head over heels for her was part of what shaped the books. I can't thank her enough for letting me take a very rough sketch of her, and shape it into a very different character. She's also so great at listening to my wild and wacky ideas and telling me if they make any sense, or if I'm going too far with it all.

Lastly, I want to thank all the people who read these books, and my other work. Without an audience, my books are just words on paper. But for everyone who reads them, they turn the words into something solid and tangible. The reader uses their own imagination to make my stories into something real. I will keep writing if you keep reading.

For Norma and Arthur Goodwin. Miss you both.

Thursday

The alley was dark, but I could read the headline beside the unmoving man sprawled out at my feet. I knew the story was getting around, but there was nothing I could do to stop the panic from spreading. These things had to be done. The Doll Maker had released countless demons, monsters and spirits onto Earth, more than I wanted to fathom. They had to be taken out one by one. The problem was, each of these creatures lived in human bodies, the original human spirit had long since vanished. Once we removed the unnatural creature from the body, there was nothing there but an empty human, with just enough brain function to breathe. If we could have brought the bodies back to the owners, we would have, but you can't put the toothpaste back in the tube, as they say.

Not that it stopped us from trying.

And failing, but at least we gave it a shot.

Ignoring the headline screaming out to me in huge, bold font about a possible disease spreading through the city, I leaned down as grey and red swirled mist seeped from the lips of the motionless man. I used a copper bottle engraved with symbols of the four forbidden realms to capture it and sealed it once the last of it had evaporated from the body. I then placed a cork dipped in the blood from a Hellion to seal it, as I had done twenty-one times before. I put the bottle in my pocket, ready to place it with the others later, and picked up the discarded newspaper.

"The mystery continues to spread," I whispered to the shallowly breathing shell on the ground. "Well, when they find you, the panic will just continue to grow, I guess. Not much I can do. Sorry we couldn't do anything more to make you whole again."

"What are you doing?"

Even though I knew the voice, the sudden breech of quiet made me jump more than I'd like to admit. I dropped the paper beside the body—not dead, yet not truly alive since there was nothing left inside—and turned to see Rouge standing behind me.

"I was just reading this one a bedtime story," I said, and stood up. I pulled the copper vial out of my pocket and showed it to her. "Another one for the collection."

"How many more do you think there are?" she asked, and we walked away from the body.

"Who knows? You saw how many dolls there were. And that doesn't even take into account the ones the Doll Maker already ate. I do miss the old days, though. When the calls were simple. Just a run-of-the-mill demon, supplies from Godfrey, then bang, it was over."

"Yeah, it almost seems like ever since you met me, nothing has been easy."

I stopped walking and turned towards her.

"Don't say things like that. Things have been so much better since I met you."

"Really?" she asked, and there was something dark in her face as she turned away from me. I don't know what was bothering her, where this came from, and I didn't know if I should push the subject. The relationship with Rouge is the first one I've had in, well, ever, really. It's not as though I'd been totally celibate since I came to Earth so many years ago, but I hadn't really been in a committed, long-term thing ever. Even when I was not on Earth. "You want to tell me that what you've gone through over the last couple of years is anything like what you had to deal with before we met?"

"I've always dealt with crazy stuff."

"Hellions, getting locked in a psychiatric hospital, meeting a doll maker, and I could go on, right? You even had another hunter hunting you. Is that normal?"

She had a point, but I never in a million years would think to blame her, or our relationship, for this. It seemed as though all the worlds, realms, and universes were having a bit of a moment these days. I've never seen this type of tension in all my years being a hunter—and I've seen some crazy things, even before I met Rouge. With the rising resistance against the Collective, it was no wonder stranger, more dangerous things were making their way into my life. Since the time the human race rose from the primordial slime, there have been creatures and demons who've wanted to come here. Some of them to escape the horrors of their own worlds, but many more to enslave, or colonize this planet to gain more power. The Collective have always stood strong against them, and most times it worked. Now, I was feeling a shift in that power struggle, and I was beginning to worry what would come next.

All in all, none of this had anything to do with her, and I let her know as much. I told her she had been the best part of these years where things had been going a little crazy, but I've known her long enough to know she wasn't really buying it.

"Let's get out of here and then we can talk about it. But I promise you, these types of cases and situations, what's happened since we met, it's not new to me. Things come and go like this. Every hunter working for the Collective has had to go on a bumpy road from time to time. You're not to blame." I knew this wasn't totally true, but it wasn't a lie either. In a way, it was all how you looked at it. Sometimes when you're right in the middle of a storm, it looks like the worst thing you've ever seen, but once the dust settles and you can get some distance between you and it, you realize it wasn't all that bad; or at least no worse than things you've already faced.

"I can't shake this nagging feeling that I'm somehow part of the problem," she told me, and took my hand. "I just worry that one day you will regret ever meeting me."

I leaned in and kissed her before we walked away from the soulless body.

"You are the one thing in all the worlds I will never regret."

🖐️·🖐️

Less than an hour later we were back at Rouge's house, which I guess was *our* house at this point. Over the last three months, after we had dispatched the Doll Maker and Don Parks, we came to a decision about our living arrangement. After all, she had the space, and I was spending a lot of money every month to use my apartment as a storage locker. If you don't know the rental rate in Toronto, let me tell you, they are over two thousand dollars for a one-bedroom apartment in an area that's about as safe as skinny dipping in iodine with a thousand paper cuts.

So, we decided to just go ahead and move in together. I'd spent a lot of time moving my meager belongings to her place. With her grandmother's house being more than ten times the size of my overpriced apartment, there was more than enough room for my clothes, boots, tools and trophies. Many of the trophies I brought over, Rouge wanted to know about, so there was a lot of storytelling time as we placed them on shelves in what was to become our office.

After getting inside, we fed the pup and then went to the office, where I took the vial out of my bag and sat it in the wall safe, which was already full of the demons and beings we'd previously removed from stolen bodies. I looked at them all and felt terrible. I didn't need to count how many were there, I was well aware how many there were. The sheer number of demons and monsters the Doll Maker had unleashed on Earth was a heavy weight on me and I walked around feeling constantly overwhelmed by it all. The whole situation was a huge mess, and I wasn't sure how long it would take to finally clean it all up. That was also assuming it would be possible to do. I never wanted to consider that we could or would lose this battle. It might take a year or two to get them all, but I was sure we could do it.

We had to do it.

The victims of the Doll Maker deserved revenge.

"Where are we going tomorrow?" Rouge asked from behind me, catching me off guard so bad that I nearly jumped out of my skin. I'd been so stuck in my whole head, replaying everything we'd done since we first found out about the Doll Maker, that I hadn't even heard her come to the doorway and get so close to me.

I felt like I was slipping a bit. Normally, I'm more aware of my surroundings than that. I also seemed a little jumpier than my usual self. I wondered what that was all about.

I turned around, ready to tell her we would be going to check the Beaches area in the east end, but when I saw her, the words were lost on my lips. She was nearly naked, dressed only in a skimpy outfit that was supposed to be Batman's ward, Robin. It had been a long time since I'd seen it on her. It was during those first days when I barely knew anything about her and she surprised me at my motel up north.

And it still looked amazing on her. Better than Robin ever looked in the comics.

"I see you like it," she said, and smiled.

"How could I not?"

"Do you know why I pulled it out tonight?"

I shook my head, but there were things I was hoping she would say.

"Tonight's sort of our anniversary. Today is the day I went up to Innisfil and met you, when we first kissed. That was followed by a whole lot more. It was very memorable for me. How well do you remember that day?"

"I dream about it," I chuckled and walked over to her. I put my arm around her waist and pulled her into me. "It was the beginning of the best time of my very long life."

"Are you sure?" she asked, and I could still hear that worry and reluctance in her voice.

"I've never been this sure about anything in my life. I love you, Rouge. And I can't imagine a day in my future that you aren't a part of."

She kissed me, hard, and then we celebrated our first night together with a replay of it. I think you can use your imagination about how that went.

Friday

There was sun streaming in through the windows when my phone woke me up the next morning. It wasn't my normal ringtone set for everyday calls, so I knew it wasn't a client. I'd set this one up for a specific person, so I knew who it was right away. So, once my brain registered it was the "Bad Boys" song by Inner Circle, made famous by the show *Cops*, I moved quickly towards it and answered.

"What's going on, Garcia?" I asked in a low voice, as Rouge hadn't even stirred.

"I need to see you as soon as possible," he said. I'd known him long enough now to recognize the urgency in his voice. Garcia only spoke to people using two main tones: quiet and yelling. He wasn't someone who emoted a whole lot, but for him, this was as excited as he got without shouting. And even though he wasn't yelling, the speed of his words told me everything.

"Guessing this isn't something we can talk about on the phone?"

"I'd rather not. But I can tell you that I was given a case, and I think you might know something about it."

Shit!

He'd gotten the cases of the soulless people.

I'd hoped he wouldn't be given these cases, that the problem of the soulless bodies we were leaving around the city wouldn't be dropped into his lap. There was no way he'd even be able to solve them. There was nothing he could offer his superiors which could be easily explained, nothing he could do to satisfy them that the case was closed. I knew Garcia had seen what happened at his station house with one of the Doll Maker's victims, and he'd put two and two together and realize we were involved. If he hadn't been given the cases, it would be fine, but with all the attention in the media this case was getting, I knew it would be a nightmare for him. I really had hoped someone else would have gotten it.

"Where do you want to meet?" I asked, and knew where he was going to suggest before he even said it. St. Jamestown.

"St. Jamestown. Meet me at the corner of Wellesley and Parliament. Text me when you're there and I'll come get you. I don't want you just showing up at the scene. We need to be a little more discreet here."

"Got it. I just woke up, so give me some time for us to get ready."

"Make it quick. This isn't going to get better with time."

I hung up and let out a long sigh.

"Everything okay?" Rouge said, her voice still full of sleep. She sat up in bed, no longer wearing the Robin costume, or anything at all, and stretched.

I shrugged. It was too early in the morning to deal with this, but Garcia was right. If it had to be done, better to just get it over with than prolong the inevitable. Yet, I sat on the bed beside her. Rouge smiled at me and squinted in the early morning light, looking as gorgeous as the first day I laid eyes on her. Her hair was a mess, she had no make-up on, and her breath had that early morning staleness to it, but I loved it. Even dishevelled, she was out of my league ten times over.

"Who was it?"

"Garcia," I told her. I was a little jealous of how easy the woman could sleep. Through a phone ring and a full conversation, nothing could disturb her if she was down deep in dreamland. "He wants to meet asap."

"Why?"

"He was just given a case and said that he thinks we might know something about it. He's in St. Jamestown waiting for us. At Parliament and Wellesley."

"Oh!" she said, and I watched as her eyes popped open wide.

It was clear she was on the same page as I was about the case we were getting called into. He was calling us to the same area we'd left an empty body in, so my guess was Garcia had been given the two of us as a new case. "Are you going to tell him what's going on?"

I should've already told him what we were doing. If I'm honest about it, I think I kept it from him because I wasn't exactly sure how he would react to us going around doing this, and how many more we might have to still do. The last thing I needed was him to freak out knowing the city was overrun with monsters hiding in the bodies of normal people. Sure, he could handle monsters and demons made up of shit, leaves, or used condoms, but I was sure the idea that there were some that could look like anyone's next door neighbor might cause him a lot more stress.

"If we have to, I guess we will. It's either that or we clam up and play dumb. We could just pretend to help and just keep doing what we are doing."

"That doesn't feel great."

"I know, but what's the alternative? We can't just let them all be. Who knows what some of these things are capable of or what they are doing here anyway. The Doll Maker was a piece of shit, and anyone who would align with them, they can't be far behind."

Rouge was nodding. Clearly, I was right about this. "Well, I guess we should go and get ready then."

"I guess," I said reluctantly, and kept playing worst case scenarios of what was going to happen as we got dressed and ate.

The news playing on the Jeep's radio was all over the place. They were talking about shootings, sports teams involved in trade disputes, issues at the Canadian-US border, but the main focus was the wave of catatonic people being found around the city. Our victim. The people on the radio were making it out like it was some new epidemic, as if it was some new virus, the start of a pandemic, and nobody was safe. They were even speculating that it could be some sort of man-made disease or terror attack. I turned it off after a few seconds and plugged my USB into the radio and hit shuffle. The first song to come on was a song by Slick Rick called "Can't Dance to a Track that Ain't Got No Soul". Skip that one, please. I just wasn't in the mood for something that light, yet some undertones I didn't want to think about. I needed music with more weight to it while we were driving towards our own crime scene, to possibly lie to someone I considered a friend. Next one was better, some nice thrash with no hidden meaning. Perfect.

"I think we should consider making a plan to hit the waterfront sometime this week," Rouge said with her nose in her phone. "I'm looking online and there are some videos of people acting really weird down there."

"How weird?"

"Some videos are of a guy eating wood chips from a planter. Another is a woman hiding behind a bench eating Vicks VapoRub like it's pudding. There's also a video of a guy wearing a Nickelback shirt. All of those things strike me as strange."

I chuckled at the last bit, but the first two did seem a little less than normal. The guy eating wood chips might be a Drazzen, or a Ghishle, but could also be just a drunk idiot doing dumb things for TikTok. The woman eating the Vick's, I couldn't imagine what that might be. I could barley breath when that stuff was on me, so the thought of eating it made me want to gag. I tried to scroll through my Rolodex of monsters and demons who might like some spicy Vaseline, but none came to mind. And then there was the guy in the Nickelback shirt. Clearly, he was the worst of the bunch.

"Well, before we go making plans on doing more of the same, lets just meet up with Garcia and see how bad things are and if we might need to take a short pause in all of this. We'll decide things after that."

"What? Why? We can't stop going after these things, can we? We can't let them just run wild and do whatever they want, or am I missing something?"

"No," I said, but even I could hear the hesitation in my voice.

"But we may have to try and figure a different way to tackle the job at hand."

"What other way is there?" she asked, and I had no real good answer for that. These creatures were living in human hosts. The original souls were long gone and there was no way they were coming back. That meant the only choice we had was to dispatch the demons and monsters and leave the bodies as empty as a two-four of Molson's at a frat party or let them wander around and just stay here. I didn't like the idea of that, and I was sure the Collective would have an even bigger problem with it. The third option, which I really didn't like and didn't want to mention, was to take the demons and monsters from the body, and then dispose of the corpse. I didn't like that one bit. To me it felt like one step away from being one of those horrid serial killers that were popping up a lot in the '80s and '90s. "I mean, you're not thinking about telling Garcia what's going on and having these things arrested?"

I shook my head.

I guess there was a fourth option I just wasn't even thinking about, but as soon as she mentioned it, I knew it was a terrible idea. What would he do if we told him, and they arrested them? They weren't committing any actual crimes. None of the ones we found were breaking any human laws the police could do anything about. Their crimes were being on a planet they were not allowed to be on. Garcia would have no way to force any of his laws on them. Not really.

I mean, sure, it wouldn't be the first time the police arrested someone and made-up fake charges to throw them in jail, but in the long run, they would end up back on the streets. Nothing would stick as far as the courts went, which would just mean they were our problem again. I didn't want to do the same job twice, so it was either do what we'd been doing, or we let Garcia in on it and keep doing what we were doing. Either way, it was going to get done.

"Well, whatever you are thinking about doing, you better be sure about it," Rouge said and motioned to the road ahead. "Looks like we're here."

There were vehicles everywhere.

Police cars; both marked and unmarked.

Emergency Medical Services.

Toronto Fire Services.

And, of course, new vans. That was the worst of it.

I looked at them and decided I wasn't just going to park the Jeep and walk up to the police tape. Garcia wanted us to keep things low profile and marching up to the crime scene wasn't going to do that. We needed to find somewhere to park and call Garcia and let him know we were there.

As we approached the scene, a uniformed officer was directing traffic and we followed the directions. Clearly, she was there to make sure the rubbernecks weren't going to try and pull over to get a better look, or back traffic up too badly. We drove past them all and half a block away I saw there was a gas station ahead. I turned into the lot.

"What are you doing?" Rouge asked as I parked and pulled out my phone.

"Garcia wanted me to text him when we got to the corner, so I'm going to let him know we're here instead. I also don't want to go anywhere near there with the media around. After the YouTube video, I'd rather be a little more inconspicuous. Did you notice anything though?"

Rouge looked back at the scene and her brow furrowed. She looked like she really wanted to see what I was seeing, but I knew it might be too obvious. She might have been looking for something very off and miss the thing that was right in her face.

"Can you give me a hint?" she asked and turned back forward in her seat.

"This isn't where we were last night. We were further south, so how can this have anything to do with us?"

"Whoa!" she said and turned back. "You're totally right. Then what do you think this is all about?"

"I'm guessing a little more to pile onto our workload. Great."

I dialed Garcia's number, and he picked up on the second ring.

"I thought I told you to text me," Garcia said, in a near whisper.

"Sorry, just thought this would be easier. We're over at the gas station. I thought it was best not to come in through the front with the news cameras and lookie-loos everywhere."

"Good idea. Stay there. I'll come and get you in a few minutes."

I hung up the phone and looked at the store connected to the gas station. I saw there was a *Tim Hortons* inside and thought about grabbing a coffee, but then realized I didn't need my nerves any more on edge than they already were. I had a good idea this wasn't about the things we had been doing lately, but there was a strange feeling deep in my gut as though whatever this was all about, it was going to be bad news for us. I've learned over the years to listen to those types of interior warnings. Better to be wrong about something and be cautious, than to ignore it and end up neck deep in a river of crap.

Someone approached the Jeep, and I rolled down the window thinking it was going to be Garcia. Instead, there was a disheveled man in a patchwork of clothing, none of which fit him at all. Before he opened his mouth and asked us something I couldn't quite make out, I was greeted by a smell that made me think he was already dead. I tried not to breath in and held out a ten-dollar bill for him just so he would leave.

"I don't need your money, my dude," the man mumbled with a thick French-Canadian accent and moved his matted hair out of his face. "I need salvation. I need a blessing and your good will."

Clearly the man was suffering from some sort of mental health condition. I felt bad for him, the way I did for so many in the city who had no real way of getting help. The province had decided decades ago not to keep people locked up in mental health wards, which was good, seeing as many of them were used as ways to mistreat the ill. Yet, when they closed them, there was little to no effort to offer actual help. It was just let them go out and fend for themselves. It was and still is a broken system.

"Well, you have that from me, as long as you take this money, buy some food and water and eat it as an offering," I told him, trying my very best to do something helpful. Seeing him get some food in himself was the best I could offer.

"And if I do, you will give me your blessing?"

"Of course."

He took the money, thanked me, and left us just as Garcia walk-ed up to the car.

"What was that about?" he asked as we stepped out and locked up.

"Just trying to be a good person," I told him, and we left the parking lot. "So, how do we get to where we are going without being seen?"

"Just follow me."

We did that. Following Garcia, we jaywalked across the street a block away from where all the media and emergency vehicles were. Garcia led us to an alley beside a *Pizza Pizza* and we walked north. It was a tight squeeze there, just enough room for a single car to drive up or down. The alley was littered with trash, old crack pipes and used syringes. It was clearly not a place most people would feel safe walking. Especially at night, but luckily it was still broad daylight.

"So," Garcia said as we went. "This is going to be a weird one, even by your standards, I think. Do you guys believe in vampires?"

I stopped in my tracks and looked at him with the question clearly on my face. He couldn't be serious.

"I know you think I'm joking, but it's a serious question."

"I certainly would say no," Rouge said. "But after all I've seen since meeting Dillon, I don't even know what is and isn't possible."

"What about you, Dillon?"

I shook my head. I told them both that while there are some creatures and demons that might resemble vampire lore, I'd never seen or heard of an actual species of vampires. If they were a thing—and to be honest, anything is possible—I had never once run into one.

"Why do you think it's a vampire?" I asked as we approached two uniform officers at the back of a what must be a store front.

"I don't really think it is, but everyone else does. This is the fourth victim who has died the same way, and it makes no sense."

"Fourth? Have these been in the news at all?"

"No. The media is so wrapped up in the other weird case, the one they think is some kind of virus, that they aren't even on the radar about this."

"What about all the media trucks out front?" Rouge asked. It's exactly what I'd been about to say.

"Once they know it's not the same thing, when they see the ambulance leave and the coroner show up, they will just report it as a homicide and move on. This is nothing to them, and I want to keep it that way. You two are keeping them busy enough without this." I was shocked and guess I didn't keep my poker face about it. "After what happened with that woman in the station, you didn't think I would see your calling card? Come on. Give me a little credit as a detective. I'm not that dumb."

"I didn't think you were. It's just you said nothing about it to us."

"I know something is going on, that it's serious too, judging by all the empties you guys are returning, so I figured it wasn't anything I needed to know about. Not to mention, it's not my case, so I don't have to try and solve that. These ones on the other hand, well, you'll see."

We got to the door and Garcia told the uniform cops we were together. They moved aside and allowed us in. I could tell right away by the smell of the place it was a restaurant, and I guessed it served Canadian Chinese food. I can smell fired rice-and-chicken balls a mile away. We were taken through the kitchen towards a bathroom, where there was a technician taking photos.

"Can you give us a second, Jon?" Garcia asked the photographer, who said he was all done anyway. "You two ready for this?"

I nodded and Rouge said she was.

"When you go in, you'll get why I asked you that question earlier."

Garcia opened the door, and I was expecting to have the regular stench of rotting death hit me, but there was nothing out of the ordinary. It was what you would expect from any typical public bathroom: strong cleaner doing its very best to cover the odor of stale urine.

It wasn't until we stepped in all the way and looked around that we were greeted with the reason why Garcia called us.

"What the hell?" Rouge said, again stealing the words right out of my mouth.

There was a body on the ground. I couldn't tell for sure if it was a man or a woman by the face, but the clothes on the body suggested it was a man. Really, they suggested a teenager, but the parts of the face and hands that were exposed made me think that was impossible. The corpse's face was a grey, wrinkled, sunken-in thing that looked like a discoloured raisin. The hands were also grey, thin skin barely stretched over a skeletal hand. The eyes were sunken so far back in the head, they looked as though they had been cleanly scooped out; just dark holes looking into nothingness. But when I got a closer look, I could see they were there. He had brown eyes.

I crouched down to get an even closer look at the body. When I was a foot away from the open-mouthed face, I could smell a slight hint of rot and vanilla, but nothing very strong. Usually when a body is found, the stench of decomposition is strong for a while. What was emanating from this body made me think he'd been here some time. I didn't see any sign of trauma to the body. I didn't want to touch him, but I did want to try and find out if there was any blood or sign of injury, something that would point to the cause of death.

"You won't find anything like that, Dillon," Garcia said, and I looked at him over my shoulder. "If this is like any of the other ones, there is no sign of trauma at all. What you see is what you get. This is why there are rumors floating around that the perp is a vampire."

"Wouldn't a vampire leave bite marks?" Rouge asked as I stood up.

"If movies and books were accurate, sure. But there is nothing to explain why this twenty-one-year-old kid looks like this," Garcia said, and I looked away from him and back down at the body.

"Wait," I gasped, as I studied the mummified body. "He's only twenty-one? How do know?"

"Wallet. But the others were the same. Young or youngish

people all turned into what you see down there. There is no trauma, and none of the bodies have any blood or bone marrow left in them when the coroner checks."

"What, all the blood and bone marrow are gone? Okay, well as far as vampire lore goes, I've heard of them drinking blood, but bone marrow? That seems a bit off to me."

"Sure, but only if vampire lore is based on how vampires really work. If all you have to go on is fiction, this won't really add up, but I was hoping you knew something that might shed light on it not being fiction, and that this is what really happens. I personally have never dealt with a vampire, have you?"

I shook my head. I hadn't even heard anything about them being real, so this was all new to me. If this was a real vampire, I didn't even know where to start. I mean, first thing I would need to know was if they were Earthbound creatures or from some other realm.

"I've read lots of books about vampires, and even syndromes that make people think they are vampires, but nothing was ever like this," Rouge said from beside me.

I agreed. If there really are vampires on Earth, who's to say anyone knows the truth about them? Unless Anne Rice was right and they were writing all the books about themselves, there is no way to know what is and isn't real.

"Is this a public or private bathroom?" I asked, looking around the very small space.

"It's for staff and customers. Anyone could have had access to this place. It's the same as the last ones. Always in a place anyone can enter."

"So, this body has been here for days, and no staff or customers noticed it?" I asked, thinking if this was the only washroom, that would be impossible.

"Body has only been here a few hours. Staff said the victim walked in here when they opened, and then they found him like this."

"Hours? How?"

He shrugged, and I shook my head. Things made less and less sense.

"Did anyone see anyone else come into the bathroom around the same time he did?" Rouge asked, and again, Garcia shook his head.

Well, that was no help. I stepped out the door and looked around. We live in a modern age and my hope was there would be a video camera system here, or close by, that might catch something that could help us. So far, I had nothing to go on that would help anything. I had never seen or heard of anything quite like this. I was almost willing to believe that Garcia was right in his assessment about our killer being a vampire of some kind. And if it was, I was screwed. I would assume that a vampire would be an earthbound monster, and technically those were out of bounds for me. Sure, I had made the exception in the recent past, but it wasn't a law I felt like bending again.

You can only test your luck so many times.

"You looking for a camera?" Garcia asked, and was already shaking his head. "You won't find one. This place has a slightly nefarious reputation with the drug trade, so they like to keep things hush-hush."

"Serious, as in major trafficking?"

"Not really. A few local crack and meth dealers hang out here. Nothing to get Narcotics to shut the place down, but enough so that the owners, who no doubt get something in return, are willing to make sure people have their privacy."

Great. I asked if there was footage from any of the other crime scenes and was told there wasn't anything good to work with. I wasn't surprised. Someone—or some*thing*—that could do that to a body would no doubt try and stay off the radar as best they could. The killer would probably scope out an area before they attacked, unless it was just sheer luck for them, but I didn't really believe all that much in luck.

"There also haven't really been any skin or clothing fibres that would help us out. There is almost no evidence left at all."

"Almost?" Rouge said before I could. "But there is something, right?"

"Yes, but I don't think it would be classed as evidence. We should go back outside and talk about this. We've been withholding certain aspects of the murders, as few people know about these last details, and I want to keep it that way. If someone heard this and leaked it to the media, it would be just the kind of thing they would blow up and have the city in a panic over by sheer speculation."

We left the washroom and head back out into the fresh air. We walked in silence down the alley, back towards where the Jeep was. When we were sufficiently away from the restaurant, Garcia told us the last part of it.

"So, aside from the first case, there has been one common thing at each of the crime scenes. The bodies are an obvious link, but this one thing also puts it all together too. And it's so weird that we wanted to keep it quiet."

"And it's not blood or a fingerprint," I interjected.

"Actually, it *is* a fingerprint. Well, finger*prints* to be more accurate."

"That's great, then. You should be able to do something with that, right? Why the cloak-and-dagger bit about not wanting others to hear about that? I don't think the media would be chomping at the bit because you found a fingerprint. Unless it belonged to someone who was high profile."

Garcia stopped and looked around nervously. I had no idea what was going on, but I was able to read from his face that even though what he said seemed simple, there would be nothing simple about it. My first thought before he explained it was that this was going to be a cop, or someone in government. He must already know who it was, and the name associated with those prints would be explosive. What the truth of it was, I wasn't prepared for.

"Each print belongs to a dead person," he whispered, moving in closer to us. "And not just any dead person. They belong to the previous victim. I know that if we find a print at this scene, it will end up belonging to the woman we found five days ago in Trinity-Bellwoods Park."

"What the hell?" Rouge said, and it was my thoughts exactly. "What is the killer doing then? Are they taking a cast of the victim's hands and somehow leaving a print behind as a game? It doesn't make sense, does it?"

Garcia shook his head, as did I.

No, it made no sense at all. The murders themselves were mysterious, making us think that a vampire was involved, and then the fingerprint of the previous victim left me scratching my head. A vampire wouldn't want to play games like that, would they? The reason they are myth rather than fact is that nobody ever finds a victim like this, and then add the evidence left at the scene and it seems more like something a comic book villain would do than anything else.

"The way the prints are left behind though, it makes it seem like a person with those fingers did it."

"How so?" I asked.

"If you take a cast of someone's hand and then make a resin or clay model out of it, you may get the prints that could transfer, but they would be a solid thing. It wouldn't move and squish the way a human finger would. So, the print would be narrow, and not full. These are full."

"Could someone make a latex or silicone glove that could transfer? Wear it on their hand like a glove?" Rouge asked, and it was a good thought.

"Maybe, but there were oils left behind as well. Oils that you would find on a hand. So, either the new victims are being killed at a place the previous victim visited somewhat recently, where there would still be a viable print, or the killer is somehow leaving a calling card behind to laugh at us. I don't know which one it could be, do you?"

I shrugged. I had never heard of anything like this before. There were ideas floating through my head, but nothing was coming together to make sense. I told him I would do some research, look up aliens and demons that had vampire traits, but if this was an earthbound monster, there was nothing much I could do. I watched him deflate, so I reassured him we would find something out that could help. I mean, I would help him track down the vampire, regardless, but if there was a way to kill it, I would have to leave it up to him to do it.

"So, there were no fingerprints left at the crime scene of the first victim?" Rouge asked. "It just seems strange that every scene had them, with the exception of the first."

"To be honest, they never really checked for the first one. The man killed was found on a subway train. The place is full of prints, so they never really checked. I wasn't on the case yet, but that's what happened. I wouldn't say the cops on the case were lazy, but they could have tried a little harder. Then again, who knew things would get so bad as they are now?"

"Give us a day or two to look into some stuff and see what we can turn up," I told him, doing my best to offer some reassurance. My current knowledge was drawing a blank, but maybe something in one of my books, or something Godfrey might know would be able to shed some light on this strangeness. "It might turn out that this is just some creature I don't know about, and if that's true we can get things wrapped up in no time."

"I hope so. Call me when you find something."

We said our farewells and once again jaywalked across Parliament Street to where the Jeep was. I took Rouge's hand and felt her squeeze mine. I turned and looked at her. She looked worried.

"This can't be a vampire for real, can it?" she asked once we were safe from traffic.

"I don't think so. In all my years on this planet, I have never seen any evidence that a vampire exists. This has got to be something else. I just don't know what. But I'm not going to close my mind to the possibility of it all. There are some things I'm just not well schooled in."

"Do you think this is it related to the Doll Maker? Could she have brought something here that could do that?"

I shrugged and answered honestly: "I don't know, but we'll find out. And one way or another we'll get rid of it before anyone else gets hurt."

"Promise?"

I nodded because I didn't want to verbally lie to her. I couldn't make a promise like that, but I would do the best I could. I learned a long time ago not to swear to anything unless I could one hundred percent guarantee it, which is something I can rarely do. This world loves to throw wrenches in the gears and turn things upside down in the blink of an eye.

I clicked the alarm off on the Jeep and as it chirped, a man popped up from the driver's side with a yelp. It was the same shabby homeless man I'd given money to before meeting up with Garcia. His eyes were wide, and he looked as shocked as I momentarily was. I hadn't expected him, or anyone else to be there. I instinctively reached for my dagger, but relaxed when I came to my senses and saw it wasn't a monster; only a guy down on his luck, who was a little mentally off.

"You scared the hell out of me," I laughed, and walked over to where he was. "What were you doing hiding down..."

The words died on my lips as I looked at where he had been and saw the front tire was deflated and there was a hole the size of a softball in the rubber. I turned my head towards him and looked at his hands, expecting to see some sort of tool or weapon he had used to do it, but there was nothing in either of them. I was more than a bit confused.

"Did you do that?" I asked and he shook his head violently but said nothing. "You sure? You were down there in that spot. So, if you didn't, who did?"

"What is it, Dillon?" Rouge asked, and I told her to stay where she was. I didn't want her near this guy until I knew what was going on.

The guy said nothing, just continued to stare at me as though he was sure I was about to beat the life out of him for cutting up my tire. I wouldn't. I try not to make a habit of going around beating humans up, especially ones that were clearly a few beers short of a six-pack. Someone suffering from mental illness already had enough to deal with without me making matters worse over something that could be so easily replaced like a tire.

"So, if you didn't do that, who did? I just want to know."

"It was the man in the long coat," he told me, his voice stuttering, and as he spoke, I saw something I hadn't expected.

As his cracked, dried lips moved, I could see his teeth. In them, aside from just looking unclean, I could see what was undoubtedly pieces of rubber. Some were flecks, but there was a long strand of one in tucked into his gums near his top, left incisor.

Was this guy so far gone, so checked-out that he had been eating my tire, ripping at the rubber with his teeth? I wouldn't have thought that was even possible, but wondered how poisonous it would be to his body.

That's when it hit me. I reached into my pocket and pulled out a coin. Not a normal one but the Ephesian coin I carried for just such an occasion. Normally I would press this to his forehead to freeze him, but instead I used my thumb to flick it in the air towards him and yelled out for him to catch it.

His eyes went wide, and he looked excited. I knew he had no idea what he was about to catch, but if my hunch was right, he would soon find out. There was a chance I could be wrong about my hunch, but I doubted it. A normal person wouldn't do something like that, even if they were mentally unwell.

The homeless man caught the coin in his hands. There'd been a smile on his face a second before he did, but as soon as the coin touched his skin, the smile faded, and his eyes nearly bulged out of his head. I waited a second to see if he would do anything else, but he was stuck there, frozen. He wasn't human after all.

I'm glad I trust my gut from time to time.

"How did you know?" Rouge asked, coming around the side of the Jeep to where I was.

"Look at the tire," I told her, and she did. "When he spoke to me, there were bits of rubber in his teeth. I figured nobody in their right—or even slightly wrong—mind would do something like that. Had to be a monster."

"Wait! Are you saying he was eating our tire? What the hell?!?"

"I know. That's because this isn't just some guy. This is a Derusha. They love eating rubbery things on this planet, but something is off with this one. Not sure if the original owner of this body was a suffering from mental illness before he took it over, or if the Derusha's diet has done something to it to make him not fully there. Either way, this must be another of the Doll Maker's clients."

"We're a little exposed here, aren't we?"

She was right. It was broad daylight, and we were doing this in a public parking lot. I looked around but saw nobody was really close to us. I looked around the perimeter of the property as well to see if there were any cameras. I saw none, so there was a chance to keep this quiet, but I needed time to deal with him and fix our vehicle.

"Do me a favour," I started and laid out my plan. I wanted her to go into the store, without her coat on, and buy us some coffee—and, more importantly, time. I asked her to flirt with the employee, so he didn't look outside and see me doing what I was about to do. I hoped it wouldn't take long, but I needed to be fast about this. After that, she could come out while we changed the tire.

"What are you going to do with him?"

I looked around again to make sure nobody could see. Luckily, where we were standing, the Jeep blocked us from anyone on the street that might be able to see, but if anyone went into the store and came out, they would have a great view of what I was about to do.

"I have three choices. First choice it to just let him go, and I'm not willing to do that. Second choice is to put him in the Jeep and deal with him somewhere else, which is good, but might be tricky if the coin falls or someone comes over. The last choice is to push him in the bushes over there and get the creature out of his body. None of them are perfect, but I'm leaning towards the last choice. I can do it fast and out of sight, but it also has tricky points."

"I don't want to put him in the Jeep. I think that's a bad idea. If someone sees him, or we get pulled over, it'll be bad. Not to mention the fact that we will never be able to get the smell out of there."

She was right. We'd have to burn the Jeep afterwards if we did that.

Since I wasn't just going to let this one off with a warning, there was only one choice left.

"Okay, go inside and give me at least five minutes. Shouldn't take longer than that."

Rouge took off her coat and even I was distracted for the moment. There are times when I see her, I wonder what I did to find someone so incredibly gorgeous to fall for me. I'm nothing to write home about, but she's gorgeous, smart as hell, and one of the toughest, bravest people I've ever met. She clearly brings way more to the table than I ever could.

"Enough of that," I whispered to nobody as she walked into the store. "Time to get to work."

I looked at the frozen man and shoved him backwards towards the bushes. He teetered for a second and then fell on his back without a sound. I looked over my shoulder and all around to make sure we weren't on anyone's radar. The last thing I needed, with the media and cops less than a block away, was for someone to see what I was doing, get the wrong idea and bring in the calvary.

There was nobody paying attention. That was good.

I went into the Jeep and pulled my bag open. I took out one of the jars I had on hand to collect what I needed from the fallen man with the monster inside. Once I had it, I walked over to the body and looked down. He was as still as a statue. That coin has a way with most monsters. I needed to be fast though, so I knelt down, put the bottle under his nose and spoke an incantation to release the monster from the host it had stolen. Black mist swirled out and into the bottle. I watched it go in, swirled darkness with flecks of magenta and green. I wished I could help the guy who had once been in the body, to give it back to him, but there was no way to reverse what had already been done. This was the best we could do: imprison the thief.

"Jesus, man! Get a fucking room! Disgusting!"

The voice of the person behind me startled me and I nearly dropped the bottle. I looked over my shoulder and saw two men walking towards the store and shaking their heads. I looked at the position of the empty body, and how I was, and realized that they clearly had the wrong idea of what was going on. They must've guessed we were up to some sexual shenanigans, but I wondered if they saw my face and had seen the YouTube video that had gone viral, if they wouldn't have made a bigger deal.

Luckily, they had no idea, and I was able to get up, shove the empty body further into the bushes so he wouldn't easily be found, and then went back to the Jeep. Rouge came out a few minutes later with the spoils of a coffee run in her hand and asked me what happened.

"What do you mean? Same as before."

"Really? There were two guys who walked in that told the clerk there were two sketchy guys playing hide the salami in the bushes. Should I be jealous?"

I laughed.

"Guess people will see what they want to see. Did the clerk do anything?"

"No. He shrugged and told them it was nothing new, and welcome to the neighborhood."

"Perfect."

"Now what?"

"Let's change this tire fast and go somewhere a little more scenic to enjoy the moment and drink coffee. Then we can see what we can figure out about Garcia's vampire problem."

Back at Rouge's house, which I really needed to start referring to as *my* house—I was having a hard time thinking of it that way—I started to do what research I could. I didn't have a lot of old books and scrolls about this sort of thing, especially when it comes to earthbound creatures. Instead, I used the one tool I normal would for this sort of thing: search engines on the computer. Of course, you look up vampires without defining anything and all you'll find will be movies and books like *Near Dark*, *Lost Boys*, *Daywalkers*, *Dracula*, and even the kind that glitter in the daylight. I needed to look for something more specific, something grounded in reality.

That wasn't much of a help either, to be honest.

Instead of actual facts about vampires, there was a lot of mythology dating back to the plague, and stories of people with fetishes, serial killers who thought they were vampires, and others with blood diseases that resembled what a creature of the night would have if they were, in fact, real. None of these things offered me anything I could actually work with. Still, I wasn't just going to give up helping, even after six hours staring at a computer screen. My eyes felt dry and strained when I finally got up and walked over to Rouge, who was sitting on the couch with her laptop.

"Any luck?" I asked, and collapsed onto the soft sofa.

"With what?" she asked, not even bothering to look away from her screen.

"On the vampire research for Garcia," I said with a bit of a laugh, knowing she was pulling my leg.

"Oh. I gave that up hours ago. I couldn't find anything useful."

"Hours ago? What have you been doing, then?"

"Lots of things. I was looking up some skin care stuff, and reading reviews on some new shoes I want, and other things."

"Really? Tell me you're joking."

"I'm not. There's nothing on the internet that isn't conjecture, myth, or movie trivia. Are you saying you've been over there all that time combing through page after page of stuff?"

I nodded, and she smiled and shook her head at me.

"You really need to know when to throw in the towel and realize if vampires are real, there is a reason nobody knows it. If these things have existed for thousands of years, have been on Earth draining blood from victims and leaving them like that guy in the bathroom, more people would know about it. It would always be on the news. But it's not. That means it's not vampires, or this one is sloppy, unlike its predecessors. Don't you agree?"

She had a point and I told her so. I felt defeated. I know I was only a few hours into looking into this, but normally I am really good at figuring out a problem when it comes to monsters, demons and other creatures, whether they are from this planet or not. I have been at this for a very long time, over two times a human's lifespan, but this was not something I had ever seen. There had been a lot of that over the last few years.

When I first arrived on Earth, things had been easy. It was all about finding a creature and getting rid of a creature. Rinse and repeat. Very little to figure out as far as things went. I wasn't much of a monster detective, that's for sure. Then, a few things popped up that were wild, and a few times I ran into monsters that nearly cost me my life. Shortly after that, things went back to normal, as much as they can when you are dealing with monsters every day. All that changed when I met Rouge and went to Innisfil. Since that happened, it has been a steady change in how things have ramped up. I know a lot of that has to do with the uprising against the Collective, the ones who sent me here. Tensions from other planets and galaxies that believe there should be no policing the Earth at all, that anyone and anything should have access here, have been clearly growing. The Doll Maker was just the latest in that. Maybe this vampire was another piece of that puzzle, but I didn't think so. I couldn't think of a single being that could leave a body completely drained like that.

"Is there somewhere we could look, like a library with old books or some occult shop that might have some better information than a publicly accessible website can offer?" Rouge asked, and I shrugged. There was an occult shop in the city I could go to, but the two of us weren't on the greatest terms, so that was probably out. I also knew there were two libraries like that in the city, another one in New York that could help, but the idea of trying to find the right book for our needs seemed like such a pain in the ass to me. The digital world had really made me lazy.

"I know there are a few, but that is a lot of work for us."

"Maybe we let someone else to do it then. Can't you pay the people at those places to look up the stuff and only give you the information you want?"

I nodded. "Now I know why I agreed to have you come on as my partner. You have a different way of looking at things than I do."

"I'm glad you said *partner* and not *assistant*. If you had slipped and said the wrong thing, you wouldn't be getting any tonight."

"But I am, right?"

"Maybe."

Saturday

It was just after ten in the morning when I finally woke up. It was nice to sleep in. With my line of work, it was something I hadn't had a chance to do in a while. Usually my phone or some noise outside will wake me up before I'm ready to crawl out from under the sheets. Since it was Saturday, I was free of any sort of city work noise, and I guess I had turned off my phone before going to bed, something I don't normally do. I restarted it and set it on the table before turning over to see Rouge. I was surprised to see she was gone, and her side of the bed was just empty.

Lately, I was getting up before her and would go make coffee and breakfast before she decided to climb out of her slumber. The fact that she was gone was a shock and I stopped and listened to see if she was out there doing my job. I didn't hear any noise, nor could I smell any food cooking. I grabbed my phone that was still rebooting and left the room to find out where she was.

The house was so quiet. Normally, I wouldn't want to think the worst, but I do have a great imagination, and after all the things that we had been through over the last few years, and especially since the Doll Maker, it was easy to think the worst. I walked down the hall towards the kitchen and living room and did my best not to imagine Rouge lying on the floor, drained of all her life, just an empty husk like the guy in the bathroom of that restaurant. I felt panic rushing through me with each step, not wanting to see her sunken face, and missing eyes, but I couldn't *not* see it.

My throat had tightened up.

My chest pounded as fear seized me.

The house was still; silent. What was going on?

I let out a small cry from fear as my phone came back to life and the first notifications started to come through. The sound broke the silence, and even though I knew what it was, my mind tried to tell me it was some sort of danger.

"Dill? What's wrong?"

And just like that, the fear and terror were gone.

I all but ran down the hall and found Rouge sitting on the couch in her nightgown, a laptop open beside her. She was fine. Of course she was fine. Why wouldn't she be? I really shouldn't let my mind play tricks on me and stress me out for no reason.

"When did you get up?" I asked, trying to avoid the question. The last thing I wanted to do was to tell her I had been worried about her safety. There should have been nothing to be afraid of. We were fine, safe. There was no Doll Maker left, no Don Parks hunting us down. We were perfectly secure here.

"About an hour ago. Couldn't sleep, so I came down here and thought I would try and look up some stuff to try and figure out what killed that guy yesterday."

I sat down beside her and gave her a kiss on the cheek, hoping she wouldn't notice the horrid smell of death seeping from my mouth. She never said anything about my morning breath, even when it tasted like I had eaten a cat turd paste.

"Nothing really. So much of it is just hearsay, myths based on fear, and mentally ill people who think they're vampires and go on killing sprees. I mean, there are a few cows and pigs that have been found exsanguinated, but those don't really look anything like our guy did. So, after an hour, nothing really to report. Now, why did you make that weird sound when you were coming down the hall?"

"It was nothing. Forgot my phone was resetting and it startled me," I told her, not really lying, just not wanting to let her know I might be worried about anything.

"A phone scared the mighty Dillon the Monster Hunter!"

"Hey, bugs scare me, so what do you expect?" I laughed. "I may chase down some weird monsters and creatures, but there are still things I can be scared of, too." I didn't mention how afraid I'd been when I was walking down the hall, filled with the idea that something had happened to her, which was the reason I let out that sad sound when the phone went off. There were things I didn't think she needed to know about.

"So, what's the plan now? I don't think the internet is going to be any help for this case."

I shrugged. I didn't have a set plan for any of this, but I did have some thoughts about what we could do. When it comes to most things in life, I prefer to plan things out as best I can for a day, but with the strangeness of this case, I wondered how much of it would be done by the seat of my pants.

"I was thinking we could run by Godfrey's first. See if he has any thoughts about what's going on, and what kind of creature could do this. If it is an off-world being, he should know what it is." Godfrey has always had a wealth of information. Whenever I am stumped on what a monster might be, he is great at figuring it out and providing the tools to stop it.

"And if he doesn't know? If this is some earthbound monster like an actual vampire, will he know what it is?"

"Not sure," I admitted, and then thought of the next best bet to him. I really didn't want to consider that, especially how things had ended the last time we had seen each other, but he would be better than almost anyone else. I figured I would have to set the past aside and just consider it after all. "But if he doesn't, then there is one other guy we can ask who might know something. Especially if this killer is from this planet."

"Is he a weirdo who lives in his mom's basement and plays a lot of computer stuff and posts on Reddit? If so, I think I've seen a movie about a guy like him."

"No. He owns a bookstore that has all kinds of stuff on the occult, demons, black magic and general strangeness. He's a good guy. I know we can trust him. He's been through a lot."

To say he'd been through a lot is a bit of an understatement.

Fifteen years ago, before he owned the *Black Spector Books*, Vjay Kajal was a detective with the Toronto Police Services. He wasn't just a young detective; he was the guy who was given the tough and high-profile murder cases. He had a reputation of being able to connect dots others would have missed, to look down avenues most wouldn't think to go down. It's how we met.

Over a weekend in July, during one of the city's worst heatwaves in years, four priests were found dead in four different churches in the downtown core. Kajal showed up at each one, and from what he told me it was the worst thing he'd ever seen. All four men of the cloth had been stripped naked, hung above the alter, and mutilated. They had been skinned, drained of blood and gutted from crotch to throat. Their insides had been pulled out and placed in the baptismal basin, and their skins draped over the thrones where the priests sit. The stomachs and heart of each were never found.

To anyone who examining the scene, it would look as though some black magic might have been at play. Kajal wasn't so sure. There seemed to be no signs of struggle and there were symbols painted on the wall in some animal blood, and a half burnt, black candle near the pews, yet it wasn't like anything Kajal had ever seen before. It didn't line up right with actual black magic scenes he had studied. He'd never seen anything quite like it before.

"Is that how you got involved? He called you?" Rouge asked, and I shook my head.

"No. It wasn't until the fifth body was found that Father Ted reached out to me on Kajal's behalf."

"Wait, the same Father Ted as..."

"Yeah. The same one."

Kajal had been interviewing some other priests in the city, getting information about each church and the victims for background. He showed up at Father Ted's church with some photos. Nothing too gruesome. I got to see them later too, but when Ted looked, he was sure there was something off about the scenes. At each of the murders, there were feathers strewn about. He said it looked like a path of them. He said it didn't look as though they had blown in, or been left behind, but rather it reminded him of the way a shedding dog will leave behind its fur as it walks. From there he began to figure out that whatever had been killing the priests wasn't some giant bird leaving feathers but was a creature from some other world that had been made of feathers that had crossed through a weak spot into this world. Ted, who I had worked with before, knew all about how creatures come to this planet. Unlike the way the Doll Maker was bringing demons and creatures through, most had to come another way. They found ripples in our world, those weak spots I just mentioned, and when they pass through into our world, they are little more than a glowing essence of their own spirits. From there, they call forth inanimate objects or dead things to make up their new forms. Some of them will pull leaves to their bodies, a few others will use discarded tissues, and some even use old paint cans. When Ted saw the feathers, he was sure he was seeing the same type of thing.

Kajal, being a good detective, and someone who has never dealt with monsters before, was reluctant. He wasn't sure some guy who claimed to be a monster dick was the type of person he wanted to be brought into an investigation. Any good cop would be a bit cautious, so I wasn't offended. Why would I be? It was rare that humans were willing to accept that there were things in the universe outside their own planet.

Father Ted somehow convinced him to meet with me, and when he did, I was shown the photos. Right away, and with the help of what Father Ted had already suggested, I knew what I was looking at and didn't need to think twice to know it wasn't human. It was a Maimeex, a demon from the outer edge of the Centurion system. They have a way of trying to be grand, thinking they are the ultimate in all species of demons. They believed it so much that not only do they do things very theatrically, but they love to leave a crest behind, a mark of their kind. This was what they had painted on the pews at each crime scene.

I told this to Kajal, and of course, he didn't really believe me. You can't blame him, I guess. If you had never seen anything strange in your life, and then along comes some guy who claims to hunt monsters, that demons are real, would you believe it? It's a hard pill to swallow when you can only see the world through the eyes of what you grew up knowing. Sometimes you just have to open up and allow the truth to come through. Not an easy task when you're a cop who must answer to the media and your higher-ups.

"But he eventually believed you, right?"

"Yeah. And that's when his life was turned upside down. Kajal became a laughingstock. After I was able to convince him that it was all real, he tried to tell his bosses there was a monster made of feathers who was killing the priests and asked for a special task force. I warned him not to, to just do things a little lower key, and I would help him, but he wanted to do things by the book as much as he could, even though there was nothing by the book about this. I'm sure you can guess how that went."

"Not well, would be my guess," Rouge said quietly.

"Yeah. We of course found the demon and got rid of it, but then the case just became an unsolved series of murders. Kajal tried to file his report, saying it was solved, but they decided to let him go, claiming he had suffered a mental breakdown. He tried to put up a fight, went to his union rep, but even they thought he should take some time off and seek help. He handed in his badge and gun and never went back to them."

"That's horrible. He must've been devastated."

I shrugged. He hadn't been that upset. Instead of being hurt by the way he was treated, he turned his attention to the dark parts of the world and universe. He began to travel, seeking out books, stories, and looking for what others might just pass off as a strange thing or unexplainable occurrence. Five years later, after I first met him, he opened his bookstore and worked side jobs looking for the kind of creatures and monsters I do. I don't know if he is happier doing what he is doing now, but he was as good at it as he was at being a cop. You tell him a small bit of what you know about some monsters, and he will open up like an encyclopedia on the matter.

"Shouldn't we just go to him first then? Especially if this is something from this planet anyway?"

"We could, but I will send him a message first and while we wait, we can go and see Godfrey."

"Why do I have a feeling you're leaving something out here, Dillon?" Rouge asked and put her hand over mine. "Is there a reason why you don't just go see him first?"

I shrugged. There *was* a reason I didn't like to go to Kajal unless I had to. I could explain it all to Rouge, but the day wasn't getting any younger. And if we did see him later, I was sure it would all be made clear then.

"Let me just message him. He always takes a while to get back, and while we wait, we can do other things."

"I'll go get dressed then."

I didn't really have a plan to send him a message, I just needed some time to try and build up the courage before we visited him. I was sure he was going to be so pissed at me, and he had every right. I could've explained that all to Rouge too, but that was another thing I just wasn't ready to deal with in that moment.

A little over an hour later we arrived at Godfrey's shop, which was also his house. After he broke some rules he never fully told me about, the Collective sent him to Earth to the store as part of his punishment. In his shop, his prison of sorts, he looked like a middle-aged Jamaican man, but if he went outside of it, left the cell he was sentenced to, his true form was revealed. He wasn't someone who would easily pass as human when he was in his true state.

I pushed the door open and was blasted in the face by hot, stinky air that reminded me of dirty socks. It was so bad. I covered my mouth and nose right away and tried to tell Rouge to do the same, but it was too late. I saw her face turn a shade of pale green before she cried out.

"What the hell is that smell? Is someone boiling diapers, or did someone die?"

"Not at all!" Godfrey laughed from out of sight, and then walked out from his back room through a sheet hanging from the top of a door frame. "That, my friends, is the wonderful aroma of whumpas. You don't like it?"

"It smells like ass," Rouge said, and it looked like she was fighting off gagging.

"I guess it's an acquired thing. I love it. Tastes just like it smells, too. My mom used to make it for me back when I was just a little one."

"And how did you manage to get your hands on that?" I asked, but knew right away how he did.

"You know me, Dillon. I have many contacts. There are so many highways connecting one world to the next. You just have to know how to make someone use the roads that lead to you. Enough of that. Come! We can go out back and talk in the fresh air if you two don't like the glorious smell of my treasure."

I was going to ask if we should lock the door in case anyone else showed up but knew there was no need. The smell of his disgusting food was better than any lock or alarm system. If a human who had no idea what this place was happened to walk in, they would run out as fast as they could or puke everywhere.

We went out the back door into the alley, his form slipping into its true self, and said some quick helloes before Godfrey asked what the unexpected visit was about. I gave him the rundown about what we saw in the restaurant washroom, making sure to tell him all the nitty gritty details. He listened and then sat down on some milk crates he had stored back there.

"Well, that must have been a horrible sight," he said, and motioned for us to sit as well.

"It was," I admitted and took a seat. "I've been scratching my head on this one. Never really saw anything like it. Garcia thinks it might be vampires."

"Vampires?" Godfrey laughed. "Are those things real and not just a myth made up by writers and scared people? I thought it was just movies and books."

"That's why we're here, Godfrey," Rouge said from my side. "We looked into it. Neither of us could find a single thing to make us think that there are real vampires here, but if not them, what?"

"Maybe *Shadow People* did it?" he suggested, and I hadn't even considered that. To most in the know, Shadow People are nearly as mythical as vampires. I had never seen one in my life, until a few years ago when I had a run-in with them and they tried to kill me. That was during the early stages of my relationship with

Rouge, and the first time I had ever heard that there might be a force rising against the Collective. I had been lucky to get out of that in one piece, but what I saw them do then was nothing like this. I wasn't sold on the idea of it being Shadow People.

Neither was Rouge.

"That doesn't seem likely," she said as she shook her head.

"You have a lot of experience with Shadow People, Rouge?" he asked her, looking at her very sceptically.

"We both did. When we were up north, Dillon was a host to one for a quick second."

"What?" Godfrey blurted out and looked totally stunned. "You never told me that."

"I also didn't tell you what I had for breakfast. And to be honest, it was after you had already messed me up by giving me a few faulty items that nearly cost me my life. Did you forget about all of that?"

"Hey, hey, hey, Dillon. That's water under the bridge. You still should have told me about that. I've never met someone who'd ever met a Shadow Person, let alone was a host to one and survived."

"Well, I did and here we are," I said and wanted to leave it at that. I hadn't ever really forgotten how that felt, when the Shadow Person invaded my body, the beginnings of the devouring only a small tickle I felt in the darkest parts of my being. I didn't tell him, because I still had nightmares from time to time that the Shadow Person was still inside of me, eating second by second. Talking about it would only make me relive the panic that set in.

"So, why do you think this isn't Shadow People?" Godfrey asked, and I was glad he was willing to move on. "Sounds like the way they do things. They go in and drain someone until there's nothing left."

I shook my head and heard Rouge huff. She wasn't liking his idea any more than I was.

"That's not really how they work, though," I told him. I didn't want to get into it, not after what I just said, but he needed to at least know why I was sure, and Rouge too, that it couldn't be one of them. "They go into a host and take over, but they don't drain them right away. The way it seems to work, Shadow People take a long time to devour the soul and life of the person they are in. It could take years for them to drain someone of all their life force. And when they are done, the body is still intact, it just has no soul in it other than the Shadow Person. This is so different it can't be them."

"Then what?"

"That's why we're here, Godfrey. You know more about the universe than I do."

"That's sweet of you, Dillon, but I don't know everything. I hate to admit that, but it's the truth. Sorry. This all seems too weird and makes no sense. Maybe it is some kind of vampire that's been hiding in the shadows all these centuries and is only now stepping out and being sloppy."

"Well, this has been a waste of time," Rouge said, and jumped up from her seat. Godfrey quickly reached over and took her wrist.

"Let's not be too hasty with saying I'm a waste of time. What I said was that I didn't know what it might be offhand, but that doesn't mean I won't be able to figure it out. Just give me some time to investigate some things, ask some question, reach out to my connections, and I'll see what I can find out. Not a total waste of time, right?"

Rouge smiled and sat back down. I wasn't so sure why she got so angry at him, but I thought maybe it was better not to ask or make a big deal about it. I don't know much about women, but I know that from my experience with Rouge it was better to let her talk about it when she wanted to, to listen to her, than it was to try and pry it out. I'm not much different to be honest. It's probably why we get along so well.

"I guess not, but still, I would have liked to leave here with something tangible," she said before I could. "I know it hasn't even been twenty-four hours, but I feel like there's going to be a lot of smashing our heads into a wall with this one."

"I get it, Rouge," Godfrey said and put his hand on hers. "None of these things are ever easy. I think in a few hours or a few days at the most, you and your ugly boyfriend here will be able to sit back and relax knowing you did some good by solving the case and getting rid of whatever it was that killed the person in the bathroom."

"Unless it's an actual vampire, right? If it is, we won't be able to do anything to stop them because of the stupid rules."

"I won't be able to," I told her, ignoring Godfrey's snarky comment about my looks. "But you still can. Since you're from this planet there's no saying you can't stop this vampire, or whatever it is."

"Really? I can do that, and you won't get in trouble?" she asked. "I thought we were both hunters now and had to follow the same rules."

"Not that I know of. But you also know how well I am at following the rules," I said, and gave her a wink. After all, it wasn't all that long ago that the Collective sent another hunter to Earth to hunt me down for all the rules I had broken.

And Rouge was the best rule I'd ignored so far.

"So, it's settled then. I'll look into a few things, and then you two will wipe it off the face of this planet and nobody else gets into trouble. Now, who wants to come and enjoy some of my delicious whumpas?"

Neither of us decided to go down that road, and instead we headed out towards Kajal's shop.

Kajal's bookstore was somewhat off the beaten path. It was in the downtown area, south of Bloor and west of Yonge Street, but not down one of the busier roads like Gerrard or Wellesley. It wasn't quite an alleyway. It was little more than a narrow, one-lane, one-way street littered with trash bags.

It had been quite a few years since I'd been to the shop, and it seemed those property management companies buying up all the stores and walk-ups in the city and turning them into condos didn't think this particular street was worth much. Why would they? It only spanned a few city blocks, was only one direction, and the stores there were either boarded up or looked as though they could only make money because they were just fronts for something illegal. Kajal's shop stood out from the rest in a way, and yet still blended into the shabby neighborhood.

The store front window was just piled with books. You couldn't really see inside because of this. There was also a thick layer of dust on the glass that would probably be greasy to the touch if someone was brave enough to try and clean it. There was a small, hand-painted sign above the black wood that surrounded the dirty window, but it was good enough to let a person interested know what was in there. It simply said *Black Spector Books*, nothing more. It would call out to those looking for it and would attract a few passers-by intrigued by the mysterious name, though the filth would no doubt keep many of them out.

"So, this is the place?" Rouge asked as we stood in front of the place I thought I would never walk into again.

"Yup," was all I said and tried not to think about whether Kajal would be happy to see me or might throw some hefty tome at me. There was a chance that Kajal didn't think about any of it anymore, that he'd simply moved on and let go of any hard feelings, but then again, I liked to go into a situation hoping for the best. Humans had a long history of holding grudges, not that I would blame him for being mad at me. I had done something terrible.

I pushed open the door and above us, a tiny bell chimed. The smell inside was old and dusty, pages yellowed and well read. It was a common smell in old book shops, and it was something I found mildly pleasing. It was familiar, and held so much promise of things unknown. There was a lot of the unknown before us, and as the door shut slowly and Rouge came up to my side, the first unknown stepped out from a back room.

As soon as our eyes met, I knew that my hopes of a happy reunion of old friends was about to be dashed. It was a small thing, just a split second, but his brow went dark for a moment. I saw his eyes narrow and flash hate for the briefest second before he turned towards Rouge and smiled.

"What brings you here, Dillon? Following a lead to a place you aren't welcome anymore? Seems like something you would do. You always had a knack of putting your own needs ahead of propriety." Kajal said, and leaned on a dark wood counter that was stacked with leatherbound books. "And did you bring a pretty face in hopes that I wouldn't jump over this counter and strangle you?"

"I'm not just a pretty face," Rouge said, and I could tell she was insulted by his comment.

"No doubt, and I'm sorry if I offended you," Kajal said and shot daggers with his eyes at me again. "But I know what Dillon is like, and it does seem like something he would do."

"I wouldn't have come here and bothered you if I didn't have to, Kajal. But I need your help. Innocent people in this city need your help."

"I don't think the people of this city care for my help, especially after the city fired me. And you need my help?" Kajal laughed and threw his head back. "Are you serious? After all the shit you did you just come waltz back here and ask me for a favour? Did I miss something? Do I owe you a favour?"

I thought things might be bad, but I didn't expect him to sound so mad at me. I hadn't come to see him in so long, or asked for any help because I had hoped time would heal the wounds between us, but clearly there were some things that would never return to the way they were.

At that moment, I thought that we should just leave and hope Godfrey would be able to turn up something, or that we would just get lucky the way we had in the recent past. I wondered if maybe things would have been better if I had reached out to him long before now, offered my apologies and tried to help him see why I did what I had. If there was a way to turn back the clock, who knows, I might've done things differently, but there was no way to do that at all.

"We should leave," I whispered to Rouge, and took her hand.

"No," she said loud enough for Kajal to hear. "We can't just leave. We need help and you said he was your best bet if Godfrey didn't know anything."

"Godfrey? You still associate with that con artist?" Kajal laughed.

"I do. He's turned himself around since nearly killing me a few times."

"Too bad he never succeeded. Not that killing you would do much. I'm sure there is a plethora of bodies lined up for you every time you abuse the one you're currently living in."

I said nothing. I knew he was angry, and to be honest, he had every right to be. What happened back then was shitty. I made a call, and looking back now I wouldn't have done the same thing. Back then, I think I wasn't really a stickler for the rules, but there were times that once I made my mind up about something, that's all there was to it. What was decided was done. I'm not like that anymore; or so I'd like to think, but it's because of that mindset back then that Kajal is still mad at me, and I was sure there was no way to say sorry enough to him to change that.

"What's your deal?" Rouge said as I once again tried to back out of there. "I know there is bad blood between you two, but seriously, there are people dying. Can't you put this shit behind you?"

Kajal stood there quiet for a second, but looked as if he was going to blow his lid. I knew him well enough to know that was anger boiling within and worried he would unleash a tongue lashing on Rouge.

"You have no idea what happened, do you? You think I'm just overreacting to something like Dillon forgetting my birthday or eating the last slice of pizza." He turned to me, his brow furrowing the same way it did when he was pissed about something work related. "Did you even tell her what happened, Dillon?" I shook my head. Of course I hadn't. In fact, I'd never mentioned it before. It wasn't that I was trying to hide anything from her, it was just that it had never come up until that moment when we needed him. "Doesn't that just figure? He has a way of not telling the whole story about things. Haven't you noticed that before?"

"He's an open book with me."

Well, there's a reason I love her. She always has my back.

"Lucky you. For the rest of us, he tells us just enough to reel us in, keeping out the important stuff that could cost us everything."

"Why don't you tell me what happened, then?" she asked and moved away from me, going further into the store. "There is something really bad going on and we could use your help. So, let's have it all out and maybe move on so we can stop anyone else from dying. Please?"

Kajal said nothing. He looked from me to Rouge and back again, but didn't say a word for over a minute. I was sure he would say no and walk away. Kajal had no reason to help us, other than the fact that he was once a cop, someone sworn to help people out. But after losing that job for solving a case that was supernatural and nobody believing him, instead forcing him to quit or go under psychiatric evaluation, did he still have that need to help flowing through him? And would that need be strong enough to allow him to get past what happened between us? I wasn't sure.

"He stole something I loved from me. Took it away, and now he wants me to forget it."

"What did he take?"

"The life of my dog, Aamir. My little guy," he told her, and sounded so sad even my heart broke. Rouge shot her head back and looked at me with a mix of shock and disgust.

"It wasn't really a dog," I told her.

"It was my dog, regardless of what you say, asshole!"

"I'm so sorry. How old was he?" Rouge asked looking back at Kajal.

"I had him for nearly fifteen years. Got him when he was just a pup. I knew kids were not going to be a thing for me, my lifestyle made it so that wouldn't really be an option, so I got a puppy I could raise and love. Named him Aamir because he looked like a little, hairy Aamir Khan. Then, I met Dillon. I worked with him for some time, trusted him even. Trusted he wouldn't betray me, but he did. He killed the one thing in this world I loved. Killed what was the equivalent of my child."

"I'm sorry, Kajal," I said quietly, and felt like utter shit. Hearing him talk like this was killing me, stabbing me straight through the chest. I was so stupid to act as though I was following the rules, doing what needed to be done. I should have thought more about his feelings before acting.

"Sorry will never bring him back. You know that, right, Dillon?"

"I do. And if I could change what I did, I would."

"What happened? Why would you hurt his dog?"

I took a deep breath and told her the story. I didn't want to. I wanted to change some of the facts so I wouldn't look like such an asshole in all of this, but I also wanted Kajal to know I was actually sorry. So, I came clean.

It was a few years after we had met, and the bookstore was already up and running. I would visit from time to time and ask Kajal for help. Since the first case we worked together, he became enthralled, nearly obsessed with the occult, magic, and what lies beyond this planet. It was a little scary to see how fast he picked up things, devouring knowledge about off-planet and earthbound monsters and demons. I was never that good at learning this stuff, and it's my job.

When I would visit him, I would see his little dog flopped out on the floor, guarding stacks of books, or laying on a raggedy blanket near the checkout counter. I like dogs, but since it was usually conked out or eating, I didn't pay the little guy any mind. He was just part of the background.

Once day I went to the shop and was going to show something to Kajal, and when I walked in, I saw the dog sitting on a small stack of books the way a human might sit in a chair, and reading a thin pamphlet. I froze, and as the bell over the door tinkled, the dog looked at me and dropped what it was reading as it gasped and said *oh shit!*

Oh shit, indeed.

Without really thinking, I pulled on my gloves, ran over to the dog and grabbed it. Of course it was frozen because there was a monster living inside it. At some point, the actual dog must've died, and a monster took over before it could start to decay. That's what I thought, and I didn't wait for Kajal to tell me otherwise. I just acted. I did what I would in any other situation like that.

"You killed it?" Rouge asked, cutting into the story.

"I dispatched it."

"You killed it," Kajal said frankly and yeah, I guess I did. Saying I dispatched it was sugar-coating it. "Don't try to paint it like it was something else to make it fit into your narrative,

Dillon. You murdered him. My Aamir."

"I didn't know. I thought a monster had taken over the dog and was hiding in plain sight in this book shop. I had no idea Kajal knew about it, and was the reason there was a monster in there."

"Wait, you knew there was a monster living in your dog?" Rouge asked Kajal, and for the first time, she didn't sound like she was mad at me about it all. That was a good thing.

"Of course I knew. Aamir passed away sooner than he should have. He had something wrong in his heart and there was nothing the vet could do. So, I did what I had to do so I would never be without him."

"Wait, wait, wait," Rouge said and threw up her hands in a dramatic way. "I'm lost here. You made it sound like you bought a puppy and raised it for fifteen years and then Dillon killed it. But now you're saying it was already dead. I think I'm missing something here."

"It was a pup Dillon killed. First it was my little guy, Aamir, and then I invited a Ghaaali to live inside him. He was so young when I brought him through and let him go into the stuffed dog. And Dillon killed him."

Rouge said nothing, but was shaking her head in disbelief.

I decided to try and explain it all without pissing off Kajal any more than he already was. It was a strange situation, and even though I knew I was in the wrong at the end of the day, I hoped if I explained it a little more, he would maybe see my side of the story and realize I made an honest mistake.

When I said that Kajal had become obsessed with the books, and demons, and monsters, I wasn't exaggerating. He would hunt down some of the rarest books, search the dark web for stories about all sorts of creature and different realms. It was during this research he found out more about weak spots and certain races of beings that are less of a menace than many of the monsters I deal with. At that point, an idea was born in his head. He knew that because of his lifestyle, the way he had been wired in the head, kids were not going to be an option. Kajal had never had a male or female partner, and never wanted one, but there was still a part of him that wanted a child. So, he went and found the cutest puppy he could find and raised it until it passed away before its time. Then he decided he wasn't just going to let the dog truly die, so he opened a weak spot, using a ritual he'd found in a book, and invited a Ghaaali child to come live in the dead dog and have a life with him.

Of course, he hadn't told me this at the time it happened. I'm sure he was worried that if he did, I might not react well. Since I had no idea of what was going on, when I saw the dog moving very un-doglike, I thought the worst. In my head, I was sure the dog had passed away and some demon had taken over the body for who-knew-what nefarious reason.

"Kajal, you have to believe me, if I had known, I would never have done it. I thought I was protecting you."

"All you had to do was ask, but you didn't. Like so many other times, you act before you think. You like to just do and then deal with the consequences afterwards, right? And even if you had waited and asked me, do you really believe you would've allowed a dreaded monster to live here on Earth when you are so dedicated to your goddamn Collective?"

"He would," Rouge told him, and stepped forward. "I've seen him let things live here, peaceful creatures that are only trying to escape terrible places. If he'd known at the time what he just told me now, I know deep down he would have seen a way to let it slide. I'm not saying it's your fault, or his. It was bad communication."

I watched Kajal as he considered what Rouge had just said. I can't say a hundred percent I would have let it slide. It was a long time ago and I wasn't in the habit of breaking quite as many rules back then, but I wasn't an angel either, so there's no telling which way I would lean. The facts were that I had done it, and now felt like shit about it, so I hoped that meant something to him.

"I still can't believe you killed him. He wasn't evil, hadn't hurt anyone. He was innocent, and you took his life as though it was nothing at all."

"Took his life? I keep telling you that I didn't actually kill him. I just sent the spirit back to his own world. The body he was in died and became unusable, but he didn't kill what was inside, Aamir's soul. I told you I dispatched him. You've read all the books, how did you not know that?"

"Not dead? But you stabbed him with your dagger. I saw him die," Kajal said and looked as though he was about to collapse a bit. He grabbed onto the edge of the desk as if to steady himself. "You're telling me he's not actually dead? All this time and I could have brought him back here? All this time wasted being without him."

"I'm sorry, Kajal," I said again as a tear rolled down his cheek. "I tried to explain it to you before, when it happened and you told me what he was to you, but you wouldn't listen to me. I'm sorry."

"No," Kajal said quietly and wiped the tears from his eyes. "It's okay, Dillon. It's better than okay. If I had asked, or read more, or anything, I would have been able to bring him back. It's been a long time, but there's enough time still to make it right. Thank you, Dillon."

I walked over and offered my hand to him. I'd been so reluctant to see Kajal over the years, had been sure he would try and shoot me, or find a way to kick me out of the body I was in. What I never expected was for him take my hand and rekindle our friendship. It made me glad that Godfrey couldn't help us.

"So, what can I do for you?"

We sat in the back room of the shop, at a dark wood table with books and scrolls scattered across it. Kajal made us some single estate Assam tea and we told him everything we knew about the case so far. There wasn't a whole lot to really go through, but I made sure not to miss a single bit of information we saw and had been told by Garcia.

"Sounds like a vampire to me," was the first thing Kajal said when we were done talking.

"That's what Garcia said," Rouge admitted.

"Garcia? As in Officer Garcia?" he asked, and I nodded. "He's working homicide now? Wow, not sure I saw that coming."

"You know him?" I asked, not thinking the two had ever crossed paths. Then again, they had both known Father Ted, so shows you how much I knew outside of monsters.

"Yeah. He was a beat cop that worked downtown. Fifty-one division. He was good, but he had a mean streak in him. Never thought he would try out for being a detective. I was sure he would get no higher than a Field Training Officer because he had a tendency of slapping people who pissed him off. Is he good at what he does?"

"He is," I said and told him a little about the cases we worked together.

"And he still has a job? That's impressive."

I got where he was going with it. Kajal had worked one case with me and had his career get flushed down the toilet. I think the big difference between the two of them was that Garcia will do his best to sway the evidence to give his bosses a case he can show the public and the Crown attorney. When Kajal worked the case with me, he tried to convince his bosses that monsters and demons were real, and that creatures from beyond this planet were responsible for the crimes committed. That is a hard pill to swallow.

"So, you think it's vampires?" Rouge asked, and didn't sound happy about the idea that it was bloodsuckers from Earth.

"No. I said it *sounds* like vampires. When you just glance at it, sure, that's how it comes off, but let's be honest, vampires aren't actually real."

"Are you sure?" I asked Kajal, because I never said never, especially when it comes to monsters.

"I'm never one hundred percent sure, but I can tell you that I have never found any real, hard evidence that vampires are among us, or ever have been. Most of the stories and history of them come from fear, both real and religious in nature. Many of the old tales involve people not understanding medicine, mental illness, and how death works. There are other times when it was virus and diseases taking lives, and people were unable to understand so they turned to the supernatural. It's the way we small-brained humans work. If we don't know something, we try and make up a bigger reason than the truth could ever provide. Even that part about vampires having hair on their palms, that's fear fed into people over masturbation. Back then, many people had fur blankets, so when they were done, they would wipe their hands on the fur, and the fur would then stick to their hands. Someone started a rumor because of that, making people think hair on the palms was a sign of being undead."

"That seems a bit much," Rouge laughed.

"So, if it isn't a vampire, what could it be?" I asked, getting us back on track and trying to scroll through my mental rolodex of demons, monsters and spirits that could do something like that to a person.

"Offhand, I don't know. I mean there are tales of blood drinkers that aren't vampires, some of them from Earth, some from out there beyond our world, but they all leave telltale signs. There's gouging, skin ripped off, heads taken or crushed, but nothing like an empty husk left behind. I'm not sure what does that, but if it is something unnatural, there should be something in one of these books here. If it's not, then someone is doing something with chemicals or drugs to leave the bodies like that."

"That can't be right," Rouge said as she shook her head in disbelief. I agreed. There was no way some chemical or drug could do that to a person, at least nothing that I had ever heard about. I'm sure on the dark web there are all kinds of conspiracy theories, and wild tales of government-tested chemicals that could do all kinds of horrible things to you, but you can't always believe everything you read on the internet.

"It can, sure." Kajal said, disagreeing with me, and went on to explain stories about places like Haiti where there were people who'd developed chemicals from planets that could turn people into what we think of as zombies. Add ideas like that to the increased technology, then anything was possible. "There is even a drug someone developed that would temporarily absorb light into their skin instead of bouncing off, and that turned him invisible for short bursts of time."

"I never heard about that," I said with a gasp. The idea of dealing with someone that could turn invisible was a horrible idea. If it was true, of course.

"It happened in the early '80s. The guy was using it as a joke and eventually the use of the chemical had some terrible side effects."

"Do I even want to know?" Rouge asked.

"Nothing as dramatic as him bursting into flames or staying invisible forever. It caused an aneurism, and he died on the toilet. Another Elvis moment." Kajal shifted a few books around on his table, opened a folded piece of parchment and then shook his head. He picked up a large leather book with gilded pages and opened it up. "There could be something in here about a creature with vampire-like traits. I'm not one hundred percent sure, but there is a little itch in the back of my mind that has me thinking it's here somewhere. I mean, there are legends of succubus and even energy drainers, but none of them do what you described. This one, on the other hand, could be something like that. It's more legend than proven fact, but the Haida people tell a story about something called the Mosquito Man, which is exactly like how it sounds."

"Who are the Haida people?" Rouge asked before I could.

"They are Indigenous people on the west coast of Canada, or 'Turtle Island' as many others call it," he told us both.

"Has there been any actual case to prove that is real?" I asked, sure that there wasn't.

"Well, like much of Indigenous history on this continent, most the stories of creatures like the Mosquito Man, or the Wendigo, Skin Walkers, and Skadegamutc are told through oral history. I know you want hard evidence you can nail down, but since this is not something you or I have ever heard of through all our research and experiences, then it's not likely this killer is one that normally leaves a lot of clues behind for you to find."

Kajal handed me the book and I started to skim through it. It sounded enough like what we were looking for, and yet it didn't. It said that usually this creature just fed on humans in a more annoying and less fatal way, and maybe that was why we had never heard of it before. Could be this creature, this Mosquito Man, had been doing this for a long time and only now had become gluttonous and began to kill.

"So, if there's normally nothing written about these legends and creatures, where did you get that book?" Rouge asked and took it from me. "It looks pretty old."

"It's from 1891. An alchemist from Germany came to North America around that time and became fascinated with the stories he was told by many of the Indigenous tribes of North America. He was amazed that many of the same legends from Europe and Asia had found their way here as well, with just slight twists to the stories. He wanted to make a history of sea creatures, demons and monster told to him by these tribes that were so reminiscent of the stories he'd heard of from Romania, Egypt, China, and other parts of the world. He just made it look older, I guess, to make it seem more important. Take a modern book, bind it in leather and edge the pages in gold and suddenly people think it's more important than it really is."

"Well, it certain has an air about it," Rouge laughed and handed it back to me.

"Can I borrow this?" I asked and he shook his head right away.

"I don't lend out or sell books like that to anyone. That is a one of a kind. He never mass published it. I had to trade some ancient trinkets I had to get my hands on it to begin with. The only book I have rarer than that one is my copy of The Anna, or The Great Nothing."

The Anna. I'd heard about that one before. It was a legend, a book full of some of the greatest mysteries of this planet, and so many other realms around it. Some said it contained the stories of the Gods that gave birth to the Gods that are known. There were rumors that the book was cursed, would cause its owner to go mad or become haunted by the words inside. I had never thought to search it out. Some things are best left unknown.

"Give me a day or two to investigate things, see if I can find something more about the Mosquito Man, or any other creature that fits into the mold. I won't come to you unless I have some eyewitness account, or actual proof. Sound good?"

It did. Anything he could do would help this get wrapped up sooner. Or so I hoped.

"What now?" I asked him as I stood up.

"With what? Us? Well, if what you said is true, I'm going to find Aamir and bring him back here. And if I can do that, well, all hard feelings are in the past."

"And if you can't find him, or he died when he returned home?"

Kajal was quiet and looked down at his feet. He obviously didn't want to think about that even being an option. I can't blame him. If I was in his shoes, I would be hoping for the best and not even be willing to consider any other option.

"If not, then this will be the last time I help you or ever see you again. I know it might seem harsh, but I don't know how I'd ever be able to look you in the face again if something terrible happened to Aamir."

After leaving Kajal's shop, I wasn't sure what the next step for us was. There wasn't a lot I could do without more inform-ation on what it was killing people and leaving them behind as empty husks. I thought about calling Garcia up and asking him for copies of the case files to go over to see if I could find something in common he may have missed, but realized that wouldn't be a great way of putting it. I didn't want to make him think I believed he wasn't competent enough to see the connecting dots, so I figured it would be better not to ask. I'm sure I could find a more diplomatic way of asking for them, but to be honest, the day was already more than halfway over, and I wasn't sure I wanted to think about the case anymore anyway.

I asked Rouge what she wanted to do, and found she was on the same page as me.

"I want to go home, curl up with the pup and watch some TV, if I am being completely honest. I feel drained today."

"Really, Rouge?"

"What?" she said, and I watched as she replayed the past thing she said in her head, and she gave a weak smile. "You know I didn't mean it like that. There was no pun intended. I'm just super worn out."

So was I. Not that we had done a whole lot, but the emotional toll at Kajal's and the disappointment at Godfrey's made me just think enough was enough.

"Should we pick up some dinner, or did you want me to make something?" I asked, and headed towards our house.

"Let's just pick something up on the way home, or have it delivered. I think slipping into some pajamas and maybe catching up on some Marvel shows on Disney+ is in order. I'm not in the mood to make anything, and I doubt you are either."

"You know me so well. Your plan sounds like a great night."

And it would have been just that if things for once could go smooth and easy, but that was not the way of the world these days.

We were more than halfway home when my phone went off. I asked Rouge to go in my pocket and pull it out, so I didn't have to struggle while driving. She did and answered the phone for me, sounding like she was my secretary for a moment.

"Offices of Dillon the Monster Hunter, how can I help you?" she said, leaving out my regular tagline of *Monster Dick* for some reason. "Yes it is... Yes he does take it very serious... No, it's not a joke... One hundred percent sure. How can we help you?"

I motioned for her to put it on speaker phone, but she ignored me, and continued to speak to the person on the other side.

"The rate will depend on the job, how long it takes, and the risk involved... Yes, very confidential... Cash or debit... That will also depend on the job. Can you give me an idea of what is going on?"

She went quiet, nodding in silence here and there as the person on the other end of the phone continued to talk. She pulled out her own phone and began to make notes on her Notes App. I tried to read what it said, but she had her phone on an angle and I needed to keep my eyes on the road.

"And can I get a callback number and your name?" she said after nearly two minutes of the person on the other end talking. "Okay. Perfect. I'll have Dillon reach out to you at his earliest convenience. Is there a time that is too late to call you back?... Okay then. Thanks for calling and have a great night."

Rouge hung my phone up and tucked it back into my pocket.

"Are you going to tell me what that was about?" I asked when I saw she had no plans on telling me.

"Looks like a run-of-the-mill case, nothing too urgent. I think it can wait until tomorrow."

"So, you're not going to tell me?"

"Don't you trust me? Don't you think I know what would be important enough to rush and tell you, and things that can wait?"

"Well, yeah, but—"

"But nothing. I'm telling you, Dillon, this is a leak, not a flood. It's not an emergency."

She was wrong.

Nearly three hours later, after getting home, eating, and starting episode four of the new show we were watching, my phone began to vibrate madly on the side table next to the couch. Rouge was in the washroom, and I had the ringer on silent, so she didn't hear it. I was reluctant to answer because I was enjoying the peaceful night. There had been so few of them, and with the new case Garcia was working, I was sure life was only going to get more hectic in the future. Still, there was a chance it was Garcia, or something else equally important, and I didn't want to spend the rest of the night in my mind, a limbo of wondering if it was serious or not, so I answered it.

"You've reach Dillion. How can I help you?"

"Did you get my message?" a woman's voice I wasn't familiar with said, her voice sounding as on-edge as any I've ever heard in my life.

"I'm not sure. Who is this?"

"My name is Rose. I called earlier about some weird shit going on in the apartment below me. I called earlier and was told you'd call me back. I left a message with your secretary."

I tried not to smile at the idea of Rouge being my secretary. I knew she wouldn't like it one bit. Especially if she knew the fantasies it pulled up in my head.

"Sorry, no. I didn't get anything yet. Normally I don't take calls this late at night, but seeing as you sound stressed out, why don't you let me know what's going on?"

The woman sighed and when she started talking, I could tell she was not happy about it.

"My friends live in the apartment below me. I mean, we're not great friends, but we hang out every now and then. You know how it is. You meet a neighbor in the elevator, start talking here and there, and then you hang out, go see movies, talk about guys you both like. It's not that strange."

"Okay. But you did say something strange is going on down there?"

"Yeah. She's been making all kinds of weird noises, like she's skinning cats, and breaking plates. I tried to knock on the door, but the woman I'm friends with just kept yelling for me to go away, to fuck off and leave her alone. She sounded…off, somehow."

"How well do you know her? Are you both really good friends? Did you have a falling out recently?"

"We're not best friends or anything, but we hang out at least once a month. She's lived there for the last six years, so I'd say we know each other pretty well and something is off with her."

"So, why call me? I mean, wouldn't your building security or the police be better?" I asked knowing very well nothing about this sounded like it was in my ballpark. As I asked that, Rouge walked in, and I gave her my best look of *why didn't you tell me about this?*

"What?" she whispered, and I held up a hand because Rose had started to talk again.

"At first, I did call security for my building. They attended, but she wouldn't answer for them either. Then they told me to call the police because it was a third party call and they can't do that, which sounds like an excuse to be lazy to me. But the cops came and since there was no noise when they arrived, they felt no need to knock. They told me I could call them back if it started again, but the officer gave me a look that made me feel like they thought I was the problem, and maybe I was. I thought I was making too much out of it all, especially since she is my friend. I would have dropped it there, but…"

She trailed off and I asked her what happened that made her call me.

"I don't want to sound like a weirdo or freak," she said quietly.

"You don't need to worry about that. I've heard and seen a lot in my day, and there is very little that I get all judgemental about. What happened?"

She paused for a second and I guessed she was trying to get herself together, to tell me the story in a way that wouldn't be too strange or shed a bad light on her. I had no idea what it could be, but I doubted it would be anything I would bat an eye at. I was wrong.

"The noise started up again about three days ago. It was eight o'clock at night and first there was the yelling and the screaming, followed by smashing dishes. I tried to ignore it for a second, and then thought I should record it so I could go to the management office and file a complaint. I mean, she is my friend, but I shouldn't have to live like that."

"I agree."

"And then I heard something really weird. I wasn't sure what it was, so I got down on all fours and put my ear to the hardwood floor. I know. It seems like a gross thing to do, to eavesdrop on my friend like that, but it was so messed up. It sounded so… wrong."

"That's not weird at all. It's normal, if you ask me. I think I may have done that back when I was living in Kensington Market and had a neighbor who used to scream and swear at the roaches in his place. At first, I thought it was a domestic he was having. Nope. Turned out it was just the bugs driving him batty."

"Well, this isn't bugs. She started to talk weird, speaking in a language I've never heard. It wasn't just that she sounded strange, like she was speaking in tongues like they do at some churches. Everything she said made it seem like her mouth was full of Jell-o when she talked. It was all squishy, and unintelligible, right up until I heard her say something about you."

"Me? How do you know it was me?"

"Most of what she did say, I couldn't understand at all, but then she said, *Dillon will never find me. And if the monster hunter ever tries to come here, I will eat his soul out of his asshole!* That's how I thought to check on your name. She said it."

Okay, there was something to all this after all. I took down her address and apartment number and confirmed her friend's name and apartment as well. I jotted it all down on a pad next to the couch and passed it to Rouge, asking her to Google Map it out so we could go there.

"When was the last time you saw or spoke to your friend face to face?" I asked Rose.

"Not in two or three weeks. Normally we even see each other in passing in the lobby or in the grocery store, but the only reason I know she's still around is because I can hear her below me."

"Can you remember anything she actually said down there when she was yelling, aside from the last part about me? I know you said she wasn't speaking English, but was there any word that stood out, or sound?" I asked this, hoping to fish a clue out of her that might solidify my idea of what was down in her friend's apartment.

"It was so hard to make much out. Just a lot of noise and grunting. I mean, after she said the thing about you, she said some weird word, like *Ash kata* or *ask kata,* something like that." That said a lot to me. It actually confirmed my suspicion that we were dealing with something not from this world, if she'd heard right. Askata was a type of victory call that creatures from Eestheal use. It's sort of like yelling out Hazzah! It meant what was living below her was not her friend, but a monster that was no doubt smashing those plates to eat them. "This just isn't like her. None of this is. The noise is terrible. The plates being smashed and the yelling. What do you think is going on down there?"

"I don't know, but I will come out to see what it is and hopefully help your friend."

"Will you be able to do anything? Like really do something to help her?"

"I will try," I told her, not wanting to say yes for sure. If there was a monster down there that had taken over her apartment, that was one thing. Or if she was housing one, the way Kajal had with

Aamir, that was something completely different. There was also the chance that the Eesthealean making noise down there was actually another one of the Doll Maker's clients, and if that was the case, there would be no way to help her in a way Rose would be satisfied. If this was one of the Doll Maker's clients in her friend's body, it was soon going to be nothing but an empty shell.

"When are you going to come here?" she asked, and there was clear impatience in her voice.

"As soon as I can. I will come see you first if you want me to, or after if I can manage to help out at all."

"Just go to her and let me know what happened. I'll pay anything it costs.

"We'll be there soon."

I said my goodbyes and hung up. I turned to Rouge and shook my head at her.

"I thought you said it didn't sound serious," I said, standing up and walking over to my bag of tools.

"It didn't seem serious the way she described it," Rouge said, and came to stand beside me. "Is it really that bad?"

"I don't know for sure. I'm hoping it is a simple case of a monster using trash and scraps to make a body, but you never know. It could be another one of the Maker's empty shells."

"I hope not. It'll be hard to stay off the radar with that since someone called you out to deal with it. If we have to leave the body empty, how do you plan on explaining it when the cops eventually come out?"

I said nothing as I checked my bag to make sure that I had everything I needed. I had my glove, dagger, empty bottles to collect souls, my coin, and even a few strains of Harpen hair, which is like a silver bullet to a werewolf for an Eesthealean.

"If that's what it is, we may have to play our cards a little more carefully. We won't do anything if it is one of the Doll Maker's empty bodies. Not right away. We will tell Rose there is nothing we can do, that it appears to be a mental health issue, and then come back and deal with the problem some time later."

"That could work," Rouge said, and tossed her dagger into the bag. "When do we leave?"

We were at the building in a little less than thirty minutes. It was already dark by the time we arrived, and I regretted not eating as much as I should've before leaving. Instead of finishing what we had got, I immediately started to pack up to go to the call. I had no idea why I felt such an urgency to come out and deal with this when we had so much other stuff on our plate. Maybe I was hoping for an easy win, something we could go to and finish in less than an hour. Nothing like a quick case to make you feel like you achieved something when things aren't going so smooth.

The Crossways Complex was at the corner of Dundas Street West and Bloor Street West. It was a strange area. Close to the subway, with some very nice hipster shops. If you cross the tracks going east you'd be in a pretty sketchy area, but if you head west you'd eventually find yourself in Bloor West village and High Park, which was a much nicer area. It really fit the stereotype of the whole wrong side of the tracks saying.

I parked the Jeep along the curb I assumed had to be visitor parking, and we walked into the lobby. There was nobody there to let us in right away, and I didn't want to stand around waiting for someone to come in or be heading out, so I gave Rose a call and asked if she could buzz us in. She seemed surprised that we were already there, but thanked me over and over again for being so quick before she finally told us the code. After that, we were in the building and heading up in the elevator.

"That's weird," Rouge said, and pointed to the buttons for the floors. "Not every day that you see a building with a thirteenth floor."

It was strange, and I didn't like it all that much. I'm not one to think about superstitious things very often, but some of them stick out like a sore thumb and make me uncomfortable. It made me feel even stranger because Rose lived on the fourteenth floor and said her friend, Mira, lived below her on twelve, but below her was the forbidden floor number.

I didn't mention that to Rouge but pushed the floor Mira lived on.

"Oh," Rouge said with more than a little shock in her tone. "And the thirteenth floor is where we're going, is it? That doesn't seem ominous at all."

I didn't say anything to that for fear our string of luck over the last couple of years, with cases that seemed easy turning to shit, might rear its ugly head. Instead, I looked up at the number call sign and watched as we slowly went up and up. I shifted the bag in my hand and took a deep breath. I tried to convince myself I was overthinking it all, worrying about what could be, instead of focusing on how I wanted it to turn out. If you go into something expecting the worst, don't be surprised when you find it.

The elevator door chimed, and we stepped out.

"What apartment is it?" Rouge asked, and I told her it was 1303. We turned left and headed down the hall.

It was quiet.

I wasn't expecting that. I thought from what Rose said we would hear the yelling and plates smashing the second we got to the floor. I walked slow, making sure we weren't making noise ourselves, but there was just nothing to hear aside from someone in 1306 quietly watching TV and laughing.

"It's too quiet," Rouge said, and I agreed. "I thought Rose said there was all kinds of noise coming from her friend's apartment all the time. I don't hear a thing from in there."

"I know."

"Do you think she was lying to us? That she's a few beers short of a six-pack?"

I shook my head. "If she hadn't brought up the words she heard her friend saying, I might think you were right, but I don't think she made that up. But I do think there is something off here. Maybe it really is on the twelfth floor, and she can hear the noise two floors up."

"Would she actually be able to hear someone say your name through two floors?" Rouge asked, and she had a point. I shrugged even though I knew there was no way that could be true. "Do you think this Mira person, or whatever is in that unit, saw us on the lobby camera, assuming this building has that set up?"

"Maybe," I said. I hadn't noticed a camera in the lobby, but if there was one, it was possible that Mira, or whatever was in Mira's unit, has seen us arrive. I didn't know if they or she would even know who I was by face. Then again, why would Mira, if she was now inhabited by a monster, just be watching the lobby and waiting for me to arrive? That didn't seem plausible either.

"So, how do you want to handle this? Do we stake it out, or just go for it?" Rouge asked me, as though I had any idea.

"I say we go for it," I told her, and knocked on the apartment door.

"Not even going to prepare, are you?"

"Nope. Sometimes it's just better to do than it is to think."

I saw someone come to the peephole and we waited a second before I heard the deadbolt turn and the door open a crack. From inside the dimly lit room, a woman of about forty-five peeked out, seeming a bit nervous as she did. She kept the chain on the door as if that would stop anyone who wanted to get it, but it struck me as strange. Would a monster be so cautious? Would they even bother to open the door for us, especially if they knew who I was by face? This didn't seem right to me.

"Can I help you?" the woman inside asked, her voice a bit shaky.

"I'm looking for Mira," I said and tried to give her as much of a friendly smile as I could to try and reassure her that we weren't killers. I was sure this woman was nothing more than she appeared to be.

"I think you have the wrong apartment. I live here alone and there's nobody named Mira here."

"Are you sure?" I asked and put my foot in the doorway in case she tried to shut it. "A neighbor of yours named Rose called and was concerned about noise coming from here."

"Rose? My name's Rose, and I didn't call anyone."

Oh, great. This was not good. This sounded like a setup and suddenly I was feeling very nervous.

"But if you're cops and you're here about the noise, you should go upstairs. Whoever moved in there this week has been driving me crazy."

"What kind of noises are you hearing?" Rouge asked.

"Banging and dragging all day and night long. The security in this building is a joke and the cops just keep telling me to call 311 and report it there. I did, and those people say they will send someone out in a month. A damn month! But since you're here now, maybe you officers could go up there and tell them to shut the fuck up before I have a meltdown."

"We can do that, but I just want to verify that you don't know the people up there at all," I said.

"I don't know anyone in this building. This is the city, not some small town where we all know what everyone is doing. I keep to myself and hope my neighbors do the same, even the assholes that think smoking weed in the stairwell is their right. I mean that stuff smells like a skunk's ass!" she said, making her voice louder at the last part as though it wasn't for me, but the neighbors in question who partook in the Devil's Cabbage. "So, please, go and talk to them and make them shut up, for the love of God!" She all but slammed the door in our faces after that. She started off being meek and mild, and then as soon as she found out we were there about noise bothering her, she put on a new mask.

"Well, this is starting to seem more than a little screwed up, Dill," Rouge said, and we walked away from the real Rose's apartment. "Any thoughts?"

"I have a few, and none of them are good for us. I mean, if that's Rose, then who called us? Clearly the caller is the issue here, but why make that story up and send us to her apartment? And if the caller is the actual monster, then we have no idea what kind of monster or demon we're actually going to be facing, if and when we find it, or get ambushed by it. This sucks."

"I agree. But I think the first place to start with all this is to head up to the unit above Rose's and see who, if anything, is there."

"If the monster isn't there, I guess we'll jump that bridge when we get to it. One thing I do know, is the caller is here in the building. She buzzed us in, so she has to be here. Which also means she knows we're here. And if she knows that, she'll surely figure out that the bluff is up and we are on to her, or it, or whatever the fake Rose is."

"Okay, then let's walk up to the fifteenth floor and wait it out a bit. If the caller is figuring we are going to find out they were lying and then come attack, we can take back the surprise by wait it out a bit. I brought some granola bars in my bag."

"You did?"

"I always pack a snack. You never know when you're going to need a little pick-me-up," she said, and we walked towards the stairwell.

"That's one of the many things I love about you, Rouge, you're always think—"

My words were cut short.

As I was opening the door to the stairwell, I was slammed in the chest with something thick and heavy. I felt the wind get knocked out of me as my feet came up off the ground and I sailed through the air. I couldn't see what was there. There were bursts of light flashing in my eyes as my brain considered giving up consciousness. When I hit the wall behind me, and I slid down to the ugly, carpeted floor, I think I did in fact lose consciousness for a second because when the world came back into focus, Rouge had snatched my bag from me and had pulled out both our daggers. I hadn't seen it happen, but there she was with a blade in each hand.

"Rouge," I called out weakly and tried to stand up, but my legs felt too wobbly to give it much of an effort. "What is it? What's in the stairwell?"

"No idea, but it's something with some octopus looking arms."

Great!

I hate tentacles.

I tried to get up again as Rouge stood at the ready in case the door opened. My body and head didn't want me to get up. I pushed though, needing to move in case the thing that hit me came back. It wasn't an easy thing to do, but eventually I made it and tried to blink the dizziness away. I asked Rouge for my dagger, and she said no.

"You worry about getting steady first. I'm not giving this to you when you look like you're going to tip over any second."

"Fair enough," I said and leaned over to pick up my bag. The least I could do was put on my gloves to hopefully paralyze anything that might come out. That was harder than I thought, and I nearly blacked out when all the blood rushed to my foggy melon.

"Take some deep breaths," Rouge said and then there was a bang at the stairwell door that made us both jump. "We need to do something."

"I'm open to suggestions."

"Me too," Rouge said and looked around. "I bet there is another stairwell down the other end of the hall."

"I'll buy that. And how will that help us?" I asked, not sure where she was going with this.

"Well, we're not going to win head on, but if we use the other stairs, walk up and over and come down, we might be able to surprise the damn thing."

"Great idea," I said, and held onto my bag. We walked quickly down the hall. I used the wall to offer some balance while I worked out the mess in my head. I needed to really work at protecting the thing. I was sort of attached to it.

By the time we were on the fourteenth floor and ran across the hall to get back to the stairwell where the monster was hiding out, I was ready to fight whatever it was. I took my dagger from Rouge and took a deep breath.

"You sure you're up for this? You were cross-eyed there for a second."

"I'm good now. Head's as clear as it can be." I took a deep breath and there was still a little bit of a fuzzy throbbing in there, but my vision and mind were clear enough. "This could be a few different monsters, or demons. For some reason, a lot of creatures that cause problems for us tend to have tentacles. It seems like a common trait for assholes in the universe."

"So, what you're saying is, you don't know what is in there, but it's more than likely a jerk. Got it. You ready then?"

"Always. You?"

She nodded and put her hand on the doorknob. I told her to open it and step aside and I would go in first. After all, I was more replaceable than she was. Literally replaceable.

Rouge opened the door slowly and quietly. Right off I could see even the floor was covered with a nest of pale, fleshy tentacles. They all moved strangely, as though they were more liquid than muscle. They pulsated and slid around the concrete steps, some of them moving up the wall as if they each had a mind of their own, searching out for prey. The sound was wet, and the aftermath of where they had been after moving on in to another place to search was a shiny mucus that I was almost sure I could smell. I watched this mass of squid-like arms of varying thickness, swirling and moving around and tried to figure out what it was, and where it's face was; or if it even had one. The longer I looked the more I was sure this was just some blob with spaghetti arms. There was no face or head that I could see. I had no idea what I was looking at, but it definitely wasn't one of the Doll Maker's empty bodies. This wasn't even something that might've come through a weak spot and collected things to make its body. This beast was in its full form, which meant that someone around the city had a porter, a human body that could be used as a gateway from other worlds and realms to this one.

Just another problem added onto a growing list of problems.

The fact that I couldn't tell what this creature was because I couldn't see its face meant there were only two ways to handle this. I could just go for it or I could run away. And I was never really great at running away from things.

With my gloves on and my dagger in my hand I rushed in and grabbed hold of the closest, thinnest tentacle I could find. The glove should paralyze the creature, even if it was only for a moment. Then, with it stuck and unable to move, I would be able to bury the dagger into it. My dagger is engraved with spells and curses that would rid this world of the creature. The problem was, since it was housed in its actual body, there was no sending it back to where it came from to reunite with its true form. It would go back to that world or realm and simply cease to exist.

Since there was no other choice here, it was kill it or possibly let it kill me or someone else. And since that someone else could be Rouge, there was no real choice here.

I reached out with my left hand and even through the gloves I could feel how soft and slimy the creature was. It felt like trying to grab a balloon full of ground meat and water. It almost pulled free before I could squeeze down on it and try to make the gloves do their job, and I felt a bit of panic fill me. I didn't want it to get loose and take another swing at me. It hit like a dump truck.

The gloves didn't seem to be working. The creature was moving and rippling in every direction, no doubt trying to turn around on me. I didn't let it go though, still tried to hold it as best I could, but man, it was strong. Since I knew it wasn't going to just hold still, and would eventually have more arms and other appendages flying at me, I buried the dagger's blade into the one I had a hold of.

"What should I do?" Rouge cried from behind me.

"Stay there for now," I called out, not sure what she could do. The thing was huge, spanning nearly two floors, and in a second it would be fully turned around.

Luckily, I was faster than it was. The creature let out a terrible sound as I quickly moved my hand back and forth so that the blade I'd put in it sawed away at the meat and finally severed the tentacle from the beast. The hacked off limb fell to the concrete floor with a wet thud, and I reached out and grabbed another and repeated the action. Hot, mucus-like liquid spewed from the dissections. The smell coming from the wounds was horrible. Like sour milk and ammonia mixed with shit. Not a great way to spend a Saturday night, if you ask me.

"STOP IT!!!"

The voice of the creature boomed through the stairwell. It was loud enough that it made my ears ring the same way they would after standing beside a speaker at a Motorhead concert. It hurt, but it was a good sign that it was screaming at me, because it meant what I was doing was hurting it, and not just simply annoying the damn thing. And if that was the case, I wasn't just going to stop because the son of a bitch decided to yell at me. It made me want to work harder and faster.

"Not likely," I said and kept sawing away at the second tentacle until it was lying severed on the floor.

The creature screamed and tried to pull its tentacles into itself to protect them from my blade. I managed to grab another and sever it, before it pulled the rest in, shrinking the mass of its body down to something nearly human-sized. When it did, it stood two steps below me, yet was nearly my height. The creature was a Creccal, and I was surprised. A Creccal is a demon from a nether region near the tip of a system with a pair of dead stars. They're usually docile. They float in their star system, eating space debris. They were kind of like space jellyfish, only not as stingy. I'd never heard a story of a violent one, or any even straying away from their home. So why this one was here and had set me up was something I needed to find out.

"Stay away from me, hunter," the creature said, and its milky flesh pulsated and throbbed as if it was about to let those appendages fly again.

"I'll stay back, if you tell me why you're here and why you set me up like that."

"I'll tell you nothing, hunter!" the Creccal all but spit at me. There was a rage building in its distorted face, which was long, wide, and looked like it was made of gelatin. As it yelled at me, the face wobbled and jiggled. "I will kill you both. I'll rip you apart and then I will earn my reward."

"Oh?" I said, getting something out of the demon without it meaning to give anything. "So, there's a reward out for me? I hope the prize is worth all the limbs you've already lost."

"The prize of you lying dead with your guts spilled out. Nothing but an empty shell. That's all the reward I need, hunter. But since you asked, yes, there is a larger price on your head. There's an entire universe out there that will hunt and kill all your kind. Not a single hunter left alive in any realm or universe. The Collective will be lost and forgotten."

"Who's paying the pot?"

"You'll learn all when you return to the universe's essence. When you're nothing more than cosmic dust, all will be made clear to you."

"I'm not the one dying here, demon. You are." At that I took off my jacket and t-shirt and showed the demon how doomed it was.

Over the years, I had covered my body in tattoos and scars. There are words and symbols in my flesh that can protect me from those that might want to invade me, but when it comes to some of these demons, what I wear on my skin is a weapon in and of itself. On the left side of my chest there is a certain symbol, a jagged circle with a vertical line going through the center and two small dashes to the right. Like a crucifix to a vampire, the sight of it was enough to get the desired effect.

The Creccal cried out and tried to cover its eyes with a milky arm that was shifting from something almost human, to a mound of tentacles. It stumbled backwards, down the stairs, and fell on the fourth one down. It tumbled like a water balloon to the landing below, and for a second I was sure the thing would just blow up into a horrible, white blood mess.

It didn't and I moved quickly down the stairs to it. I put my boot to its neck as it struggled to look away from the marking on my chest. It couldn't.

"You going to tell me who is paying you and others to have me killed?" I asked, and bent down towards the demon's face. "Or maybe I should just start carving you up until you're ready to talk."

"It's not just you they're paying for. It's all you hunters. Anyone the Collective has sent here is fair game at this point. All you hunters are fair game. There is a price on every one of your heads until you're all gone."

"For who? Who is behind it?"

"There is no one person behind it, but the one here helping out will do far worse to me than anything you can do. You can hurt me, even kill me, but if he finds out I told you something, I'm doomed. He will damn me to a place worse than torture or death, somewhere I can suffer for a millennia for betraying him. So, go ahead, hunter. Do your best at doing your worst."

I was at a loss for words. I had no idea who was behind this, or what could scare this Creccal so bad it was worried about being damned somewhere inescapable. What the hell was going on here? We came to the building, sure this would be just something nice and simple to deal with, and here we were, uncovering an even bigger pile of shit for us to plow through.

I opened my mouth to try and offer some sort of deal to the Creccal, about to fly from the seat of my pants and offer up some false glimpses of hope. If I played it right, I could serve up something so tempting and perfect that the Creccal would give me what I wanted and uncover who was behind it all.

Before I could even get the first word out, Rouge was next to me, and then rushed past me, nearly knocking me over. Before I could stop her, she buried her own knife in the thing's neck. I gasped and jumped back and watched as she tore the blade across and clean out. The Creccal made a horrid sound. Milky blood bubbled from its lips for a second before there was no more blood in the demon's severed head.

"What did you do?" I asked and stood up, unable to believe she had done that so fast. It was so violent, so brutal.

"It wasn't going to give us anything. Why waste any more time trying to sweet talk it while it tried to figure out a way to hurt you, or me?"

"It couldn't do anything. Not with this on my chest," I said, and pointed to the symbol. "I was going to try and find out who was behind all of this, who has put a hit out on all us hunters."

"You think it would've actually said anything?"

"I certainly had hoped so. I wasn't just doing all that talking to waste my own breath."

"Well, I'm sure this won't be the last one to come after us. My guess is, whoever sent this one here, has sent more, and they're all out there somewhere waiting for us to find them. Maybe one of them will be more forthcoming with information than this pile of Jell-O."

She had a point.

I looked down at the dead Creccal, lying there in an ever-growing pool of blood and saw it as hope draining away. I wasn't really mad at Rouge, but for the first time I wished I had been alone when I came to do this job. There have been times I'd been face to face with something way more dire than this, and not only did I manage to walk away from it, but was able to get something I needed as well. Whether it was information, a tool, or just where

I could find the person or monster who would be able to give me what I wanted, I had a way of coming out ahead, no matter how dangerous or hopeless it seemed. This wouldn't be that. And that was all on Rouge. Usually, she was there to save my ass, but standing in that stairwell in the Crossways building, I worried she might have just screwed us over.

Sunday

I woke up the next morning with late morning sunlight streaming into our bedroom and my phone ringing. I lazily reached for it, and missed the phone, and missed the call too. I groaned, sat up, and grabbed it off the side table and saw I'd actually missed three calls. They were all from Garcia. It was already after ten in the morning, but for me it was too early. I was sure he might think it was an emergency, but he knows I do a lot of my work later into the night, so I hoped this was worth pulling me out of a good dream for.

I considered simply turning the phone off and going back to bed. My chest still hurt from the little dance I had the night before, and I wasn't in the best of moods. It was no surprise that I was in a bit of a dark place after all that happened. Not that someone was trying to kill me, that's all part of the job. It was how for the first time in our relationship I felt like we weren't on the same page about something. I knew I would get over it, that maybe I was making a bigger deal out of it than I should, but after all this time together, it was the first real hiccup over something kind of major.

The phone started to ring again.

"Are you going to get that, or silence it?" Rouge asked before she pulled the covers over her head and turned over.

In the end I decided to answer it.

"I hope you have some good news for me, Garcia," I said as I hit the little green icon. "Tell me you solved that little case of yours and all is in order."

"I wish."

"So, is this a social call then?"

"I had two reports dropped on my desk about two bodies found last night. I feel like you might know about one of them."

"Was one of them a humanish thing with milky white skin with arms and a back covered in a bunch of tentacles?" I asked.

"What the fuck was that? I'm lucky that case didn't get dropped on my desk, but I saw the photos. I nearly lost my breakfast. I've never seen anything like that before, and people here are a little freaked out. Do we need to be concerned about this? What the hell was it?"

"It's a long story, but it's something called a Creccal. And you won't have to worry about it anymore. Forget about it. It tried to kill me, so I did what I had to. We had no choice."

I didn't feel like going into it all over again, but if I needed to bring him in on it, I would. There was no reason he needed to know about the hit on all the hunters, or anyone who worked for the Collective. The only other one I had to warn about this was Godfrey, though I was sure he could take care of himself.

"I don't doubt it. Are you guys clean on this, though? Did you get seen by anyone, or get caught on camera?"

"Maybe. But still, I doubt anyone will look too deep into this once it goes to the morgue. A creature like that, they will want to keep it all quiet. They always do."

"Who does?"

"The people above you. Your bosses. The city. Government. No way they will want this sort of thing to go public. The taxpayers don't want to know that there are things like a Creccal out and about in the world."

"Are you saying there's been things like this left around before?"

"Of course. When something's come through a porter, or find another way to get here, it's a little hard to clean up. You should have seen the state we left Innisfil in. Long story short, I'm not worried."

"Well, if you're not worried, then neither am I."

"So, what about the second one?" I asked, wondering if it was the guy I'd left in the bushes the other day.

"Another vampire victim. Body was found this morning around eight-thirty this morning at Kipling subway station."

"Same condition as the last one?" I asked. I shook Rouge awake, and then put Garcia on speaker phone.

"To a T. Nothing more than a husk found lying in the accessibility stall. Cleaners were doing their thing and noticed someone was lying on the floor. They looked under the door and called us. You want to come down and see for yourself?"

"I guess we should," I told him. "We can be there within the hour."

"Call me when you get here. There won't be a way to sneak you in, so dress like you're not two monster hunters. Low key is the best way to not get noticed."

I hung up and sat down hard on the bed. Not even ten minutes of being awake and I was already at work. This monster hunter needed a vacation, but I knew there was no way that was going to happen any time soon. With the Doll Maker's mess still to clean up, our apparent vampire, and now creatures hired to kill us, our plates were full.

"What time is it?" Rouge asked, rubbing her eyes. I told her and she let out a long moan. "Why do we have to get up? I feel so drained today."

"Didn't you hear what Garcia said? There was another body found."

"Vampire victim?" she asked, sitting up and letting out a long yawn as she stretched.

"Yeah. At Kipling station. Once again, the body was left in a public bathroom."

"And I guess we're going?"

"Didn't you hear anything we were saying?"

She shook her head. "I wasn't really paying attention. I was trying to get back to my sweet dream where we were sitting on a beach drinking fancy drinks and barely wearing any clothes."

"That does sound nice," I admitted, but knew we needed to stay focused on the job at hand and not go swirling down a fantasy, no matter how much more I'd prefer to be there with her. "We should really get ready and get going."

"You sure you wouldn't rather slip under these sheets with me for a little bit and see if we can make part of that dream come true?" she asked, pulling the blanket down just enough so that I could see she wasn't wearing anything at all under there. She rarely did, but the way she was looking at me and showing off her skin was driving me nuts.

"You know I would love to, you temptress, but we should really do this. When we find out who or what is doing this—"

"Yeah, but there will always be another case we will have to take care of, won't there?" she asked, cutting me off in mid-sentence.

I slumped a little. Obviously she was right. Since we had first met, which was also on the job, I had not really had much in the way of time off. There was always a case to work on, some monster, demon, or spirit that needed attention. And not just some run-of-the-mill thing either. Since I met her, the amount of serious cases over standard ones was way off-kilter.

"Maybe we should make a promise to each other then," I offered.

"What kind of promise?"

I sat down on the bed beside her and ran my fingers over her shoulder, watching as goosebumps broke over her skin. "Once this is done, as soon as we figure out what it is killing these people, we take a break. A well-deserved break."

"What about all the Doll Maker's customers running around? What about the things coming through because someone's put out a hit on all hunters?"

"They won't be going anywhere, and how much worse can things get if we take a week or two off to just get away from it all? You know, I've never had a vacation in my entire, very long life doing this."

"Never?"

I shook my head. I hadn't really thought I needed one. Well, I guess if you think about times I recovered from bad injuries, or had to wait until a new body was ready for me after I destroyed the one I had been in, I guess those could be considered a vacation if you wanted.

"What do you say we take care of this and then take off on a cruise, or go to Cuba, Mexico, or somewhere with a beach and no major city?"

"I love it! But I think I will need a new bikini. The old one I have might not fit great anymore."

"Maybe we can go somewhere bathing suits aren't the set rule, but more like something optional," I said, winking at her and giving her a kiss. "Now, let's get ready before I lose all sense of control and just rip those sheets off of you."

And just like that, I had forgotten about everything that happened the night before. It's funny how that works.

Forty-five minutes later we met with Garcia and were led through the taped-off crime scene. There were a lot of people standing around on the non-police side of the tape trying to get a look at what might be going on. No doubt they wanted to see a gurney being wheeled out of there, a human body shape under a sheet, when suddenly, an arm slips out that is torn up or covered in blood. Humans are so strange the way they are drawn to death, yet are terrified by the idea of their own mortality.

I knew if that was what they were waiting for, they'd be standing around for a while. Forensics doesn't move as fast in reality as they do on TV shows. CSI and shows of that nature make evidence-gathering seem like some wild, fun adventure, which it really isn't. There was a lot of meticulous work to be done. It isn't something you could rush.

Rouge and I walked past them all, dressed like the most normal people ever. I wore some terrible, beige slacks with a dress shirt, tie, and suit jacket. It felt like I was wearing someone else's skin. I was glad I had these clothes though, something I'd picked up to go out for a dinner with Rouge which required a jacket and tie, but I felt like an imposter then, and now as well. On a good note, I looked like two of the other suits that were working the scene, so nobody paid me much mind.

Rouge had her red hair pulled back in a ponytail with a silk scarf covering it. She wore something resembling the business attire Scully might have worn in an episode of the X-Files. The outfit and hair made her look like she was all business. She was still getting some attention, partially because she was still very shapely in her outfit, but I'm sure there were some there that were just curious about who this woman being brought to a crime scene could be. Some people had not gotten over the notion that women could be great at anything, just like there are people that thought dark chocolate tasted better than milk chocolate. Who are you even?

"So, we have some information on the victim," Garcia said as we walked into the horrible-smelling bathroom. I couldn't believe how much the place reeked of old piss and stale cigarettes. I avoid public washrooms whenever I can. Some smells are hard to get out of your nose once they get in there. "His name is Freddy Hughes," Garcia continued. "Thirty-two years old. Works evening shifts at some building downtown. Cameras have him getting off the last train of the night, and then heading up here to the washroom and buses."

"Anything on this level, or near the washroom?" I asked, but I'd looked around when we arrived and seen nothing.

Garcia shook his head. "There are cameras on the bus platforms, but not a lot, and the TTC supervisor I spoke to said that none of them catch this area."

"Well, I had to ask."

There were people standing at the far-right side of the washroom where the accessibility stall was. As the three of us walked over, they moved aside as though we were Moses and they were the Red Sea. I looked inside and there was our victim, a husk of what he once had been. He was a shrivelled thing, looking frail and broken there on the ugly, tiled floor.

"Why bathrooms?" was the first thing Rouge said to break the silence. "Is it always bathrooms, or just the last two?"

"No. They were all in washrooms, aside from one. Our third victim, the only one that was a female, was found near a park bench in Trinity-Bellwoods Park. Aside from that, all the victims were male, and found in washrooms, mainly very public ones. Do you think that means something?"

Rouge shrugged.

"I don't think it does," I offered, but I didn't know for sure. "The places the killer's picking are all quiet and offer some privacy, I guess. I think what we need to figure out is the motivation for the killing and the means."

"It's obviously a vampire," one of the uniform cops said behind us, and when I turned around, I saw he wasn't joking or trying to be a smart ass.

"We need proof before we jump to conclusions, Castle," Garcia snapped. "And if you walk out there and start spraying off bullshit like that in ear shot of anyone else, I swear you will be stuck on traffic duty for the next twenty years. If one single newspaper prints some bullshit about vampires, heads are going to roll. We crystal clear on that? Got it?"

The cop named Castle blushed and looked as nervous as anyone could. Garcia didn't seem to want to let it go at that, though. He turned and looked at everyone standing in that room as he crossed his arms, clearly trying to look as menacing as he could. It didn't do much to me, but I wasn't someone who had to answer to him.

"If anyone in this room thinks they are going to go out there and start telling the press, or their friends, or anyone they share a bed with, what they see in here, I will tell you this: there are worse things than an unemployment line waiting for you. This case isn't just some gang banger, or angry drunk who killed someone. We don't know what this is, and until we do, our lips stay sealed. Any questions?"

One of the uniforms timidly raised their hand and Garcia chuckled a little at that.

"What is it, Yuri?"

"Who are these two? Are they with RCMP or something?"

"They are experts in cases like this. That's all I will say. If we have any hope at solving this mess, it'll be thanks to them. And if anyone out there asks who they are, you tell them what, Yuri?"

"Uhm, that it's a…uh…need-to-know…uh…thing…and they don't…need to know?" he said, more of a question than it was a statement.

"Exactly. Nobody outside these walls needs to know anything unless I tell them personally. That means if your supervisor asks, or your FTO, you tell them they need to come see me. The only way we keep a lid on this damn thing is to keep a tight lid on the thing. Now keep making your notes and mind yourself."

After he was done, Garcia turned back to us and shook his head. I whispered the word "kids" and that gave him a bit of a laugh and he shook his head.

"You see anything in here that gives you any clues?" he asked, and I stepped into the stall and knelt down next to the dead man. Again there was no sign of trauma, nothing that showed how the person could have been drained. I looked at the fingernails as well to see if there was any skin, a sign of a struggle, but from what my eyes could see, there was nothing there to make me believe the victim had been able to fight off whoever, or whatever, had done this to them.

"There's not much to go on here that I can see," I admitted, and looked up and around the stall. I checked the walls, the back of the door, and even the ceiling overhead thinking if this was a demon, there might be some kind of symbol left behind. Demons loved leaving a tag like some sort of thug or graffiti artist. Sign it as a little bit of a *fuck you* to whoever might find the body. "It doesn't even look like the guy put up any sort of struggle. Who gets this done to them and doesn't even put up a fight at all?"

"It's like that with all of them. No sign of wounds or struggles," he said and walked out of the stall. "It's so frustrating. Usually there's a clear sign, you know? A hint at what and who could have done something like this. But these bodies are a husk and a mystery."

"We have two people looking into any stories of actual vampires that might be floating around," Rouge said, whispering very quietly as she leaned in towards Garcia, clearly not wanting the others to hear what she was saying. "We also have them checking on any otherworldly things that could do something like that to a body."

"So, you two still have nothing?" he asked, sounding very disappointed.

"We're working on it," I told him, and that was the best I could do. "I personally don't think it's a you-know-what, but we want to keep our options open on this. If we get something, even a thin lead, we will pursue it and let you know right away."

"Thanks, but I really wish—"

"Uh, Detective?" Yuri called out from behind Garcia.

"What now?" Garcia asked, and turned to the uniform officer looking pissed off and short tempered.

"I think there's something here in the garbage can. I…don't want to touch it." Yuri looked at us, his eyes wide, and his pallor had taken on the colour of slate.

"Good. Don't." Garcia rushed over and pulled open the metal door cover of the garbage can mounted in the wall. He pulled out the can, and from it a black, shiny bag. He lowered it to the tiled floor as Rouge and I stepped up beside him. "You have a light on your phone, Dillon?"

I nodded and pulled it out. As soon as I turned on the light and aimed it into the abyss of trash, I saw why the uniformed cop had looked so pale when he told us about what might be in there. It was something alright, I just didn't know what it was exactly. My brain had an idea of what it was looking at, but couldn't make sense of it. It was familiar and yet strange. At first my mind processed it as a discarded snakeskin, but why was it so big?

"Is that what I think it is?" Rouge gasped from my side and I shrugged.

"I need some gloves," Garcia called out and let go of the bag. One of the other officers, whose name I didn't know, passed a pair of blue latex gloves to the detective. Garcia slipped them on and reached into the bag. "You've got to be fucking kidding me."

"Holy shit!" Rouge said, sounding a little breathless and taking the words right out of my mouth.

It was a snakeskin, or at least looked like one. Only instead of it being a long, cylindrical husk, the whole thing had a human shape to it. It was moister than a snake skin too, with clumps of clear fluid here and there which resembled hair gel. I had never seen anything like it before.

"I need someone to go get me an evidence bag," Garcia called out, and then shook his head. "No. Wait. This won't fit in that. We're going to need another body bag for this. Shit."

I leaned in with my light aimed on the shrugged-off skin. I looked for some sign of a face shape, whether it was a man or a woman, anything that might stand out. It was disgusting and smelled a bit like dirty socks. I couldn't see anything that looked male or female, and because of how transparent it was, I wasn't even sure if I could determine what race it was, but there was no doubt it was human skin. I could see little hairs, the texture of follicles, and on the hands, I was sure I could make out the swirls and ridges of fingerprints.

"I'm guessing you know what this is now, Dillon?" Garcia whispered to me, holding the discarded skin suit.

"No. Not at all. But I think at this point we can rule out the idea of it being a vampire. There is nothing in any lore about this."

"Great. So instead of vampires, we have something that drains people and sheds skin. So much better than Count Dracula."

"Was anything like this found at any of the other scenes?" Rouge asked, and Garcia shook his head.

"Nothing that was brought to my attention, but if this is here, I think we can assume there was something like this at or near the other crime scenes. Not that it will still be there." Garcia turned towards Yuri. "I think you may be getting a letter of commendation for this one, Yuri."

"We should probably let Kajal and Godfrey know about this," I whispered to Rouge, and took a few photos of the skin. "If they have any leads, or ideas, this might connect the dots to it even more."

"Should I even ask who they are?" Garcia said when he heard the names.

"Better not to," I told him, and we left shortly after.

We were back in the Jeep and heading towards Godfrey's shop. We were both strangely quiet on the drive over. I didn't have much to say because my head was trying to wrap around the idea of something that could be killing people and then walking out of its skin. I'd never heard of any creature other than some reptiles or spiders that did that sort of thing, and those were small things from Earth, not demons or monsters from another planet or galaxy. There are all kinds of strange things in the universe and the realms that surround it, but never in any of my experiences had I seen something like this.

"What are you thinking about?" Rouge asked me, finally cutting through the silence in the car.

"Just about what we saw, and wondering what it could be. What about you?"

"Just wondering if you're still mad at me about last night," she said quietly, staring out the passenger's side window.

"We don't need to worry about that right now." To be honest, I'd let that go before we left the house, and I really didn't want any of those stressful, nagging feelings getting in the way of what we were doing. "We can just let it go for now."

"Can we?" she asked, and looked at me. I was surprised to see she seemed mad more than anything else. "You didn't seem like you were going to be able to let it go last night. You barely talked to me when we got home before bed."

"It's fine. It's done, and we can just let it go." I wanted it to be fine, to just be something we could forget about, even if it did rear its head in my mind now and then. Some things are better left buried; even if you have to keep throwing dirt on it as it tries to rise from the grave.

"It's not fine. You think I did a bad job. You clearly think I acted too rashly, and instead we should have kept talking to that thing that wanted you dead."

"I would have just liked to try and get more answers, but if there are any to get, we will find them on our own. For all I know, you saved us some time just being done with it. Who knows?"

"But you still think I made a mistake, right?"

I felt like I was walking into a trap. Did I feel like she had made the wrong decision? Yes, I did. Did I think it would help to dwell on it? Not at all. It was done with, and if there was more to come of it, we would deal with it in the moment. I would have liked to find out if there were others hunting us down, where the porter was that was acting as a gateway to Earth, and who was the one or ones behind the move, but that wasn't in the cards. When she cut the Creccal's head off, the time to get answers was cut off.

"Well? Do you think I made a mistake?"

"Would I have done it at that moment? No, I think I would have tried to get more answers first, but eventually, it would have all ended the same way," I told her, and figured it was better just to smooth things over than to try and fight over something that was already done and couldn't be undone. "In the end, you might've just saved us the hassle. There's no saying the Creccal would have given us any answers anyway, and in that case, it would have been a huge waste of time and energy. Things happen for a reason, so I'm sure this is the way it should have been."

"So, you're not angry with me?"

"Not at all," I told her, hoping it didn't sound like I was lying a bit, even if it felt that way. "But maybe we come up with a word or a gesture so we can let the other know that we're going to cut a monster's head off next time."

"Like a safe word?"

"Sure, only not so safe for them. How about Saskatoon Berry?" I asked and laughed a little, thinking about a kids' show I'd once watched where a character named Russell ate too many of them and got sick.

"Why that word?" she asked, also laughing, a good sign.

"How many times in your life will you ever say it in normal conversation?" I asked her. "Unless we are excited about going home to watch *Teepee Tales*, there's little or no reason to say it at all, especially if we are fighting monsters and demons."

"Good point," she said, and reached over to turn on the radio. She started to bop up and down in her seat as The Ramones came on the radio asking if we wanted to dance.

That seemed to improve her mood, which was better. I preferred us on good terms, even if I still was a little uncomfortable with how things had gone. I wanted to be honest with her, and wanted to let it all go, but there was something in the back of my head that I just couldn't shake. It was over and done with, but still, seeing her like that, so angry and violent had been a shock. It was just something I needed to keep an eye on.

Fifteen minutes later we parked the Jeep and walked through the door of Godfrey's shop. He was sitting behind the front counter, a hot cup of something steaming in front of him. He didn't even look up at us as his nose was buried in a thick, old-looking book.

"Whatever you're looking for, you won't find it here," he said with his thick, Jamaican-like accent.

"What if we're looking for you?" I said and tried not to laugh, even if it was a bad joke.

Godfrey looked up and closed the book. "You really are in a hurry for this information, aren't you?"

"There was another body found, so yeah. But we also have some new information I think might come in handy."

I walked across the shop and pulled my phone out. I showed him the photos of the skin found in the trash at the crime scene. His eyes went wide for a second and I didn't think that was very promising. I wanted more of an "ah-ha" moment, less of an "oh-my-god" look.

"What is that?" he asked, and took the phone from me. His fingers went to work zooming in on the image as his face moved through an array of disgusted looks.

"Body was found at Kipling station, and this was found in the trash a few feet away. Looks like someone shed their skin and dumped it either before or after the killing. We were hoping this might fit into place with something you would know."

"Shed skin like a snake? What the hell does that?" he said and handed the phone back. "There is no species I can think of that drains a body of all blood and fluids and sheds skin like this. But I guess the vampire theory is out now?"

"Vampires out and giant snake-monster is in," Rouge said, sounding as dismayed as I was.

"I'll keep looking though and add the skin thing to my parameters." He took a sip of his drink and leaned back in his chair.

"But seriously, that is some messed up shit, Dillon. I've seen a lot of weird things, but that is in the top ten for sure."

"It's probably in my top twenty," I told him, because as a hunter, I had definitely seen things much stranger than that.

"For me, it takes top spot," Rouge admitted, and I found that hard to believe since she had seen a talking doll, a living sex doll, a wig that was alive, and the monster we dealt with the night before. Those were stranger for sure. Even the Hellion we had run into in the early days of our relationship should have ranked higher than this.

"How is everything else going for the two of you?" Godfrey asked and slid the book across the counter, closer to the register.

"Oh, you know, same old same old," I said and then told him about the squishy adventure we'd been involved in the night before. I broke it down from the original call, to finding the Creccal in the stairwell, and everything we were told by the monster about how all hunters were on a hit list.

"You think I'm added to that list since I help the two of you out?" he asked, and was I really surprised that his first concern was for himself?

"If I were a betting man, I would be betting against your safety. If they are after us, they are after anyone involved with the Collective, and that means you."

"Wow. Thanks for being gentle and offering a little false hope," he said, sounding sad. "Are things ever going to be nice and easy like they used to be?"

"I've asked myself the same question more times than I care to remember over the last couple of years," I admitted. "What I want to know is who is behind this, and where is the porter they are using to get here?"

"You think they're using a porter?"

I nodded. "They have to be. The Creccal was in its real body. It wasn't just a spirit with things pulled to it, or in the body of someone dead. This was a Creccal in living colour. The stuff of nightmares."

"Well, this makes things more fun. So, not only do you have to hunt down the rest of the Doll Maker's customers, while also finding out what strange creature is sucking the lives out of humans, but now there is someone around with a porter letting monsters and demons come to Earth in their true forms."

"And now you're all caught up," Rouge said with a laugh, even though there was little humor in her voice.

"I have to admit, I'm not very stoked about someone having a porter," I told him, and was about to admit something to Rouge for the first time. "The last time we had one of them, a Hellion had been let through, and I nearly died. That's not something I want to face a second time."

"I don't blame you," Rouge said. "I was there and remember how scared we both were."

"And porters aren't something you just stumble upon or find ads for on Kijiji. They're people who have something special living inside them, and most times they're unaware of the gift or curse. Not every person can become one. If you were to take a regular human and just try and make them a porter, the gateway would just tear them to shreds. These are people who are searched out and harvested. You're lucky to find one every hundred years, and yet here we are only years away from the last one we had, dealing with the same situation again. I don't like it."

"What's to like about it?" Godfrey said and drank more of his steaming drink. "We don't even know for sure the porter they have is human. It could be a creature from somewhere else that was brought here for this."

"I never thought of that," I said, and it was true, I hadn't. I'd just assumed it was a human because how hard it would be to bring something for another planet or realm here to use as a porter. Unless this was another one of the Doll Maker's customers which was given a body specifically for this purpose, which only made everything else more fucked up. This would mean they either tracked down a human with these traits, stole their soul and gave it to a monster to become a gateway, or during the process of taking the soul out, the Doll Maker found someone who was more than just an empty vessel.

I shared my thoughts with them, and Rouge groaned like she had just been told some terrible news about her dog.

"What are you going to do about all this?" Godfrey asked, and to be honest I wasn't even sure how to answer that. "Is there one thing you are going to focus on more than another?"

I shook my head. "Until I can figure out what it is killing these people, I think I just have to sit and wait. There is no way I can hunt down something when I don't know what it even is, and it seems to have no killing pattern that I can figure out."

"There's nothing?"

"Not that I can see. Five victims in all. Four of them are men, one is a woman. Four were killed in bathrooms, one killed in a park. First was killed in a shopping mall in Etobicoke, next in High Park, third in Trinity-Bellwoods Park, fourth in a restaurant in St. Jamestown, and this last one at a subway station in Etobicoke. They're all over the city. Only thing in common is the way they were killed."

"And the skins, right?" he asked and made a creeped out, shivering motion.

"They don't know that for sure. This was the only scene where the skin was found, but they weren't really looking in the other places, and now it's too late to go back and try to find anything."

"So, you're going after the porter then?"

"No. I don't know where the source is."

"The Creccal wouldn't say?" Godfrey asked, and before I could say anything, Rouge jumped in.

"I messed up. I saw what it did to Dillon, and I was so mad that I cut its head off before Dillon could interrogate it."

"Damn! You cut a Creccal's head off because it hurt *him?*" Godfrey said and burst out laughing. "Dillon, you have the most badass girlfriend-slash-bodyguard I've ever seen. Wow! You get 'em, Rouge!"

I couldn't believe it. Godfrey was siding with her. Was I wrong here? Was I the one who was mistaken in how we handled the situation? I took a breath and thought about it. If Rouge hadn't been there, would I have bothered to listen to lies from the Creccal and tried to get answers, or would it have turned out the exact same way as it did because I normally don't take a lot of bullshit from monsters?

Well, there you go. I was the one in the wrong.

"Well, Dillon thought we should have questioned the monster more. He thinks I reacted rashly."

"Like the thing would have told you anything close to the truth, Dillon," Godfrey said as if he was scolding me. "What would you have been able to offer a pale, squid, ugly-ass Creccal to make it tell you anything you wanted to know?"

"I get it," I admitted and wrapped an arm around Rouge. "She was right. I might be getting soft in my old age."

"Soft in the head, maybe," Godfrey said and cackled an old, witchy laugh. "But at least you have this woman here to keep you on the right path. Maybe you should follow her lead instead of trying to dictate how you guys hunt."

"You might be right."

After leaving Godfrey's I thought it might be a good idea to head over to Kajal's book shop. I thought that if we showed up and gave him the information about the shed skin the cops found at the crime scene, he might be able to narrow down the search, even a little bit. I parked and headed to the door, but when we got there, we found the shop was closed. I knocked on the glass door.

Nothing.

I called his number, but I only had his old one, and it seemed to have been disconnected. Who knows how long ago he'd done that, but I had no way to get a hold of him otherwise. I wish I had thought to get his new one the last time we'd been here.

"What now?" Rouge asked when she found out I couldn't get a hold of Kajal.

"Guess we go home and wait for something else to happen," I told her. There was little else to do but wait for more information, or something else to go wrong.

Monday

The next day seemed like it was going to be very uneventful. *Seemed* being the important word here. We got up and went about our day as though there wasn't a worry or care in the world: no monsters, no porter, nothing but the domestic life we so seldom seemed to enjoy these days. We took our time and enjoyed a nice breakfast while we watched some YouTube channels we're subscribed to, went for a walk with the dog around the neighborhood, and then headed to a local restaurant that had opened up earlier in the month that apparently made some of the best ramen. The best, I wasn't so certain, but it was for sure some of the priciest soup I'd ever bought.

After that we drove home and as we pulled into the driveway, my phone rang. I groaned. I was positive it would be Garcia with news that another body had turned up. It wasn't. It was an unknown number.

"Dillon here," I said.

"The monster hunter?" a woman asked on the other end in a near hushed voice, as though she was whispering so her mom or dad wouldn't hear.

"Maybe. Who's this?"

"I...uh...this might sound weird, but do you do exorcisms too?" she asked me, and the question took me back a bit. This was a first. Out of all the calls I've received over the years, I've never been contacted for an exorcism.

"Tell me what made you call me, and I will tell you if I can help," I said, and put the call on speaker phone so that Rouge could hear too. She tried to ask me what the call was about, but I motioned for her to not say anything; just listen.

"Okay. I can't believe I'm calling you about this, but I'm at my wits' end, and I'm really worried about someone I know. I live in a rooming house near Bathurst and Bloor, just north of there," she began, sounding a little less nervous, but there was still a bit of hesitation in her voice. "I've been here for about two years, know almost everyone who lives here. Well, I thought I did. Someone here is acting so strange, and well, I think there is something in him that is...how do I say it without sounding nuts...evil."

"How long has he been living there?" I asked, needing more information.

"He was here before I moved in, but I don't know how long."

"How old is he?"

"Not sure. I'm not so good with trying to figure out how old someone is, but if I had to narrow it down, my guess would be that he's in his fifties. I don't know him super well. We don't hang out or anything, but I see him almost every day and there's something really messed up going on here."

"Okay. So, your neighbor, not a great friend, has been acting a little strangely as of late. Why do you think he's in need of my services? What is he doing that makes you think he needs an exorcist?"

She said nothing, but I could still hear her breathing heavy. I looked over at Rouge, who made a shrugging gesture, showing me she was as lost as I was on what was going on with this woman and her neighbor.

"Over the last month, he looks at me and other people here like he doesn't know us at all. I've tried to say hi to him and he passes me by like I'm a stranger," she started, and to me that didn't sound all that strange. This city was full of people who preferred to be left alone. Even if someone had been social before, the city has a way of turning people into hermits. "If that was the only thing, I might be able to ignore it. Like I said, we aren't best friends or anything. I did try to just let it all slide, to just assume he was going through something, maybe stopped taking meds he was on, but there's something else. This is going to sound strange, and gross maybe, but I think…I think he might be killing and maybe even eating stray animals."

"Okay," I said slowly, not wanting to blurt out a huge *What!* at that statement. It was better to just stay composed with people reporting weird things. Better to let them assume no matter how off something might seem to them, for me it was no big deal. But someone eating stray animals, not an everyday thing in my line of work. "What makes you think he is killing and possibly eating strays?"

"I don't want to sound like some noisy neighbor or a Karen or anything," she said, and I was starting to wonder if this was just another setup. Was it all going to turn into the same type of call that we got with the Creccal? Two cases in a row that were just something trying to set us up? I had to keep an open mind about this and try to hear if there was anything that sounded like it was another trick.

"Just tell me what you saw that makes you think that. I don't judge," I said and smirked at Rouge. I do judge, very much, but she didn't need to know that.

"Once or twice a day I see him come to the building with a ratty-looking cat, one you can tell has been living in alleys for some time. He takes them to his room, and every single time you can hear the cats make some weird-ass sounds. Kind of like crying, but it doesn't last long. And then…"

"Then, what?" I asked as she trailed off and went silent.

"Uh…you ever sit in a room with someone who eats food loud, smacking their lips and making *yum yum* noises" she asked, and made a sound as though she was gagging at the thought of what she was telling us.

"Yeah," I told her, admitting I have heard some nasty sounds like that before.

"Well, that's what I hear. And then, a few hours later he goes back out and sometimes comes back with another one. The rooms here are small. There is no way he has thirty or forty cats living in there. Cats smell. If someone has a cat in their room, which is not allowed here anyway, you can smell that horrible ammonia smell seeping through the walls, and from under their door. But there is nothing coming from there. No cat smells at all."

"Okay, but why would you think he was possessed and not just some weirdo who is killing cats?" I asked, because that was a possibility. People can have all kinds of breaks with reality, and when they do, there is no saying what they are capable of. In my experience, humans are just as capable of horrors as a demon is, given the right circumstances.

"On top of that, he keeps speaking something that sounds like Latin. Repeating it over and over again like he's in his room chanting it. I recorded it, just so I could run it through Google translate, but nothing comes back. I don't think it's gibberish. It sounds like he is saying something."

"Do you still have the recording? Can you play it for me?" I asked, and if she did, it would make me trust this a lot more.

"Hold on," she said, and I could hear her fumbling around. "I don't want to play it too loud. I'm at my place and I don't know if he's home, so I don't want him to hear me."

"That's fine. Just play it quietly and hold the phone to the speaker."

"Okay," she said, and it was followed by more shuffling sounds and then it started.

I put the phone closer to my ear and Rouge leaned closer to it as well. I slowed my breathing and waited for it to start. When it was over, I asked her to play it again. When she did, I knew for certain the man living next door to her wasn't possessed. He didn't need an exorcist. The man living next to her was a K'Unlin. I knew the language well enough but hadn't seen one of them here for over a hundred and twenty years or so. My guess was that it was another one of the Doll Maker's customers, yet another one to deal with. Unless, of course, this was another setup, but because the speaker was a man for sure, and the caller was a woman, I hoped this one wasn't another asshole wanting to kill me. With the recording she had, I really doubted she was trying to set me up, but you never know. We had to be more cautious going into this one.

"So," she said when she stopped playing the tape, "he's possessed, right?"

Rouge was nodding but didn't say anything.

"Well, I don't know about possessed, but there is something off about this, so yes, I can look into it for you," I told her and motioned for Rouge to grab a pen and paper from the glove box. "Can I get the address and his apartment number, as well as a description?"

She quickly shot off all the information to me, and Rouge jotted it down. When she was done, she asked me how much something like this cost, because she didn't have the best job, hence why she was living in a rooming house. I explained that in a case like this, unless we find something, there is no fee. The truth was, we wouldn't charge her anything if this turned out to be a K'Unlin. If we showed up and found it was another of the Doll Maker's problems, we would get him outside and deal with it and pretend as though we never found him at all. When the cops went sniffing around, which they may or may not, they would speak to her, and more than likely she would tell them she hired me because she thought he was possessed. If we were ever questioned, I would just say that I never ended up finding him and hope that would be that.

That was thinking very far into the future, though. We still needed to go there and see if any of this was true.

There are times when we are on the job, and back in the day long before I'd ever met Rouge, that I'd be bored out of my mind waiting for something to happen. Doing a stakeout, alone or with someone you like, gets to be a brain drain. I'd be stuck in a car, or hiding in an alley, or waiting in someone's basement for a sign that the monster I was called for would show up. This time, sitting in the Jeep with Rouge, it was a little tougher. Instead of being bored, looking out the window waiting for something to happen, we didn't even know exactly what we were looking for. Normally it was a monster or demon made up of all kinds of trash, but instead we were looking for an older man with a thin white beard, who dressed liked a guy who shopped at an army surplus store. Who knew there were so many people in the area who dressed like that in the area?

"Did you bring any snacks?" Rouge asked while she looked in the back seat where my bag—and nothing else—sat.

"No. I forgot to pack anything, but we're close to a lot of stores over there near the subway station. Want to make a run for us?" I asked her, because I didn't really want to do it.

"How could you forget treats?" she huffed and held out her hand. "If I have to go, then you're the one who's paying, so hand over some cash, Dill Pickle."

I handed her my credit card, but she wouldn't take it.

"No. That's not going to work. There are so many little shops around here. Most of them won't want to take a credit card. So, it's cash or you settle on getting Pizza Pizza, that's it. You want some good coffee and snacks, or cardboard covered in low quality cheese? Let's be honest, we both work better on coffee and pastries."

She had a point. I handed her two twenties and told her to get anything she could. She promised she'd buy only the best and left me there in the car alone. I turned the radio on when she shut the door, and tuned in to a country music station where someone was singing about pants being painted on, a pickup truck, and cold beer. Country music wasn't my usual cup of tea, but the songs could be catchy, and they offered nothing so deep or heavy that might distract me from what I needed to focus on. So instead of bobbing and singing along to something I loved, I was able to give my full attention to the small, three-story red brick building in front of me where our suspect was supposed to live. So far only two people had come or gone from it, and they were both dark-skinned, and didn't dress like DeNiro from *Taxi Driver*.

While I watched the building waiting to see our guy, I started to ponder the case—no, the cases—we were already dealing with before the call came through. The most pressing one, of course, was the killer who was draining people. I wanted to do my best to look at the case with a clear head, so I'd notice anything that might pop up. I didn't need to see a file, or to look at the reports on my phone. I just had to go back through everything we already knew about what had happened and see what fit, what was the common thread, and what could be the single thread that would unravel everything.

The first thing was to think over the areas each of these people were killed at. Was there anything about them that was connected? A parking lot, three bathrooms, and a place where there was a lot of bushes to provide ample cover. Obviously the three bathrooms were easy to connect, but the other two broke the connection. The next part was the fact that all five victims were found in very public places: two parks, a mall, a Chinese restaurant and a subway station. Why was this killer willing to do it somewhere they could get caught? Why not in a dark alley, in a building stairwell, or in someone's apartment? Was the killer not just a killer but a thrill seeker? Were they just as attracted to murder as they were to the feeling of nearly getting caught? Every single case had a real chance of someone stumbling in on it as it was going on. I had no idea if that was a key, but it seemed as though it could be something to keep in the forefront of motivation.

There was also the timeline of each killing. I wished there was something more obvious with that. Like someone who kills every full and new moon, murders once a week or month. At least there would be a pattern to follow, something that made sense. Yet, this killer was all over the place with the killings. Sometimes there was a week between one to the next, others it was a day or two. There were no two the same, and that made them almost impossible to make a timeline for when they might strike again. For all I knew, they were getting ready to kill someone right now, while I was staked out waiting for a cat-eater to show up. Not that I could just start the hunt for our fluid-draining murderer. I still had no idea where to start in order to hunt the killer down.

Nothing aside from the skin it left behind.

I wanted to hold on to that evidence as being a huge key in solving this. It was so strange, and so out of the ordinary from anything I had dealt with before. In all the years I'd been on Earth, I'd seen many strange, and horrific things, but the skin was one of the weirdest for sure, and I had to believe it was the key to finding the monster behind it all. It wasn't just a small piece of the puzzle. I was sure it would be the thing to take us to the finish line. The problem was, I had no idea what it meant, but I was certain it meant something.

If only I was able to get my head around what that was.

I jumped a little as I was pulled out of my thoughts when Rouge opened the door and slid into the Jeep.

"Miss me, stranger?" she asked, and I was greeted by a rich smell of coffee and baked goods.

"I did, and not only am I happy to see you, but my stomach is anxious to see what you brought."

"That might have to wait," she said and motioned out the windshield to where the building was. I followed and saw our guy. At least, I was pretty sure it was our guy. He was dressed just like she said he would be: ratty jeans, a discoloured army coat, and mud-caked work boots. Even more, he had an equally ratty cat in his arms as he walked into the building.

"Shit," I whispered. "I had been hoping we'd get here and see him coming out and then follow him."

"Okay. So, what are we doing now?"

"Now we have to wait for him to go back out. Hope you brought a lot of snacks from this place."

"Well, there's no change, if that lets you know."

I smiled and took the bag and my coffee. It was time to sit and wait.

It was nearly five hours later when our guy came back out of the rooming house. I looked at the clock on the Jeep's dashboard and saw it was almost ten-thirty, and the nightlife in the area didn't seem to care that it wasn't the weekend still. There were groups of people stumbling around, probably coming from or going to a bar or party, others were walking along solo puffing on huge, greasy looking blunts, and all in all, most of them looked like they were holding on to the way a weekend rolls.

Our guy looked normal, as far as the area went. He was wearing the same clothes as when he walked in with the cat. He hadn't changed clothes, didn't come out with a suspicious garbage bag. Nothing out of the ordinary. But we knew better, or at least I hoped we did.

"How are we going to handle this?" Rouge asked as I sat the remnants of the snacks down.

"I will go first and start to follow him. You wait forty-five seconds, and then start to trail me. Not too close."

"Why not go together?"

"You kind of stand out a lot, and I don't want him to notice us at all. I look like any old Joe Blow, so I will blend in and be a ghost. But stay kind of close. Don't let me get out of sight."

"Well," Rouge said with a shrug. "I guess you know best, right?"

"That sounds sarcastic," I told her, and opened the door.

"It's not sarcastic, it's just the truth. How many times have I saved your ass since we met?"

"Point taken. Okay, just make sure you follow close by and be ready for anything."

"I think I can manage. What's the worst that could happen?"

She was right. She was more than capable of protecting herself. The most she might have to deal with was some drunk that wanted to try his luck with her. I remembered what she did to Don Park, twice, so I knew I shouldn't be that worried. Maybe I was more cautious about ensuring she had my back than watching her own. How many times had she saved my ass already in the last few years?

I shut the door and then began to trail our suspect. I wanted to get a little closer to him, but not close enough to spook him. I knew that as soon as he turned from the main drag into a side street it would be harder not to be noticed, but I had to try.

As he moved north, I peeked over my shoulder and saw Rouge was already out and following. She had put on a hoodie and used it to cover her hair and shadow her face. It was a good idea. She looked like she belonged to the area more than I did, that was for sure.

Three blocks north from the rooming house, the guy I was following turned west onto another side street. I didn't bother to look at the name of it. It wasn't like I was going to write a report on the incident. I wasn't even going to call back the woman who hired us. If this guy was in fact a monster, and wasn't just some sicko who liked to kill and maybe even eat cats, we'd deal with him our way, and if the woman called back, we would tell her we couldn't find him at all. She might go to the cops after that, but eventually his empty body would get found and he would be added on to the list of people found in the same state. I was sure we would be in the clear, just like with all the others.

I would be really glad when all the Doll Maker's bodies were dealt with and we never had to leave another empty shell of a person laying around for the cops to find.

The street we were on was tree-lined and quiet. It was nice here. Not lit very well, but well enough so that I could see he was still on the move. He was looking for something. Maybe he didn't just hunt down stray cats in alleyways, but actually went to where families let their pets out to roam free for whatever reason they did.

I wasn't sure what this guy might be, but I had enough on me to deal with a doll maker special. There were plenty of monsters and demons that would eat a cat, if that was what he was doing. There was no way to know if he was a monster or a dirtbag, unless I got close to him, preferably when he had a cat, and tossed the coin at him. Once it made contact with his skin, I would know for sure and deal with it. Nothing, other than a creature in a human host, would be affected by the coin at all.

Our guy stopped.

I did too.

He crouched down and put out a hand. I couldn't hear anything, but I was sure he was making that little noise to get a cat's attention. I moved off the sidewalk and stepped onto the road, moving towards him without bringing attention to myself. I peeked over my shoulder again and saw that Rouge was doing the same. I loved that she was able to figure out what I was doing without me needing to say a word.

I turned back to where our guy was and saw a fat orange-and-black tabby waddling over to the suspect. I was closer and could hear him talking baby talk to the animal. He looked like he had something in his hand, probably some sort of food he was using to lure the cat to him. I moved quietly, not making any sound, and reached into my pocket and pulled out the coin. I wanted this to go nice and smooth, easy as easy could be, but I was a little worried because of our track record.

I walked off the road and stepped across a small patch of grass towards the sidewalk and the crouching man. The cat was purring loudly. The man was still doing the whole baby-talking to it. He didn't seem to know I was there. Good. I moved forward. Only three feet away and I reached the coin out towards him.

"My friend here says you have something in your hand," the crouched man said, but didn't even turn towards me. I should've been more surprised, even jumped a little when he started to talk, but these days, I'm always ready for something messed up to happen.

"So, you speak cat?" I asked, looking at the tabby, who was still purring and eating the bits of whatever the guy had given him.

"Don't you? Doesn't everyone here speak cat, or do they all live in ignorance of the creatures around them?"

I shook my head, but he couldn't see me. "That's the problem with humans," I told him. "They tend not to hear anything aside from what they want to."

The man chuckled and turned his head towards me. "So, I'm guessing you're not human either?" he asked.

"And by that I see that you're not. That's what I thought. I figured anyone who eats cats must not really be from these parts," I told him and crept a little closer.

"Eat cats?" he all but barked at me, and even in the dark I could see his brow furrow. "Are you crazy? Why would I eat one of my brothers?"

"Brothers?" I said, taken a little aback. I was sure I knew what he might be, but calling a cat his brother changed everything. Yet, it also meant I knew right away what he really was. "Let me guess: you're a Maanx?"

He nodded and stood up to face me. "And what might you be, that would figure that out so easily?"

"Just someone who knows a thing or two. And if I had to go out on a limb, did you come here with the help of the Doll Maker, because I know that a Maanx looks a lot different than you look right now."

"Well, that makes sense, doesn't it? You're a hunter," he said, not really asking. "I'd been warned about you. So, what's your plan? You know that I can't just let the person who was in this body go back into it, right?"

"I'm aware of that, but it doesn't matter. I can't have any of you running around and killing animals."

"I told you, I'm not killing anything. I would never harm a dear creature that is related to me. We might be from different galaxies, but we are cousins of sorts."

"Then what are you doing with the cats? You seem to take a lot of them into a very small space with you, and then they are never seen again."

"That's not true. They *are* seen again. I don't take cats like this into my place. He has a home. I was just saying hello."

"And what about the one you took in a few hours ago?"

"You were watching me?" he asked, and looked offended.

"Yeah. We were hired to," I admitted, and heard a footstep close by and knew Rouge was coming up on me. I held my hand up, hoping she would get that I was signalling for her not to make a move yet. When I didn't hear her step again, I hoped she had gotten the hint. "So, what are you doing with the cats then?"

"I take those cast out, dirty and sick, and take care of them. I usually have six or seven in there at a time. I clean them up, make them better, and then find them somewhere new to stay."

"So, you're a regular Mother Theresa."

"I don't know who that is, but judging by the tone of your voice, I can tell you're being an asshole."

"Maybe I am, but I have a job to do," I told him, and raised the coin so he could see it.

"But what if there is a better job you can have than me? What if I tell you of something that is an actual threat out there? I don't hurt humans, or animals. The food I eat is from a can. So, in the grand scheme of it all, I'm a small fish. So, what if I tell you about a much bigger, more dangerous fish? Would that be enough for you to let me stay and help these poor creatures?"

"What is it you're offering?" I asked, feeling more intrigued by what he was suggesting than I would've guessed.

"There's a lot of monsters out here. Ones the Doll Maker has let through. Most of them are as pathetic- or even *more* pathetic- than I am. But a few of them are horrible. Even I'd be scared to be in a room with them. But I'm not going to tell you anything until you and your friend make a promise that you will leave me alone."

"My friend?" I asked, trying to play it off.

"The girl hiding in the shadows. I can smell her from here. Is that citrus body wash you use, miss?"

"Citrus and sandalwood," Rouge said, and came up to my side. She leaned in and whispered in my ear: "What's the plan?"

"I want to hear what he has to say," I said loud enough for our Maanx to hear. "So, tell us…"

"Not so fast, hunter. I will tell you, but first I want your word."

"And you would trust the word of a hunter?" I asked. Usually, these monsters and demons wouldn't believe anything one of us said, and it might be for a good reason. I couldn't count the number of times I double-crossed one of these things after I got what I needed. It wasn't my job to make a deal with creatures. But there was always that one special circumstance…

"What choice do I have Although, if you do something against our deal here, my friend will be a witness and you will never be safe near another cat again."

I looked at the fat tabby next to him that looked like it was listening intently to what we were saying. Was I supposed to be afraid of some cat network? As though if I killed the Maanx, this one next to him would start spreading the word to every cat in the city, and then what? They would claw my ankles? Spray me with their stinky butt spray? I didn't feel too threatened by what he was saying, but in all honesty if what he said turned out to be something good, I would let his being here slide. As it turned out, it seemed like he wasn't all that much of a threat after all.

"You have my word, but I will need more than just what you are going to offer. You say these cats have a little network that you can join in on?"

"They do. Why?"

"Well, here's the deal. I want something good right now. But not just a one-time thing. That lets you off too easy. What I want is info now, and if there are any other dangerous monsters or demons out there, you have your little network put out their feline feelers and pass that on to me. I don't care if it's the Doll Maker's creatures or something else, if I come to you with something later, you owe me information. If you do that, you will have a free pass. Sound fair?"

He looked at me and squinted a little. I wondered what he was thinking. He said nothing to me, but turned to the cat by his side and made some strange noises at it. I wondered if this was what the woman who called in had heard. I personally didn't think it sounded like Latin, but what the hell did I know? I'm no language expert.

"I think we can work with that."

"One more thing," Rouge said, cutting in before he could drop the dime on the particularly bad monster he hinted at. "If you step out of line and start causing problems, the deal is off and we won't even bother to just send you home. Instead, we will rip you out of that body very painfully and jam you into an itty-bitty jar and leave you on a shelf for an eternity. Got it?"

He nodded, even though she came off a little harsh on that.

"I would never hurt anything that wasn't trying to hurt me," he said, and offered a hand for us to shake. "So, you have my word to. I will help any way I can if you allow me to stay with my friends."

"Thanks, but I think we can just take each other at our words. No need to give me your paw," I said, and tried not to chuckle.

"Okay then. I will keep up my end if you keep up yours," the Maanx said and turned again to the cat at his side and said something I couldn't understand.

"Good. Then it's a deal. So you've got something for us?"

"I will give you two. The first is two sisters that the Doll Maker has put in some weird doll bodies. They are actually—"

"We know them already," I said, cutting him off. "They're no longer in play. You better have something else."

"You know about them?" he asked, and seemed shocked by that. Guess he thought two monsters in silicon sex dolls was something I might miss.

"*Knew* would be more accurate," Rouge told him. "They're long gone. What else you have?"

"Do you two also know about the Baucis?" he asked, his voice lowering as he spoke, and he looked slightly more nervous. I'm sure he realized that if we did and had already dealt with it, he would have no cards left to put on the table, so he would be out. Lucky for him, I had never even heard of a Baucis, never mind already dealt with it. I shook my head and said as much. "Oh, thank the Mistress. You hear that, Leaf? They've haven't dealt with it, so I'm okay."

The cat meowed something and the Maanx returned the sound, only it was a bit different.

"I asked him to stay, just in case you two lied to me, but if you're really looking to get rid of bad things from this planet, then this one is the worst."

"Okay, act like we don't know what this Baucis is," I said, because I had no idea what a Baucis was. Never heard of one in all my years. "What is he or she doing here, and just how bad is it?"

"A Baucis isn't a he or a she. They are whatever they want to be. I don't know much about them other than the fact that if this one is still alive, then there are either dead bodies around, or you're going to start to find them soon."

"That's it? That's all you got?" I asked, wondering if that was enough. "You know where this thing is staying, how it kills, who it kills, why it kills? Anything other than the type of monster it is. Just saying the type of monster that is here and nothing more doesn't fill your side of the bargain."

"I know those Baucis are like parasites. They feed off whatever beings are near them, even their own kind. They are horrible and hard to keep track of. You never know when you're dealing with one," he told us.

"How can you not know if you're dealing with one or not?" Rouge asked.

"They're changers. They never look the same. What an actual Baucis looks isn't something many living would even know. Most just see the last face it wore and have never seen how they started."

That gave me pause, and a thought came to me.

"Are you thinking what I'm thinking?" Rouge asked in a hushed voice.

"This could be the killer Garcia is looking for," I said back and knew it had to be. I turned back towards the Maanx. "Do these things drain a body, like a vampire? Leave the body like an empty husk?"

"Maybe. I don't know exactly how they do it, but I've been told that they are parasitic in nature. I do know they steal the face of whoever they kill. This is why most don't know what a Baucis actually looks like. So, if that's true, then what you're asking makes sense."

"Please tell me you have some sort of idea where it is."

He shook his head. "I wouldn't want to, if I'm being honest. But if you want me to put the word out to my brothers and sisters, I will try and find out as much as I can for you."

"Well, I'd say you are buying your ticket to stay here for sure. If you can find that out for us, it will be set in stone as far as I'm concerned."

"I will do my best. I don't know what body the Doll Maker gave to it, or if it has switched faces, but I will check what the cats have seen and let you know."

"I'll give you my phone number," I said, and jotted it down on some paper. "What's your name, anyway?"

"And please don't say it's *Whiskers*," Rouge said, and I wasn't able to hold back the laugh.

"I know a few friends named Whiskers, but that's not my name. Where I'm from they called me Myst, but here I prefer to be called Doc. That's what the cats know me as."

"Okay, Doc. You call us when you know anything at all," I told him and handed over my number.

"I will. And thanks," Doc said and tucked the paper into his dirty pants. "I've always heard you hunters were an unreasonable bunch, but you two seem only slightly unreasonable."

"I'll take that as a compliment," I told him. I guess it was one. Usually all we heard was what assholes we are, that we are heartless and unkind. Anything positive is a good thing, I guess. "One more thing, Doc."

"Please don't make me regret saying something nice to you," he said and looked a little sad, as though he was sure something bad was about to come.

"You might want to move out of that rooming house. Some of the people there think you are either a serial killer or possessed by a demon. I could tell them the truth, but I think if you move and do it soon, it'll be better."

After that, he left us, and we went back towards Bathurst and our Jeep. On the way, we didn't say much. I wasn't sure what Rouge was thinking, but I was grateful to feel like we were one step closer to helping Garcia solve this case. The best thing was we knew what the creature was called. We could check in with Godfrey or Kajal tomorrow and see what they could dig up. If we were lucky, they would add a few pieces to the puzzle, and we could close the book on this.

"Where to now?" Rouge said when we got back to the car.

"It's nearly midnight, so I think we head home for the night and then go see Godfrey and Kajal tomorrow."

"Not tonight?"

"No. It can wait."

In the end, it turns out the Baucis wasn't as patient as we were.

Tuesday

Another day, another wake-up call to my phone ringing off the hook. I mean, it's a cellphone, and not an old school phone that is actually on a hook, but you know what I mean. The ringer blared and I grabbed it after I don't know how many calls I'd actually managed to sleep through, and wasn't surprised to see it was Garcia.

I groaned before I answered it.

"Dillon, are you awake?"

"I answered the phone, so obviously I am. What's going on?" I asked, and rubbed my eyes vigorously until the sleeping blurs were gone.

"How fast can you come down to Police Headquarters?" he asked. He sounded excited.

"I don't know, fast? What's going on?" I asked and Rouge started to stir in bed and slowly sat up. She mouthed the words for *what's going on*, and I shrugged.

"I think we may have a break in the case. Turns out the TTC supervisor was useless, because they did have video footage at Kipling station aimed right at the washrooms."

"Why didn't they tell you before now?"

"My boss is dealing with that. Not my problem. I'm just glad we have some video to watch so that maybe we can get a hand on what's going on here."

"Me too. Have you watched it yet?"

"No. It just arrived on my desk. Thought I'd see if you two wanted to watch it with me. So, how fast can you get here?"

"We're on our way," I told him and hung up. As soon as I did, I told Rouge what was going on and she was just as confused about it all as I was.

"You didn't tell him that we may have a lead on what's doing this," she said as she got up and the two of us got dressed.

"We can tell him later. I'd like to find more out about this thing before we start celebrating and giving him anything. Who knows, maybe this video will give us even more to go on as soon as we see it.

"We can hope."

Less than an hour later we were in Garcia's office drinking bad police coffee and nibbling on free donuts. I'd say the donuts weren't great, but I'll be honest, there's no such thing as a bad donut in my book. Fried, sugary bread is as perfect as humans have managed to get as far as I'm concerned. And the one I chose had sprinkles. I love sprinkles. Life is just more fun with colourful bits on them.

"Is anyone else coming in to watch this?" I asked as I sat down in one of the four chairs in the office and pulled up to the monitor. Rouge joined me, and then Garcia sat.

"No. It'll just be us. I want to see if you can find anything before anyone else gets a hold of this."

I nodded and Garcia went to work on setting up the video. I had some high hopes about this. I know it would have been easier if we saw the killer in the act, but there was no chance there would ever be a video of something like that from inside the washroom. Not legally, at least.

Still, getting to put a face on whoever this killer was would be perfect, and it would move us a step closer to ending it. Anything more than the nothing we had would be good. I mean, I've solved cases with less, but that was more dumb luck than actual work. I'm the king of dumb luck.

"Okay," Garcia said as the video played. "So, we know the last time he was seen down on the platform. I'm going to scroll to that time."

"How busy should it really be there that late at night?" Rouge asked.

"My thoughts exactly. That time of day we should be able to see him easily. If it was rush hours, all bets would be off. Ah, there he is."

We watched as the victim walked into the bathroom. It wasn't very busy there at all. He opened the door, went in and we waited. The camera time jumped, and a woman walked into the Ladies' Room. I asked if the cameras were motion activated and Garcia said they clearly were. I knew it should be obvious but had to ask.

Another time jump and the woman walked out of her side, and in the same frame a man walked into the men's room. I couldn't see his face, but wondered if it was our suspect. Garcia must've thought the same because he went back and moved the video frame by frame and took a photo with this cellphone.

"Just in case this is our guy," he said and put it back on regular play.

The video paused a moment, and then the guy who'd just gone in left the washroom, and I was beginning to wonder if our victim was already dead. He'd been in there for nearly nine minutes with our victim by that point, and it really felt like he might have already had his run in with the Baucis.

"What the fuck?" Garcia said. I'd clearly missed something because I'd been stuck in thought.

"What did you see?" I asked. I leaned in to look at the screen but had no idea what he was seeing.

He played the guy leaving again, rewound it back to where he entered, and played it again until the guy came out a third time. He paused the tape. I had no idea what he was seeing, but I didn't notice anything out of the ordinary.

"I don't see anything," Rouge said, also leaning in towards the screen.

"Me neither. What is it?" I asked and Garcia pulled his phone out again. He scrolled through something and turned it towards me. I was expecting to see the photo he had taken of the guy going in, but instead it was a photo from a driver's license. "That's the same guy. How did you get his photo?"

"That's the photo of the victim, the guy we found dead on the floor."

"What?" I looked at the phone and then at the screen. It was for sure the same guy, but how was that even possible? I tried to make sense of it. Was the guy on the floor not who we thought he was? Was the killer this guy all along? But then why leave his ID in the dead man's wallet, assuming that was where Garcia found it? I asked and he confirmed, and I was so confused.

"What is going on here?" Garcia asked, clearly as lost as I was.

"Do you mind?" Rouge asked the detective, and took the mouse from him when he said it was fine. I didn't ask her what she was doing, I simply sat back and watched her. She obviously saw something we didn't. I had no idea what she caught that we missed until she rewound it past where the woman was to the point when the victim first walked into the washroom. She paused it as he was in front of the door. "Take a photo of that," she told Garcia, and he complied. Rouge then fast-forwarded it to the next guy walking in, but past it because Garcia already had that shot. She moved instead to where the man we thought was the victim exited and paused it there. "And take a photo of that," she directed again, and Garcia obliged.

"What are you seeing?" he asked her before I could. "Holy shit!" Garcia said as he flipped through the three photos. "How the fuck is that possible? What the hell is going on here?"

I was still in the dark on it all until Garcia turned the phone towards me and went through the photos. Three shots. Shot one, two and three. One was our victim, two was our suspect, and three was our victim again. It was still just as it had been and I had no idea why they were both so...

"Holy shit," I gasped as I realized what they were seeing. It was easy to miss, so there was no point in beating myself up, but now that I had seen it I couldn't believe how obvious it was. I had been so focused on the faces I hadn't looked anywhere else for a clue. "The clothes," I said as though it was a great revelation.

"The clothes," Rouge said and nodded.

It was an easy thing to miss when you were so focused on the face. The man who walked in dressed like our victim, was not wearing the same clothes leaving as he had been when he walked in. He had the face of our victim, but was wearing the jeans and the hoodie of the man who walked in after the woman. We didn't know the face of the man who walked in there who had come out with the victim's face, but I wanted to find out.

"Do you have the footage from the platform, too?" I asked, and Garcia quickly pulled it up. We started from the time we saw him go into the washroom and played backwards. I wanted to know what he looked like. I thought there would be an answer to it there.

I was right.

"Holy fuck," Garcia blurted out and leaned back in his seat. "This shit just keeps getting stranger."

"I'm guessing that's the face of the victim from the *Tender Trap*?" Rouge said, coming up with the answer while my brain was still working.

"It is. But how? What the fuck is this...thing?"

We knew what it was. We had found out the night before, and now we had an idea of what it was doing and how it was killing people. I think I was also formulating an idea as to why it was killing. This wasn't just to be mean, because it had a taste for human flesh. Our killer was doing this to steal the identity of the victims. Was it possible the Baucis was not just stealing blood and fluid from these people; it was stealing their identity as well because the faces only lasted so long, or maybe it became bored with the stolen mask? I guess we didn't need Godfrey or Kajal in this after all. At least, not for the moment. We were doing pretty well on our own. Things were coming together nicely.

"I'm going to take a photo of the victim," I said and took out my own phone. "Right now, until there is another body, this is who we are looking for."

"But how?" Garcia asked.

"There are a lot of strange things in the universe. Maybe when we catch this thing, we'll have time to ask it some questions, but I won't hold my breath. There might not be a whole lot of talking between us and it."

"And what am I supposed to tell the cops here, my boss? I can't put out a BOLO for a guy who has the face of a dead man."

"If anyone asks, show them the video," I said, even though I knew that wouldn't do any good. "There is no good way to go about this. Last time someone tried to tell the truth about what's out there, they lost everything."

"You talking about Detective Kajal?" Garcia asked. I hadn't said his name because I thought it was before his time, or at least that the two hadn't really crossed paths. I knew Kajal mentioned that he was aware of who Garcia was, but I had no idea it went both ways.

"Yeah. I feel responsible for that," I told him. "When he told me he was going to make a report and tell the truth about it all, I should've stopped him. I didn't, and he lost everything. I don't want that for you, so the best thing you can do is show them the video and say you have no idea what happened. There's nothing else to say about this."

"Until you get a hold of them?" he asked, and I nodded. "And what then? Is this one going to be like the others recently? Just an empty body with nothing going on? Then what am I going to tell them? 'Oh, that body we found, even though it belongs to this guy, here is another version of him in a comatose state'?"

"Yeah. I know it is going to be hard, but you don't have to try and explain it. Just look as lost about it all as they will."

"That's it?"

"What else could you do? There's nothing to explain that people would be willing to accept. Humans don't want to see things like this. If you live your life thinking up is down, and then someone tries to tell you that up is up, you're not going to believe them. Human minds aren't ready to understand the things that are out there in the universe."

"Not all aliens or monsters are ready for real truths, either, Dillon. It's not just a human thing, I'm guessing."

I nodded. "But where I might not be able to grasp some things, humans here can handle a lot less. No offense, Garcia."

The detective knew it was true, but that didn't make anything better. It was shitty, and there was no way to clean it up and package it in a way that would make sense to anyone other than people who knew what was really out in the universe.

Before we left, I asked to see the video played back a few more times. I wanted to know if there was anything else that stood out. If there was a particular walk, some sort of swagger or limp, anything to help. It was so weird to watch it all unfold again and again. Seeing one man walk in, followed by another, and then the first man walk out with the second man's clothes. Other than that, we had nothing.

It really sucked.

At least we had the name of the species killing people and knew that the current face of the killer would be the face of the last victim. That was something. It was huge. It meant one way or another, this thing was done.

We left the police headquarters and for the first time in a long time, I felt like we were about to have a huge win. This was a massive case. It was the kind of thing that could snowball into a hell storm if we sat on our hands and did nothing. Now, with everything we'd uncovered, this would hopefully get solved before anyone else had to die.

We drove to Godfrey's after that, but saw a few weird hippies going into the shop so we thought better against it. There was still the chance one of those idiots would look at me and remember me from the YouTube video. They seemed like that age, and I really didn't want to have that kind of run-in. I suggested we head to Kajal's instead, and she agreed when I explained why. It wasn't a long drive, and there were ample places to park. When we got there, the door was locked again, and the "closed" sign was in the window. I knocked on the glass and waited. I hoped he was actually there.

Nothing.

I knocked again and waited a few minutes before all-out banging on the door. What was going on with this guy? He was here fine the first day, and then since he's been a ghost. I thought I would have heard back from him too after I had seen him, expecting he'd call within that first twenty-four hours with some sort of news about finding some sort of creature that might be close to what we were looking for, but there had been nothing. I took out my cellphone just to confirm, and like I thought, there was nothing at all.

"Are you getting worried about this?" Rouge asked as she leaned her face towards the door and tried to peer inside. "You don't think something happened to him because we visited, do you?"

"I don't know, but I hope not."

Was that even possible? I hadn't considered something might have happened to him. I just figured he had reached out to his old friend and was busy catching up. Also, maybe he was avoiding me because he had nothing. The idea that some sort of harm had come his way hadn't even entered my mind.

That all was laid to rest as the yellowish-stained curtain moved back an inch or so and someone peered out from the inside. A second later I heard the deadbolt click and the door opened. A very tired-looking Kajal was standing there, welcoming us in.

"Sorry," he said as we walked inside, and he locked the door. "I've been a bit under the weather for the last couple of days."

"Hopefully it's nothing serious," Rouge offered, and I gave him a good look. He seemed a bit grey around the gills, and the small dark spots under his eyes had grown quite a bit. He didn't look good at all.

"I'll be fine. I think I just need some really good sleep," he told her, and we walked to the back room where his office was.

"Did you have any luck finding Aamir?" I asked him and he spun around fast and looked mad. I put up my hands in a surrender gesture, not sure what it was that had set him off. "Sorry. Did I say something wrong?"

"Why are you asking about Aamir?" he barked, and suddenly didn't seem so under the weather. His cheeks flushed and his eyes went wide.

"Because when we left you the other day, you said you were going to try and find him. I just wanted to know how that was going?"

"Oh," he said, and all the rage died in him. "Sorry. I don't know what came over me there. I forgot what we talked about last time and thought... I don't know what I was thinking." I watched him and he twitched for a split second. "Only that you're a killer and wanted to do harm to him again. That's the type of asshole you are."

"Wow," Rouge said and stepped back a second. "What's with the attitude?"

"Sorry," he repeated, as he balled his fists and put them to his head. "It must be the flu I have."

No. Not even close.

As we continued to walk, I very carefully pulled my gloves out of the back pocket of my jeans. I knew something was off, and I wanted to see if I was right. I wasn't one hundred percent sure about what I was thinking until I reached out and touched his exposed wrist with my gloves. These gloves may look like regular deerskin work gloves to many, but on closer inspection you can see writing etched into them. They are formed with spells, curses, and ancient rites that cause paralysis in almost any creature not from Earth. I wasn't positive that something was in Kajal, but I had a suspicion he wasn't alone in there.

"What are you doing, Dillon?" he asked, but his feet stopped moving forward. "Why can't I move?"

"You tell me, Kajal. Assuming you are who you look like."

"It's me. But why...can't...I move?" he asked, and was clearly struggling to go forward or to at least pull away from me. There was no use. If he was just Kajal, he could have, but there was something inside him that was not of this world. Whether or not he was still in there was yet to be seen.

"You can't move because you seem to have a guest. Want to tell me about it?" I asked, still holding on to him. "Don't be shy."

"There's nothing in me," Kajal said, his voice straining as he tried to fight against the spells freezing him to where he was. "I'm...alone...here."

"They why can't you move?" I said and spun him to face me. I looked into his eyes and could see something in there, something swirling in the brown and black of his iris and pupil. What was it?

"Let...me...go...Dillon," he strained and pleaded.

"Or what? You can't do anything. And if you don't tell me what's going on, Rouge here is going to pull out a dagger that is blessed and cursed and she will cut the truth from you. So, what's it going to be?"

"Please, Dillon. I don't know...how...why..." he fought with his words, and then his voice changed and his eyes narrowed. There it was. Whatever was in him was showing itself. But at least I knew Kajal was still there. "Release me, hunter."

"Thank you for joining us," I said to the unknown creature inside him. I wasn't sure how something was in there. Monsters and demons could only enter something not alive, or had the soul removed from it, as in the case of the Doll Maker's victims and the horde of monsters she gave those bodies to. Normally, when a monster comes through a weak spot, it forms a body from things like piles of dead leaves, discarded cans, or if they're lucky they might find a recently deceased person. What they didn't do was try to enter someone that was still living and breathing. If they did, all sorts of havoc could ensue because the human body cannot normally hold two souls at the same time. Of course, there are some demons that know how to enter a living body, but in those cases it is a specific demon and there are ancient words that must be spoken to allow the demon to enter. And let's not forget the Shadow People. "What are you?"

"One of your victims, but I won't be one again."

"That doesn't help. Want to give me some sort of idea as to who you are?"

"No. I don't...want...stop it, Kajal!" it growled to the man who owned the body it was in. "Don't...tell him...anything."

"Kajal, tell me. What is inside you? You can do it."

"NO!" it yelled to me, and to Kajal as well. "Don't do...it... stop...fighting me."

"Don't listen to it, Kajal. Let me know what it is and what I can do to get it out of you."

"Don't...tell..." it started and then the swirling stopped, and Kajal's head dropped a bit. "No, Dillon," he said, sounding like himself again. "Don't harm him. You know who it is."

"Aamir?" I asked, but there was no way Aamir could be in there.

"I didn't want to tell you the last time you were here, Dillon. I wasn't sure how to explain it."

"Start from how the hell he is in you when you are alive for starters," I said and let go of his wrist, figuring that if they were both in there, I really didn't have anything to worry about. This wasn't some monster holding a dead body hostage like I've dealt with before.

"After you destroyed Aamir's body here, I did everything I could to bring him back. I read books, found chants and spells in order to open a weak spot here. I even looked into the idea of finding someone I could turn into a porter."

"And did you?" I asked, suspicious because there was clearly one somewhere in the city.

"No. I couldn't make that work. As you know, making someone into a porter is no easy task." I nodded and waited for more. "I did mange to open a door, though. Not a weak spot but using an incantation from the *R'Yzilian Book of Spells* I opened a door of sorts to allow his spirit through, but I screwed up."

"I don't even know where you managed to get your hands on that book," I told him, and then turned to Rouge. "This book is from a galaxy quite far from here. This is not something someone easily gets their hands on."

"I was lucky to find it, because I managed to bring Aamir back home to me."

"But you said you screwed up. Do tell."

"I didn't want him back in a dead animal, or clumps of trash. I was worried you'd come back and do the same thing all over again and traumatize me all over again. So, with the book and the door open, I used a different spell to intertwine our beings together so he could live with me in secret."

"Why would you do that?" I said, shaking my head, because I knew how dangerous that was. He was lucky the process didn't kill him right off the bat. Human bodies are strong to a point, but if you try and put too much in one, especially spirits, or souls, they have a tendency to burst. It's why some say that humans only have a half of a soul within them, because they would explode if the soul was complete.

"I thought it would be fine. There is nothing in the books about this, and until you showed up here, there was no problem. But then we tried to separate so that he could be free to be in his own body and live with me, and that's why I look and feel like I'm dying. I'm not though, am I?"

I shrugged. I didn't know. I had never met anyone stupid enough to do something like this. It was a bad move, so dangerous, and to then try and separate was clearly ripping him apart. I sat down on a stack of very thick books and looked at his off-coloured complexion.

"I would love to tell you 'don't worry about it, you'll be fine.' But in all honesty, I have no idea. You look like you've already died."

"I feel like I'm coming apart at the seams. I don't know what to do now."

"I think it's obvious," Rouge said and walked over to him. She put her hand on his shoulder and gave him a soft smile. "You two will just have to live together, unless someone else can figure out a way to separate you."

"Dillon, there has to be some way out of this," he pleaded, but I knew nothing to help.

"It can't be so bad living together like that, can it? I mean you each care for one another, right? I mean, if I had to share my body with someone I loved, I wouldn't try to fight it, especially if it was going to hurt one, or both, of us," Rouge said, and I shook my head.

"It's not that easy. Human bodies aren't meant to house two souls, spirits, or whatever you want to call them. I'm sure there is something in one of those books, maybe even the one you found the spell to get him in there in the first place. I'd try to find it as fast as you could."

"But in the meantime, at least you two have each other," Rouge added.

Kajal's head drooped, but Rouge was right. These two cared for one another. Kajal felt like Aamir was a child of his. He loved him so much that he did everything he could to bring him back to Earth, even offering his own body as a home. This was going to be his life until he could find something in one of his many books to change things.

"Well, if you're here about information regarding your monster, I haven't found anything out for you. Clearly, I've been preoccupied with other matters."

"Well, there's some good news on that front," I told him, and he perked up a little. I broke it all down for him, from the information we received from the Maanx, to the video tape we watched. "We know what we are looking for, and how he's killing. The only thing I need to find out now is how to kill a Baucis, and maybe how they choose their kills."

"A Baucis? I know I've seen that name somewhere before," Kajal said and moved towards a wall of his books. "I don't know where, but I'm sure I have."

Kajal ran his finger over the book bindings, mouthing the names of one volume and then another. He started to take one down, slid it back into place and went for another. I watched him as he quickly flipped through pages and whispered inaudibly to himself. Or maybe he was talking to Aamir. I couldn't tell at this point.

After a minute or so, he grunted and slammed the book back into place and then began to scan the shelves again. He grabbed another, scanned again, and put it back. I realized this could take a while. Kajal had to have thousands of books in there, and he clearly didn't know which one it was in for sure.

"We can come back later, if you want," I told him, knowing I didn't want to just sit here while he went through all the books he owned.

"I know it's one of these ones in this section, Dillon," he told me and pointed to three shelves with over a hundred books crammed onto them. "I'm just trying to remember which one it is exactly. It must be this one, right?" he said to nobody in particular and took a thinner, dark leather book out. He started to scan through those pages, and I looked over at Rouge.

Want to leave? I mouthed the question to her without speaking out loud.

She shrugged and then mouthed the words, *I don't want to be rude.*

I didn't either, but if there was anything I was one hundred percent sure about when it came to the research side of monster hunting, I knew it was *so* boring. Unless Kajal had a book titled *How to Kill a Baucis*, this would be brain-meltingly dull. The thought of searching through book after book after book, hoping to flip through pages until you found what you were after, was as appealing as going to a poetry slam. I have nothing against people who like that kind of thing, I just couldn't wrap my head around it. Book research is the same. If you like it, you love it. Me, I'd rather go for a twenty-minute run with a leg cramp than do it.

"Ha!" Kajal all but yelled and made me jump a bit. "I knew it was in one of these. Here it is in the *Chronicles of the N'aanie*."

"What is or are the N'aanie? Is it anything like *The Chronicles of Narnia*?" Rouge asked as Kajal walked over to his desk and sat down.

"Not at all. The N'aanie are information gathers," I told her. "They travel through the universe and into other realms to record information and statistics on all kinds of beings they encounter. They are watchers of worlds, and record keepers for those that want to seek knowledge."

"Like a Census worker here," she said, and I nodded. It wasn't exactly like it, but it was close enough not to need to mention the differences.

"They usually share tales of their encounters as well, pass along myths and legends of different species, along with weapons they use, inventions they are known for, and things that are a weakness to them. In other words, how to kill them." Kajal explained when I didn't. "Usually their chronicles are very large, but some of them in the more distant realms contain very little to put out there, and hence why this one is so small in comparison," Kajal added without looking up from the pages he was skimming. "It's always fascinating to read, though, and see how different things are in these other places."

"I'm sure they see here the same," Rouge said, and she was

probably right. Earth was a strange place to anyone looking in from the outside. Even if you go from one country to the next, it seems like you are looking into something so very different. Food, clothing, language, even ideology here are so different from continent to continent, and even if you go to certain parts of the same city. It was one of the things I love about being here. So many other planets and even galaxies fall into line with one central way of thinking and being. If there is a god they believe in, they all believe in it. If there is a language spoken on a planet, everything that can talk will speak the same tongue. While it seems like the worlds beyond Earth are so different, at least Earth offers variety in a way others don't.

"Is there anything in there about killing a Baucis?" I asked and walked over to him, looking over his shoulder to see if I could read anything. "There has to be something in there, right?"

"Maybe. I don't know for sure, but there could be something... Wait," he said, and put his finger on the page. "It says something here about a type of iron that all Baucis are severely allergic too. To the point where in most cases it is fatal. Okay. That should be it then," Kajal said and continued to run his finger over the same lines again and again.

"So, we just need to use iron on this killer?" Rouge asked and smiled as though that would be no problem. "We can go to Wal Mart and grab a cast iron pan and beat the shit out of this monster with it."

"That won't work," Kajal told her. "This must be a very specific type of iron used. The kind is something from their planet and a few of the surrounding ones as well. It's called S'Borouth iron, from ore dug out from volcanic oceans. You have any of that kicking around, Dillon?"

I shook my head. I hadn't even heard of it, but I was hoping Godfrey had. And if I was lucky, he might even have some with him, or know how to get his hands on it. Even when I thought it was unlikely, he would have something; Godfrey had a way of coming up with the perfect tool for a given job. That wasn't always true, of course. There was a time, not even that long ago, when Godfrey was a bit of a snake in the grass, giving me fake weapons to go after some truly dangerous creatures. I'm glad those days are over, but the memory that he once did that always lives in the back of my mind.

"You think Godfrey would have something for you?" Rouge asked and I winced. I didn't like her using his name in front of people, even if they were someone I trusted. The less one source knew about the other the better, in my opinion.

"We can go and ask," I told her, and wasn't surprised by Kajal's curiosity.

"Who is Godfrey?" Kajal asked us.

"He's—" Rouge began but I decided to cut her off.

"You don't need to worry about who he is," I told him. "Just like he doesn't need to know about who you are, and he never will unless something bad happens."

"Something bad?"

"Don't worry, Kajal. Nothing bad is going to happen to you," I assured him. There was no way for me to keep that promise, but I knew telling him would make him feel more at ease.

"Unless that Baucis finds out I'm helping you out, right?" Kajal asked and put his hand to his head as he winced. Aamir must've been causing more havoc in there.

"That won't happen. I've never let anything happen to anyone who helped me before, so I won't let anything bad happen to you." That was a lie. There were plenty of people I had known over the years who'd died trying to help me. I didn't want him to worry. I felt like it was easier to offer a small amount of deceit to make him feel some sense of hope.

"Are you sure you can make that promise, Dillon?" Kajal asked, looking up from the book and seeming so sad.

"You have nothing to worry about. There is no way the Baucis can know you're helping me. Promise."

"You want what?" Godfrey asked, seeming more than a little shocked by the request.

"We need a piece of S'Borouth iron, and sooner than later," I said again, knowing right away that this wasn't going to be as easy as I was hoping it would.

"Oh, sure, and while I'm at it would you like me to get you the Holy Grail, or nude photos of the Queen of Rezzik? What you're asking for is just as hard, you know. There isn't an easy way to even get that type of iron, and whenever you can find some, it's either fake or costs more money than you can imagine."

"Well, money doesn't matter to me," I told him as we stood in his store, near the front counter. All around us there were all kinds of tools and weapons I could use to kill or at least stop all sorts of demons and creatures. Godfrey was able to get things that didn't belong on Earth as easy as I can order a pizza online. I wasn't sure why this was so hard.

"It might not matter to you, but I'm telling you, the way that ore needs to be mined is not only really difficult, it's downright dangerous. So many have died just to get an ounce of that, and for what? There is no practical use for it, other than to kill a Baucis."

"You know what a Baucis is?" I asked, and no doubted looked as shocked by this as I felt.

"I know that many looking to kill one use S'Borouth iron. But that's about it," he said, as though the information was something we all should've known.

"Well, that's the thing that is sucking the life out of the people around the city. This is what we were asking you to help us out with," I told him.

"Sucking their life and stealing their identity," Rouge explained, and it was Godfrey's turn to look shocked. "When it's draining the body, it also steals the face and body of the victim and then sheds its old identity like a snake."

"That is a lot to take in," Godfrey said and slumped against the counter.

"If you think it's a lot, well, you should have seen what we had. Now, can you help us out with the iron?"

Godfrey mumbled to himself and walked around to the other side of the counter where his register was. He leaned down and came back up with something that looked like a laptop. Looked like one but didn't at the same time. This thing wasn't housed in plastic, a little apple or HP logo on the front of it. The outside of it looked almost organic. It seemed wet, made of something alive. I could swear it was breathing.

"What the hell is that?" Rouge asked, and leaned close into it. She bent closer, and then jumped back a bit. "Oh, wow, it smells too," she said and covered her nose.

"This is something the Collective gave me when they put me here for my sentence. This is how I can get into the database and order the things I need. What, Dillon, did you think that I just called up my alien and demon artifact guy who brings over suitcases of things I need? This is how I get my stuff."

He opened it just like a laptop too, and it made a cooing sound. He moved his fingers out of sight from me. I had to get a better look at this. In all the time I had known him, I had never seen him with this thing, and I had no knowledge of what it was.

His fingers weren't on a keyboard. They weren't touching keys the way I am as I write all this down. There were things on the so-called "keyboard" that looked like organs, plants, and flesh. His fingers touched, pressed, and caressed these areas and the living computer, continued to make a cooing sound, along with some chirping sounds. This was like something out a nightmare, or a drug-induced bender. It was fascinating to watch. Rouge was right there with me. She was watching it with a disgusted look on her face, as though she were smelling a fart. It might've been the rotten egg smell emanating from the living machine, or it might just be how wrong it all looked.

"Is it alive?" she asked, lowering her voice as though the computer would hear her.

"It is made up of living beings. It is no one creature. Each one is unable to do this on its own, but as they come together with the computer parts, they are able to work in connecting to the networks in other worlds and realms."

"That's so cool," Rouge whispered. "And nasty at the same time. I love it."

"You might need some help," I laughed nervously, thinking this might be something that would haunt my dreams for a long time.

"You have to admit, it is a little cool, Dill," Rouge said and reached out to touch it. Before she could feel it, Godfrey smacked her hand as though she was a child about to take a cookie before dinner. "Ow."

"Sorry, but you can't touch them," he told her and pulled the machine closer to him. "It's not that I don't trust you, Rouge, it's just that they don't know who you are. If a stranger tries to use them, one that doesn't know how to touch and work them, they will release a toxin and you will die. And not a good death, either. A very painful, messy one."

"This just gets better and better," I laughed, and moved a little further away from the computer that might want to kill me. "Can we just bring this along and throw it at the Baucis when we see it?"

"No. And watch what you're saying or they won't help you anymore with what you need."

"Okay," I said and nodded, before leaning a little bit towards the mucky machine. "No offense. Sorry if I said anything out of line."

The computer seemed to chirp at that and Godfrey began to nod. His fingers darted quickly along the many different surfaces, and then he looked at me.

"They won't hold it against you, but from here on in, you need to watch your mouth. I know for you that might be hard, but you need to try." I apologized again and Godfrey returned to it. I sat back and watched him and tried not to get the heebie jeebies while he did it. There was almost something sensual about the way he touched it, as though it was a little bit of intimacy I was peeking in on, and that made it even worse. I looked over at Rouge and she seemed utterly enthralled by it all. What a weirdo.

"Okay," Godfrey said after a few minutes of touching the meaty machine. "I think I found something here. It's not on this planet, but I can get it brought here."

"How long?" I asked.

"Four or five days," he said, and then leaned in to where the screen was. "I think six at the most."

"Six days?" I gasped, feeling a little deflated. "There's nothing faster?"

"Sorry, Dillon. Amazon doesn't do same day delivery on inter-dimensional artifacts. That's the best I can offer you. Six days is the far end, but there is a chance it will get here sooner, depending on a thing or two."

"What could it depend on?" Rouge asked. "Is there bad weather or a holiday that can slow service down?"

"Not the way you're thinking, but something like that, yes. The way it can be transported, there can be...static that can interrupt its arrival. You know what I mean, Dillon."

I did and didn't, but in the end, I just didn't care anymore. It would get here when it did, and we would just have to hope there wasn't a line of bodies left in the wake of it all. We could only do our part. Without the iron, there was little we could do to kill the thing. If we ran into it, we might be able to slow it down, but there was no way to even know how strong a Baucis was. Were they anything like the vampire myth, with the strength of one hundred men? If we tried to stop it without the iron, would we be like two people trying to face an entire army?

I didn't want to find out.

"Will you call us the second you get it?" I asked him and he nodded.

"As soon as it is in my hand, you'll know, Dillon."

"Thanks."

"Thank me when it's all over."

Friday

The next two days were uneventful. There were no calls from Kajal, or Godfrey. Nor were there any from potential clients or people trying to set us up to kill us. The latter was a nice thing. With the free time, we did some spring cleaning, went to the store, stocked up on food and drinks, and took the pup on plenty of walks. For two days it felt like we were just living a normal life, as though there weren't monsters out in the world wanting to pull our heads from our bodies and bury us as deep as the earth would allow it, or others walking around in bodies they stole and killing people and stealing their identities. For those days, it almost felt like we weren't monster hunters, just something people might call regular folk.

Then, on Friday, just after noon, my phone rang. I was hoping for something good. Instead, all I got was the real world calling to bring me back to reality.

"We have another one," Garcia said, not even bothering to offer a greeting. "Do you want to meet me at the crime scene?"

Did I? That was a good question. I wasn't sure what seeing another dead body would help. The only information we would be able to get from this to further the case on our end would be seeing the identity of the new victim. Knowing what the current face the Baucis would be wearing would be necessary to catching and killing it.

"Is there anything new with this one? Something that we might need to know that changes things?" I asked, and after a moment of silence, he spoke up.

"Not really. But the fingerprints made it to my Captain, and he is very confused at what's going on. I told him I had no idea what it meant. I thought it was better than telling him the truth and having him put me on leave, or worse, firing me. So, I shrugged and told him that maybe it's a serial killer who is leaving behind the prints of the previous victims because he thinks he's smart and is playing some kind of game with us. It was the best I could come up with."

"It's not far from the truth, and it keeps you out of trying to explain the truth to him." I admitted. "Just play it like that and if he jumps to any bizarre conclusions, that's on him, not you."

"My thoughts exactly."

"Now, can you send me the ID of the new victim so I can know who we are hunting down when we have the item that can stop it?"

"So, you actually know how to stop this thing?"

"We do. I just have to wait until we can get our hands on the weapon to do the job."

"I hope it's soon, because eventually, something is going to pop up that I won't be able to just shrug off as though I have no way to explain it. Someone is going to witness something, or there will be good footage that makes the whole story exploded and then shit will hit the fan. I know this is not easy to just squash, but the sooner you can the better."

"We're working on it. I even have an army of cats keeping an eye out for him," I told him and heard him chuckle.

"You know what, I don't even think you're kidding about that, are you?"

"You never know."

I hung up and told Rouge about what had happened. I let her know we weren't going to bother going to the crime scene, that Garcia was going to send me the details and the photo of the latest victim.

"I really can't wait for this one to be over, Dill. There's something about this case that just makes me feel so damn defeated."

I sat down next to her on the couch and put my arm around

her. I knew exactly how she felt. There were few cases in my life that took so much time and left so many hurt or dead in the wake of it. Knowing that this Baucis had now killed six people. I couldn't remember the last time one monster or demon had killed so many in such a short period of time. Of course there had been others that had killed way more, but not in this manner. Garcia was right that the Baucis was more like a serial killer than anything else we had ever dealt with. I wondered if it was stalking its victims, or were these all just crimes of convenience? Did it just see an opportunity or was there more to it than that?

My phone pinged and I opened it to look at what Garcia had sent to me.

Here's the photo of the victim. Her name is Susan Peterson. She was thirty-six, five-five, and about one hundred and thirty-five pounds. The killer got her at the Toronto Reference Library, in the third-floor washroom. No witnesses, but there is video footage. It's not the best, but I think when my bosses see a guy walk in, and then a woman walks out that is an exact match to our victim but wearing the guy's clothes, there will be a lot of questions coming my way. I will play dumb because if I don't, they'll lock me in a rubber room.

As I was finishing reading the message, another one came through.

Also, there was another skin stuffed into the garbage bin, and a single, bloody fingerprint near the sink. I think we know what will come back when we run them.

After that, the photo came through, and I showed Rouge. I hated seeing old photos of the faces of the dead. The faces in those photos held such promise, so much hope. You could see dreams in their eyes, hopes. And now, they were gone. There would never been another joy to see, a dream to live out. They were gone, taken by something that shouldn't even be on this planet. I hated that part so much.

"I want to kill this one myself," Rouge whispered as she stared at the face of the woman. "I don't want to trap it in a fucking bottle. I want it dead."

"That's the plan. I don't even know if we could trap it in a bottle, or if it is even one of the Doll Maker's customers. Better to end the thing and deal with whatever happens after that."

"Sounds good but let me do it. I want to look past the face it stole and into the thing's eyes as the life drains out of it. I want to know that I did it, and I want it to know who took its life."

She sounded so harsh again, like she wouldn't just kill it, but savour it. I knew she must be as frustrated as I was, but I just wanted to kill the thing. I never thought of doing it slow, making it suffer, or looking into its eyes as the life seeped from it. That seemed a little too much. It felt personal, and I wasn't good with that. You had to keep the type of work we did at arm's length. You didn't want it ever to be personal. It was a job, work. Sure, what we did helped the people of Earth, or at least that's what I told myself since I got here, but I never took joy in rooting out something vicious, or even evil. I had to just work at doing it and not let it be something I allowed to get too far under my skin.

Yet even I wanted to kill this one badly. I just didn't want to take any particular pleasure in it at all. I would be happy to know that nobody else would die, and that was all.

But, to each their own. I wasn't going to scold her or tell her she was wrong to be so angry.

My phone rang again, and I answered it before the first ring had finished, figuring Garcia had something else to tell me. It wasn't him, though. It was our new friend, Doc.

"I think one of my friends might have found who you are looking for," Doc said after I realized it was him.

"What do you have?"

"There is a man, who is also a woman sometimes, who is living in an abandoned house near Pape and Gerrard. My friend, Tickles, meowed to me that they always seem to be the same person, but their face changes. They smell the same though."

"You have an address?"

"Yes and no. Tickles doesn't know his numbers really, but he described the house and the area. The windows are boarded up, so there is no way you won't be able to figure out which one it is. There are no other houses boarded up there," Doc told me, and then gave me the layout of where this house would be situated. "I will also tell Tickles to sit in his window, so you know that you are in the right area. My friend lives right next to this house."

"And how will I know your friend?"

"He is an albino Afghan. He is quite striking and manly."

"I'll take your word for it. Thank you, Doc. And when I get the tools to fight this killer, I will make sure to visit there."

"Call me when you are so I can let Tickles know to be by the window for you."

"Will do. And thanks again."

I hung up and passed on the good news. Now all we needed was the S'Borouth iron to finish this up and make everything safe. I crossed my fingers that it would be sooner rather than later.

Sunday

O n Sunday morning, Godfrey called me to let me know the iron had arrived at his shop. I was thrilled and told him we would be in within the hour.

"So, this is it, eh?" Rouge asked as she was getting dressed. She picked out a great outfit for staking out the Baucis' house if you ask me: some very tight, olive leggings, and a burgundy top that would keep me entertained while we waited. To say the top was a bit low would be to say summers in Toronto are a little humid. If you know, you know.

"I hope so. Once we get the iron, we will set up to watch the house until we see the Baucis and confirm it has the face of the last victim. I don't want to be rushing in there with guns blazing only to find some drug addict hiding out the place. And if it is the Baucis, we'll kill it quick and easy. After that, it's a quick stop at a drive-through for some takeout and close the case."

"You think it'll be that easy?" she asked, and I shrugged.

"I certainly hope so. If it doesn't know it's being hunted, we should be able to get the drop on it easy enough. And with it all said and done, I'm sure Garcia will be happy."

"Are you going to call him and tell him that we're heading after the killer tonight?"

"No," I told her, and explained that I would rather wait until we had finished before we mentioned it to him. I didn't know for sure if we would catch the Baucis tonight or not, so I didn't want to be hasty and have Garcia getting too excited before we got the creature.

I did have high hopes for it all, though. I was confident that before Sunday turned to Monday, we would have wrapped it all up and have this strange case closed and sealed in a safe and thrown in the lake. There were six bodies tied to this monster, and I knew there would be no more if we could get it fast. First thing though, we had to go pick up the S'Borouth iron from Godfrey.

After we were both dressed and caffeinated, we headed over to the shop and met up with Godfrey. He had clearly been waiting for us, because as we walked up to the shop, he unlocked the door and swung it open for us. We went in and he shut and locked the door behind him, something he never did.

"Everything okay?" I asked, a little concerned about all of that.

"It's fine. I'm closed on Sunday, and I don't want anyone even trying to come in when we have this. It's worth a lot to people who might know it's here."

"Seriously? Then how have I never heard of it?"

"I'm sure there are a lot of things in this universe you haven't heard of before, Dillon. The number of things you don't know could span several planets. But I'm telling you, this is not something you want others to know you have unless you have an army behind you."

"I get it," I said and followed him to the back room with Rouge. "It's a big secret. Shhhhh. Not sure how anyone else would find out it's here at all, but I'll let you have your big James Bond moment."

"Don't joke about this, Dillon," he said, almost as a warning.

I said nothing more. We went into the back room and nervously he opened his safe on the west wall and pulled out a wooden box. It was about the size of a cigar box, but was made of dark, reddish wood and had a silver medallion in the center. It looked fancy as hell.

"Does it always come in a box like that?" Rouge asked he sat it down on the table between us.

"I don't know. This is the first time I've ever come into possession of S'Borouth iron," Godfrey said and slowly opened the box. He did it with such precise movements, you would almost think he was expecting it might explode if he did it too quick, or that it was booby trapped. "Oh, the Gods!"

He spun the box towards us, and there on a bed of fine white sand sat the most unassuming weapon you could imagine. It was small. It was a little longer than twelve inches, and thinner than a screwdriver. I don't know what I had been expecting, but it wasn't this thing in the box. I wanted it to be a weapon with more substance, like a giant iron stake people used to kill vampires with in the movies. I asked him if I could touch it, and when he said yes, I picked it up.

I was instantly surprised by how heavy it was. For something so small, it felt like it weighed about as much as a bag of sugar would. It was hot, too. Not blister your-skin hot, but more than being just a bit warm. I passed it to Rouge and looked at the surprise on her face.

"That's way heavier than it looks like it should be," she said, and I nodded. "Feels like it would burn me if I held it in my hand for too long or squeezed it."

"It won't," Godfrey said as Rouge put it back down on the sand in the box. "But when you pierce the Baucis with it, do it fast and move away. I don't know for sure what will happen, but I would assume it will be warm there."

"Like burst-into-flame warm?" I asked, imagining it would be like Christopher Lee in one of those old Dracula movies.

"Maybe. Or maybe it just kills him dead, but I hear that when someone has a reaction to this that leads to death, it's never clean."

"Good to know. Oh! Does it have to be through the heart or brain?"

"You watch too many movies, Dillon," Godfrey said, shaking his head. "Anywhere on the body will work, just be quick and get away."

"I'll do my best to make it fast," I assured him.

"No, you won't, Dillon," Rouge said and crossed her arms, giving me a stern look. "This one is mine, remember?"

"Sorry. Almost forgot," I admitted, shutting the box and passing it to her. "You get the honor of this one."

"Taking it personally, are you, Rouge?" Godfrey asked.

"This one, yeah. Very. I don't like the bad name he's giving to...well, you know, the whole thing he's doing. I just don't like it," she said, stammering a little with her thoughts, and I wondered what she was going to say. What was he giving a bad name? The Baucis species? Impossible. These things are all known for the same thing, from what Kajal read to us. Maybe she just meant aliens in general, knowing that she was in a room with two of them that were not anything close to being as evil as this monster was.

We left the shop, and I called Doc as we headed back to the Jeep. I didn't want to waste any time with this. If we did, others could end up dead, and I didn't want that on my conscience. The phone rang through and went to voicemail. I didn't want to leave one, so I hung up and tried calling back. He picked up on the last ring before it clicked over again to him saying he couldn't get to the phone.

"I'm in the middle of something," he whispered, instead of offering a greeting.

"I have what I need. It's going to be tonight," I told him before he could just hang up on me.

"What? Wait. Is that you, Dillon?" he asked, sounding confused.

"Last time I checked. Don't you have call display?"

"Sorry, I didn't even bother to look. Give me a second," he said, and then he muffled the phone. I tried to listen to what was going on. There were no voices, just a rustling sound like he'd put me in his pocket while he walked. After nearly a minute, he was back. "Sorry about that. I just was helping out a friend with a project. Now, what were you saying?"

"I have what I need. We're going to go to the house where your friend Tickles thinks the Baucis is and we're going to end this. If we do, you're not just safe and free, but I will owe you a favour in the future. I don't owe a lot of people anything, so this is a big deal."

"I know it'll happen. Tickles is sure that something is wrong with the people there. Again, he said the person always smells the same, but looks different."

"Okay. I will call you when it's done and let you know that you're one hundred percent safe in my book. Thanks again for the help."

"If it means getting to stay here with my friends, I'd do absolutely anything I needed to do."

"We will be there around six tonight, as soon as it gets dark, so let Tickles know we'll be showing up in a green Jeep. Two of us, male and female. He'll know us by her red hair."

"It stands out. I'll tell him."

I hung up and then it was time to prepare for the night.

We were packed up within the hour and decided to eat before we headed over to the house. I had my gloves, our daggers, an enchanted rope that was regular hemp twined with the hair of something similar to a unicorn, my coin, a few empty bottles to remove souls, and some other weapons that would work on a number of creatures in case the Baucis had friends. You can never be too safe. The last item, the S'Borouth iron, stayed with me, close by so we would be ready to access it and use it fast. I know Rouge wanted to be the one to kill it, but as long as it was dead, I knew she would be happy.

We ate in relative silence. Normally we are both very chatty, but there seemed to be something in the air. For me, personally, I wanted to stay in the right headspace for it all. This was not a simple task of tracking down some illegal monster or demon; this was a killer. The Baucis was both dangerous and vicious. It killed not for need, but for some sort of sport, or pleasure. At least I didn't think it was for need. Stealing the life and identity of the victims seemed to be some sort of game to it, and tonight, it would get thrown out for bad behaviour. I couldn't wait to do it.

When we were done with our food, I changed into some fresh clothes. Nothing special. Just my regular uniform of jeans, a t-shirt, a hoodie, and a jacket over it. I threw on my skate shoes, which were good for running short distances in, but also for just sitting around and being comfortable. Who knew how long we might have to sit in the car and wait for the Baucis to show up?

Rouge had the same idea. She changed into some leggings and a burgundy hoodie. No high heels for this, either. Instead she threw on a pair of her Brooks shoes she only wore when she was going jogging every other day.

"You have a superhero name?" I asked, gesturing to what she was wearing.

"I'd go for *Kick-Ass*, but it's already taken. So, I guess my burlesque name will have to do."

I laughed at that, imaging a hero in a comic book whose name was about her hair colour and breasts instead of the sum of her abilities. It was ridiculous. Then again, there were ones named *The Whizzer*, *The Badger*, and *Spot*, so who was I to judge?

"I would have suggested the name *Red Thunder* because after all that chilli you just ate, it might be the very power you use to defeat your foes. Or me in that car with you," I jokingly said, and she punched my arm for it.

"You ate your fair share too, *Ass of Gas*," she shot back. "That's your name, even before you eat the chilli. You fart way more than I do. Did you know that you snore with your butt at night? You do realize that, right?"

I felt my cheeks turn red. No, I hadn't known that. How would I know I fart in my sleep? I'm asleep. I've never ripped one so loud that it tore me out of my slumber. That I knew of, at least. Well, she won that round, I guess.

"You don't need to be embarrassed. I love you, no matter how gassy you are, Dill," she said, and kissed me hard on the lips. I offered the same back and wished we weren't heading out to kill a monster. I could think of something I'd much rather be doing.

Yet, I knew this was what needed to be done, so we grabbed the bag, two thermoses of coffee, and some food and headed out to the east end of the city to find the Baucis and end it all.

We drove to the area, skipping the highway because I could tell on the GPS it would be a nightmare. It was rush hour, the time of day where everyone rushes to move at a snail's pace on an overcrowded 401, DVP, or Gardener Expressway. I decided to take College across, which then turns into Carlton. Once we got near Pape, I drove south to Gerrard and headed to the side street where our Baucis was supposed to be.

Those streets it turned out, were a bit of a maze. Some of them were one-ways, and some of those turned into dead ends. It took some time to get around. It was also very unlike where Rouge and I lived. Some of the streets had just houses, while others looked like businesses in older buildings, and then some of those older buildings appeared to have been turned into loft spaces for anyone who was willing to pay or rent these places that cost an arm and a leg.

After five minutes or so of driving from one street to the next, getting turned around because of all the one-ways scattered about, we finally found a boarded-up, run-down looking house on a dark street that didn't seem overly populated with people or even parked cars.

"Is that it?" Rouge asked, spotting it before I did.

"It must be. Right now, it's the only one I see that looks boarded up around here," I said and looked for the cat in the window of the neighboring house. I squinted and slowed down and there it was. It pawed the window as though it was trying to wave to me. At least that's how it looked, so I waved back.

"What are you doing?" Rouge asked.

"Waving back to the cat Doc told me about."

"It was waving at you?"

"Yeah, I think so. Anyway, this is the place," I told her and parked on the side of the road. "And now, we wait."

"How long would you guess that we'll be waiting for, if you had to guess?"

"You know how these things work. You never can tell how long it'll be."

As it turns out, it was just over five hours after we parked that something moved near the house. We were well into our snacks and coffee, listening to something a little lighter than normal— Etta James, I think—when I saw a shadow move from the side of the house and into a window that wasn't as boarded up as we thought. Rouge saw it too and grabbed for the bag.

"How do we do this?" she asked and pulled out her blade. She tucked the sheathed weapon into the front pocket of her hoodie and passed the bag to me.

"One takes the window it went in; the other goes through the back. Hopefully there's a way to get in there, but if not, we make one."

"You have a preference?"

"Lady's choice," I offered.

"First, I'm no lady. Let's just squash that one right now. Secondly, you have all the experience here, old timer, so you pick."

"Ouch," I chuckled, and took out my knife and gloves. I tucked them away and then took out the coin and a bottle, just in case. I hadn't seen any other movement around, but still I wanted our I's dotted and our T's crossed. I also patted the front pocket of my pullover hoodie where the S'Borouth iron was to make sure it was still there, and it was all good. "I'll take the window it climbed through, and you take the back. If you see anything out of the ordinary or need help, you scream your ass off. Okay?"

"Usually, you're the one that needs saving, lover. But I will. Just make sure you do the same."

We hopped out of the Jeep and moved to the house. I looked over at the neighbor's house and saw that Tickles was still sitting in the window, watching us. I waved again, and felt weird doing it, but what the hell. The cat knew what we were there for. He was our little informant after all, so how weird could it be?

Once we were at the house, I waited and watched as Rouge moved along the side and disappeared around the back. Once she was out of sight, I made quick work to climb up and through the same window the Baucis had. I wanted to be fast to avoid anyone seeing me and maybe calling the cops. The last thing I wanted was to try and explain to some uniform new to the force why we were carrying weird knives and an iron rod while crawling through windows of an abandoned house. Worst still would be if we killed the Baucis and were standing over the body when the cops came to find us because a nosy neighbor called 911. Assuming of course there would even be a body, that it wouldn't be like a vampire movie where once they died, they crumbled to ash and blew away.

I guess we'd find out soon enough. I just wanted to be quick about it.

The house was pitch black and smelled terrible. It was mould and mildew and a very hot animal smell. I wondered if that was the Baucis that smelled like that, or some cats or rats were nesting somewhere close by. I could easily ignore it, especially as I fought to get my night eyes working. I didn't want to use the light from my phone to see what was around me or where I was going, because I didn't want anything being able to hone in on me.

I moved slow. I slid my feet across the uncarpeted floor more than just taking steps. I didn't want to make the floor creak, and let the Baucis know I was there. Listening and slowing my breath, I went to the wall and moved along it to the next room. I couldn't hear anyone in there. Not a sound other than my own steady heartbeat in my ears. I had seen the Baucis go through the same window I did, so where was it?

I was in another room. The wall felt oily, and the first thing other than a wall my hand came into contact with was cold and felt metal. My eyes still weren't full adjusted, but I was able to tell that I was in the kitchen. It smelled even worse there. It wasn't like old food. It was rot. Rotten wood, decayed drywall, and something more organic. Maybe I should be glad my eyes weren't fully adjusted.

Something moved.

It was close and to the left. I stopped dead in my tracks and swung my head around. It was gone, but I could hear more movement. It was quiet, but now that I had heard it once, I was able to pick it up. Whatever it was, it was moving fast.

There was more movement in front of me.

Shit.

There wasn't just one thing here. There were two.

Movement behind me, and I knew that I had made a huge mistake. I had assumed I was dealing with a single Baucis, but that was a stupid thing to assume. Now I realized there were at least three of them here and I was alone. I needed to warn Rouge not to come in.

I pulled out my phone to call her, and as the screen lit up, there was even more movement. I was being surrounded. Since they knew I was already here, I clicked on my flashlight and spun around to brighten up the darkness.

"Rouge!" I yelled out. "Don't come in here!"

I said the words, and as I did, I saw that I had made another mistake. It was full of them, it seemed.

My light immediately caught the creatures stalking me. I had been so sure they were all Baucis, or maybe even other monsters like it brought to be the thing's minions, but as it turns out, this was some sort of setup. Instead of monsters hiding in human skins, my stalkers were all cats. A lot of them, too. What the hell was going on?

"Hey, guys," I said, and backed away as the filthy kitchen began to be swarmed by the sea of felines. "I don't know what you're all doing here, but if you leave now, I won't call the Humane Society and get you all locked up in kitty prison."

The cats didn't move or back off. They stood their ground, hissing at me, and then slowly they began to move forward. I threw another warning at them, but they were cats. Could they even be reasoned with at all? By the looks of them, I put my money on *no*.

This was quite a pickle. I mean, they were just cats, but there were a lot of them. At my best count, as far as I could see, there were at least one hundred of them. I didn't know how much of a threat a cat could be, but with this many, I thought of it like bees. One bee, no big deal. A sting, a little burning, and unless you were allergic to them, you'd be fine. A hundred bee stings were a different story altogether, as were hundreds of cat clawing at me. I felt as though even half of them getting at me would be too many scratches for my liking.

The real question wasn't how I would get out without getting torn up to hell and back, it was who had sent them in the first place. Doc, the Baucis, or maybe both of them. Was Doc working with whoever had found the porter, and this was all a setup to—

what, scratch me to death? Was this all some fucked-up double cross by a damn man-cat and a skin stealer?

I pulled out my dagger and kept the light on them. I didn't want to have to use the blade on a cat, or a hundred of them, but I needed to get out of here in one piece. If it was me or them, I would turn them all into pulp if it meant I got to walk out of here on my own.

"I really don't want to have to hurt or kill any of you, but be warned, I'm more of a dog person anyway. Just thought you should all know that before you think about doing anything stupid," I told them, knowing it was a strange thing to be standing in front of a horde of cats and trying to reason with them. That was, assuming they were all actually cats and not just the housing units of monsters and demons.

I still hadn't heard a peep from Rouge. She hadn't called out to me when I told her not to come in, but I figured doing that would just make her change her point of entry. There was no way that me yelling would keep her out. She was determined to be a hunter. How many times had she already disregarded what I said, and saved my ass for it in the end? More than I would admit to her.

I was about to call out to her again, when the first wave of the attack came. Between twenty to thirty cats ran and lunged at me, straight into the kitchen, making a horrific howling sound as they did. I tried to block them off, but felt claws digging into my thighs, calves and stomach. I cried out and felt the sting of their little cuts. I kicked out, but wouldn't use the dagger on them.

Then the second wave came and my reluctance to truly harm them went out the window.

An all out brawl between me and the feline army erupted. I was scratched and bitten more times than I could count. Blood ran down my body and face, but not all of it was mine. I kicked, stabbed, and grabbed these attacking cats. The ones I grabbed I would throw at the rest, using them as bowling balls with hopes of taking out as many of them as I could. There was a cacophony of howls and meowing, sounds of cat pain. The more of them I took down, the more of them seemed to come at me. If you had asked me any time before if I thought I would be killed by a bunch of cats, I would have laughed it off like it was the worst joke ever, but then here I was, fighting a battle that seemed to have no end. If ever there was a time Rouge could swoop in and save me, it was now.

"Now would be a great time to save my ass, Rouge," I yelled out as the ongoing attacks continued.

They kept coming and I continued to fight them off. Their little dagger claws were ripping my clothes and skin and as harmless as a cat scratch might seem, thousands of them would be bad. The old saying of death by a thousand cuts was not lost on me. I needed to get out of there, whether or not Rouge came to save the day or stay where she was.

Then something hit me that put me into hyper gear. What if there were more of them out there? What if she was having her own war with these menacing monsters while I was in here fighting them as best as I could? The idea of them ripping her skin and hurting her gave me the push I needed. It wasn't a pretty sight to see, I'm sure of that. I was kicking, stomping, slicing and punching my way through the four-legged attackers. There were horrid howls coming from them, as the sound of their bones being crushed under my skate shoes set my nerves on edge. I didn't care. I needed to get out of there and find her.

They were still slicing me with those razor claws of theirs, but I wasn't going to let them stop me from getting outside and making sure Rouge was okay. I was fighting a growing wave of them. At some points there were three of four on me, claws dug in, biting at my clothes as they tried to find flesh to eat. Three were on my back, so I slammed backwards into a wall and felt them go weak and let go. I didn't want to do this, but they left me no choice.

When I finally pushed and kicked my way through them to a door, it was locked. I couldn't get the lock to disengage so I used my foot to kick it outwards. Luckily it was a cheap, not very well-built door and it gave way on the second strike. The cats continued to attack as I got out into the fresh air of the back yard. They followed me as I spun around looking for Rouge.

She wasn't there.

I called out her name and kicked at more attacking animals. She didn't answer. I ran through the back yard, back to the front of the house, and hoped to see she was there, hiding in the Jeep that might be surrounded by cats. But she wasn't there either. Had she gone into the house while I was coming out? I hadn't heard her, but then again, I wasn't really paying attention to that. I knew I had to go back in and see if she was there.

I groaned and then just did it.

More cats charged at me and fought to bring me down. I was so mad. I didn't care anymore how bad I hurt them. I didn't even think of them as cats. They were now just an obstacle to my finding Rouge; a very annoying one. The good thing was, there were less of them. The more I sliced and kicked and punched, the smaller the feline army became. Back in the house, I turned my flashlight back on, and saw many of them licking their own wounds or the wounds of the fallen. I didn't feel bad for them. I had warned them not to do it. They should have listened.

I called out to Rouge and saw a few of the cats perk up, but at this point it seemed like the fight was out of them. I was cut and bloody, but many of them were in worse shape and I guess the rest considered their own survival was at risk. I called her name again, and when there was no answer, I left the injured alone and went back to the Jeep. On the way there, I called Rouge's phone. It went straight to voicemail.

Shit.

Where had she gone to?

I got in the Jeep and just sat there, waiting to see her, or for her to call me. I tried not to worry, to be patient, but that was not my specialty. I tried her number repeatedly. My mind began to play on all the horrible things that could have happened, never once imagining a scenario where she saw the Baucis leave and began to follow it. Instead, I saw the cats killing her and dragging her off, or some other animal sent out to get us. I shook that idea off by thinking of other questions.

Who had sent them?

There was no way the Maanx could have really been behind it, so who was it?

The Baucis?

Whoever has the porter?

It could be any of them, but one thing I knew for sure: Doc was the one who was the go-between in setting us up. When Rouge popped up, the two of us would go find him and make him tell us exactly who got him to send us to that house. I would beat it out of him if I had to, but one thing was for sure: there was no way I would let the Maanx stay on Earth when it was all over.

Where was she?

I was more than a little worried when I realized I had tried to call her eighty-six times, and already an hour had passed and there was still no word from her. I knew she was more than capable and able to handle herself, but that didn't make it any easier for me. I loved her and the last thing I wanted to do was to just be sitting in a Jeep, twiddling my thumbs while something terrible was going on.

I didn't even know what to do.

I stuck around there for another forty-five minutes and called her more times than I care to admit. There was no way she was around here anymore. She must have chased something, maybe she damaged her phone. I would have to go home and hope she showed up, or called me, or something. I even tried to think that maybe her battery was dead, and there was nothing more to it than that. She had seen the Baucis, chased it, but couldn't call me because she had no battery life left. Maybe she was halfway home, figuring that was the best thing to do. I had to hope and go and check if she was there.

It took a lot out of me to start the Jeep up and drive off. I was feeling this cold pull in my stomach like maybe I was making the wrong choice. It was a choice between staying there and seeing if she showed up, or going home and seeing if she had just gone there and something was wrong with her phone. Neither choice seemed like a good idea. One didn't make me feel surer than the other, but I couldn't stay there all night. I had to do something.

I looked at my watch and saw that it was already after—

Monday

—midnight. I wasn't sure how the time had gotten so far away from me. It was enough to let me know there was no point in staying on the side street in front of the boarded-up house full of injured and dead cats. I had to leave and hope she was safe at home.

Reluctantly, I drove off. I turned through the maze of side streets until I got to a main road. Once I was there, I realized I was very low on gas, and headed to where Google said the closest station was. I made sure it was self-service and would take a credit card at the pump, because I didn't want to go inside in the condition I was in. Even in the low light I could see just how shredded my stuff was, that my shirt and jeans were soaked with blood. I didn't feel weak at all, so that was good, but I was sure if someone got a look at me this late at night, looking like I had been in a fight with a lawn mower, it would raise some eyebrows. Still, I would just have to be stealthy getting out of the car and filling the tank.

When I pulled into the gas station, it looked like a ghost town. Inside where the store clerk was, I could see he was alone; not a single customer in sight, and his eyes were glued to his cellphone. There were no other cars at the pumps, so I could do this fast and easy, and nobody would see the messy shape I was in. I zipped up my coat to hide the damage to my upper body and slid out of the car. I making quick work of filling up the tank when another car pulled in and dinged the pumps next to me.

Of course, someone would show up now.

It was a young couple, maybe in their early twenties. They were all laughs and kisses as they both got out of the Honda Civic and eventually the guy started to fill up his own tank. I kept my head down trying to avoid them looking at me and seeing the state I was in. The woman said she would be right back and skipped off in the direction of the store attached to the station. No doubt she was going to get some food and drinks, or maybe even something to make their fun time later a little safer. The guy began to whistle some popular tune to himself and then I was all topped up and ready to get out of there. I hooked the nozzle back up and paid. When I raised my head, I saw the guy was eyeing me, and I didn't get to look away in time.

"You okay there, man?" he asked.

"Oh, this?" I said, motioning to my torn, bloody jeans. "Yeah, it's nothing. I was working as an extra on a movie set. Some new zombie thing."

"They didn't even clean off your face. How ratchet is that, dude?"

"The lowest budget you can imagine," I laughed, and was impressed by how easily that lie came to me. "Hopefully this will be the last day of—"

A scream cut off my sentence.

"Molly?" the guy called out and ran towards the store.

I followed with my eyes and saw she was near the washrooms connected to the building. I ran over to see what it was as she flung herself into her boyfriend's arms and sobbed aloud. I came up beside him, expecting there to be something in the bathroom. The doors were closed, but I saw what she was screaming about.

Beside the washroom doors, there were two dumpsters: one was for trash, the other was blue for recycle. Poking out from between them was a hand. If it was just a hand, I would've been fine and not tasting bile in the back of my throat. I wasn't afraid of death, but what I thought I was looking at made my heart sink. And yet, I stepped towards it, even though I didn't want to. I wanted to turn around and get back into the Jeep. I knew what I was about to see, but I couldn't stop myself. I needed to know for sure.

The hand was grey and shrivelled, the body a mere husk. It was another victim of the Baucis. I knew this and I knew something else, even though I didn't want to acknowledge it; when I saw the hoodie, the tights, the red hair, I realized why Rouge wasn't answering me.

I opened my mouth to say something.

Nothing came out, and the world spun around me. Maybe it was weakness from the blood loss, mixed with the devastation I felt looking at Rouge's body, but either way I couldn't stand anymore, and I fell backwards. The guy came to my rescue, just as he had come to his girlfriend's, and caught me before my head could smack against the concrete.

"Holy shit, dude. Are you all right?" he asked, and lowered me to the ground.

"Call...Detective Garcia..." I managed to croak out. The I lost consciousness.

I must've been out of it for a while. There were no dreams, no worries; it was just the darkness surrounding me. Later, I was told I was unconscious for nearly twenty minutes, but for me it was just a blink. One moment I was being lowered to the ground by a helpful stranger, and then next moment I was in the back seat of a car with my cheek pressed against a window.

My head was full of cobwebs, and I tried to shake it off and blink away the confusion. I thought maybe I had been put in the guy and girl's Honda by them, but when I went to rub my eyes, I found my hands were cuffed behind my back. There was a second of wonder at what had happened, but when I looked outside, saw all the cops and medical people hustling about, I knew what had happened. They'd looked at Rouge, and then the condition I was in, and put two and two together. They were wrong, but it was the only thing that made sense. They had no idea who she was to me. They couldn't even fathom what I had just lost.

I was gutted all over again.

Rouge.

She was gone, out there with a bunch of nobodies standing around her and looking at her. They would no doubt be making jokes, and soon someone would be coming by to take her photo because to them she was just another victim. No different than the others because they didn't have a clue who she really was. I wanted to get there to her, see if there was something I could do, at least cover her up and make all those vultures get the hell away from her.

God!

How could I have let this happen? What was I doing in that house fighting those stupid cats when I should have been with her? I know it sound sexist and all, but I should have been there to protect her, and no doubt she would have felt the same if it was me there and her in the cop car. We should have been there for each other, the whole *us against the world*. But now I was alone, and I had lost the one person in this world, on this planet, that I truly loved. I felt so cold inside.

I felt even worse when I realized that if I'd never come into her life, hadn't taken her first call all those years ago, hadn't ever met her, she would still be alive, and I wouldn't be sitting handcuffed in the back of a cruiser feeling like my world had just crumbled. I was an idiot to think I could bring a human into my world. I was an asshole who had gotten a beautiful person killed.

It was all my fault.

I felt the sudden urge to get out of there, away from the vultures. I wanted to go take Rouge away, stop them all gawking over her, and give her peace and dignity. I was stuck in the cruiser, though, with all of them out there. I wondered if Garcia had shown up yet. I looked out at the group but couldn't see anyone who looked like him. I needed him to be here. I could see two detectives on the scene, judging by the suits they wore, but no Garcia. I had to get one of them to call him.

I shifted in the seat and felt the scratches and punctures on my legs and chest and stomach reopening. That was fine. I would rather feel that pain than to focus on the real pain I would have to face later. When my mind even started to slide towards thoughts of Rouge and her body lying between the dumpsters, I felt the darkness calling back to me, wanting to swallow me whole. Part of me wanted to let it, and maybe that would be better, but not here, not in the back seat of a cop car. Freedom would be allowing the darkness in, to swirl around me and suck me down into the nothingness.

Someone must've noticed I was awake. A uniform cop perked up when she looked over at me and I watched her walk over and tell the two detectives in the suits. One of them headed my way. He was short, and wide, but not fat. He looked like the kind of guy that decided since he couldn't grow in height, he'd choose girth instead. His face was stern, and his brow furrowed. He didn't look like he was someone who was going to take me too seriously or put up with any bullshit. There was no way I was going to able to tell him what had really happened and make him believe it. I could just read that all over his face.

Great.

Instead of opening my door, he opened the front passenger side door and sat down. He didn't bother to even turn around in his seat, choosing to simply move the rear-view mirror so he could look at me that way.

"You're in some serious shit, son. You know that, right?" he asked and pulled a pack of Juicy Fruit out of his pocket, unwrapped one and folded it into his mouth. "But before we get to all that, why don't you start with giving me your name."

"Is Detective Garcia here yet?" was all I offered.

"Who's that? Can't say I know him," he said, and I wasn't sure if he was playing coy, or if he really meant it.

"He's already on the case of the other murders like this," I explained and then offered his cellphone number. "Please. Just call him and let him know what you found. He'll tell you everything you need to know."

"Sure. I could do that for you. I'll ring him up right after you tell me your name," he said and didn't even bother to write down the phone number.

"My name is Dillon," I told him, not wanting to prolong all this. "Her name is Rouge Hills, well, I mean, that was her stage name back a couple of years ago. I still call her Rouge, because you know, it's easier for me to call her that when it's the same as what everyone else calls her too," I told him, and realized I was rambling, sounding nervous. And to a cop, that's always a sign of guilt. Shit. "She is—or was—my partner."

"And she's the one who cut you all up like that?" he said and gestured towards all the cat damage. "She did this to you, so you did that to her? What was the fight about, Dillon? Money? Women?"

"You're joking, right?" I wanted to yell, but I didn't have any real fight left in me. The questions just made me feel more drained. I also knew getting angry wouldn't fix or help anything. If I showed signs of that, it would just be an excuse to continue putting blame on me and wasting both our time. "I loved her. We were working together on a case. She didn't do this to me, and there is no way I could do that to her. You can tell that, right? You're a good enough detective to know there is no way I could do that to her, aren't you?"

"Maybe, but if not you, then who?"

"Or what, more like it," I said, and saw his eyes narrow at me. I could tell he wasn't going to be the type of cop that Garcia was. He wouldn't look at what was happening and then hear the strange truths and believe any of it. He wanted his crime vanilla: something easy to understand, and even easier to accept.

"What the hell is that supposed to mean?" he asked me, and chewed his gum like a cow.

"I don't know how to explain it at all, to be honest."

"Start with why you killed her," he offered, and changed the tone of his voice as though he was offering me an olive branch to my own freedom.

"I...I would never hurt...her... I loved her," I said, my voice as weak as my body felt. I leaned my head against the window and just wanted to go to sleep. I wanted to close my eyes and hope the darkness would take away the horrible feeling in my heart and stomach. But every time I closed my eyes, I saw flashes of her face—alive, and then the way she was between those two dumpsters. I looked over again, the vultures still circling her, and I felt the tears streaming down my face.

"You going to just sit there and fake those tears, or are you going to answer my damn question, Dillon?" he barked at me, finally turning around in his seat.

"I didn't hear you," I said quietly, and I hadn't. I had been thinking about my own failures, not paying attention to him.

"Oh, bullshit!" he yelled and slammed a fist on the head rest of his seat. "I've been at this job for fifteen years and I know fake tears when I see them. We have a woman dead, and you were found at the scene covered in cuts. Just so happens the two of you know each other, and you even said she was your partner. You said that I'm good at my job, and I am. Good enough to know that you're a killer. The spouse, or boyfriend, is always the killer. So, stop playing games with me. Something happened, and I want to know what you did to her."

"Nothing. I would never hurt her. But..."

"But what? Come on, Dillon. Tell me. You know, all this will go easier if you just come clean. Get it off your chest. I'll even put in a good word with the Crown Attorney for you."

"It's my fault, even though I didn't do it," I told him, because it was the truth. It was my fault. I failed her. I should have been there. We should have been together. But we weren't and I failed to help her, to stand by her side and fight the monsters she was forced to face alone.

"Well, if you say you didn't do it, who did?"

"I don't even know how to explain that in a way you would believe."

"What about the cuts all over you? Is that as impossible to understand?"

"It was cats that did this. Not her."

"A cat did that to you?" he laughed, and looked me up and down.

"No. Not a cat. Cats. Plural. We were following a lead to an abandoned house where someone we were looking for was apparently hiding out. It's a few blocks from here. I went in the house and...Rouge...went into the...back yard...and she...fuck... I don't even know what happened. Shit!"

I broke down again. I closed my eyes and pressed my head against the window. What was I going to do now without her? What was I supposed to do with her house, and her dog? Oh shit, her pup. I can't imagine how that poor baby was going to feel when her mommy didn't some home.

"So, you went inside and then what? You were mauled by a dozen cats?"

"More like two hundred or more," I whispered. "If you don't believe me, go check it out. There's a boarded-up house not far from here, next door to an obnoxious yellow house. Only one like it on the street. Place will be full of hurt and dead cats."

"You killed a bunch of cats?" he asked and smirked like he had just caught me with my hand in the cookie jar. There was a big leap from killing a cat to the woman I loved, but he didn't see it that way.

"Have you had a good look at me? Do you think I wanted to kill any of them? They were going to kill me."

"Cats? Little kitties were going to kill you?"

"There were a lot of them."

"Right. Two hundred cats were going to kill you? Okay, this is one for the books. I gotta give it to you, Dillon, this is a way different story than I was expecting. Do you have any history of mental illness?"

I didn't answer that. I didn't have any, but I had spent some time in a mental hospital not all that long ago. If I told him about that, or the Baucis, or anything else about my life and job, I realized I was going to get locked up in a rubber room instead of a cell. I wished Garcia would just get here already.

"No? Yes? Give me something, Dillon," he asked, and still I said nothing. "You just going to ignore that one? Well, I think that's pretty telling. But, since you don't want to answer that one, tell me about this instead," he said, and held up an evidence bag with my bloody Tincher in it.

"Nothing to tell. Test it. It's not her blood. It's feline."

"Back to being a cat killer, huh?" he said and put the bag on his lap. "Well, we are going to test it, and if we find her blood on it, even a drop, you're fucked, and I think you know it. Just come clean with me right now, and I can tell the Crown attorney how you helped our investigation. This can be hard or easy, and I'm telling you, you want it to be easy, Dillon. Just admit what really happened and we can move forward with getting you the help you need."

What I needed was something to turn the clock back. I needed Rouge to be okay. I had to wake up from the nightmare I was trapped in. There was nothing I could say that would make any of this easier for him, or me, or Rouge.

"So, are we going to move forward and make this easier, or —" he started, but a woman in a suit, another detective no doubt, knocked on the window and then opened the door. "What?"

"You need to come with me," she said, and I could hear it in her voice: something was wrong.

"I'm in the middle of something," he told her, and she peeked her head in to look at me. She wasn't as stern as he looked, but I could tell by the suspicious glare she was giving me that she didn't trust I was innocent in this.

"He's not going anywhere, and before you ask anything else, you need to see something."

The detective questioning me let out a grunted breath and then without a word to me, he got out of the car and slammed the door. I watched the two of them walk over to the store that was part of the gas station and they disappeared inside. Even though I didn't want to, I found my eyes drifting back over to where she was. They still hadn't moved her. Occasionally someone moved a bit and I saw a flash of her hand and it sent me spiralling down again. I couldn't stop seeing her face, lifeless, grey, staring at me with vacant eyes that blamed me for what had happened.

It was hard to breathe. I leaned my head back against the headrest and tried to breathe in deep through my nose, and then slowly out of my mouth. Instead of closing my eyes to where Rouge was waiting for me, I looked up at the roof of the car I was handcuffed in and began to count all the stains up there. I decided to try and focus on why they were there, what had caused them, anything to keep me away from thinking about her out there. I think it was working with calming me down too, because I didn't even notice the detectives coming back to the car until they opened my door.

"Let's go," the male one said and stepped aside. "Get out and tell us what the hell is going on here."

"I don't really know myself," I said and struggled to get out of the car without using hands. "What do you want me to try and explain?"

"Come with me," the woman said and took my arm. "Actually, hold on a sec." She got behind me and removed the handcuffs that had been put on a little too tight. I hoped this meant they knew I didn't have anything to do with Rouge's death, but it also meant they had seen something they couldn't explain. As we began to walk towards the store all together, I looked up at the top of the building and saw there was a camera near the garbage bins. That explained everything.

Shit.

This was going to be a hard one to make them believe.

The two of them led me to the back room, where a uniform cop was sitting at a desk. In front of him was a computer screen with multiple cameras on it. The male detective all but barked at the younger beat cop to pull up the video again. I took a deep breath. I didn't know what I was going to see here, and I worried I wouldn't be able to handle it.

"Before you press play, can I get a chair? If you're going to show me what I think you are, I need to sit down or there is a high percentage that I'm going to faint."

"You were in love with her, weren't you?" the female detective asked and put a hand on my shoulder as I sat down on the chair she slid across the floor for me.

"More than I've ever loved anything before," I said quietly, and then they started the video.

I squeezed my knees and tried to keep my shit together. I didn't want to cry. I needed to see this. I had to watch and allow the grief to be washed away and anger to take over. I wanted to be filled with the want and urge to find the Baucis and kill it, strip it of its skin, and make it suffer. This video could be the very fuel for my fire, and as much as I knew it was going to decimate me, I had to let it in.

The clip started with the clerk bringing out a bag of garbage. He clearly hated his job. His shoulders were slumped, his head down, his feet barely leaving the ground. After dumping the heavy-looking black bag, he left the shot. Less than forty seconds later, Rouge came running into view.

She looked terrified. She didn't have her knife, which meant she either lost it when she was running, or there had been a struggle in the back yard I wasn't aware of. She ran straight for where the dumpsters were and lifted each of the lids, paused briefly before coming to a decision. After a quick look over her shoulder, she ducked between the bins where she still was, and would never walk away from again.

I took a breath. I knew I needed to see what came next, but I didn't want to. I asked them to pause it for a second and worked on my breathing again. The female detective offered me a bottle of water, and I took it. It might not help, but at least I could fiddle with the bottle and have a slight distraction.

"Are you ready to keep watching?" she asked me, and I nodded, but didn't say a word. I wasn't ready, but I knew there was no way to prepare myself for it either. How do you watch someone you love have their life torn from them and not be gut-torn doing it?

They pressed play again and after a few seconds a shape in the distance came into view. They were running, dressed in jeans and a black sweatshirt. I didn't need to see her face to know exactly who it was coming towards where Rouge was hiding. It would be the woman who was the last victim found in the Reference Library. Sure enough, as she came into better view, I recognized her face as the same one Garcia had sent me.

The killer, the Baucis, came up to the gas station and slowed down. Like a dog trying to find the scent of some food close by, she looked to be sniffing the air. It only took a second for her to turn her attention to the dumpster and begin to walk over to where Rouge was. I could feel sweat dripping down my back, hands clenched as I watched, knowing how this would end. I took a deep breath and tried to stay calm. The woman's mouth was moving. I wondered what she was saying, if she was taunting Rouge as she approached. I would make sure to remember that when I found it. I would taunt and torture it until I felt revenge had been dished out.

The Baucis moved fast suddenly and dashed to the area where Rouge was, making me gasp like it was a jump scare in a horror movie. She was half in between the bins and half out of them, but lucky for me I couldn't see exactly what was going on. Whatever it did to her, it happened off camera, and for that I was thankful.

It took one minute and three seconds. That was all. You couldn't even tell there was a struggle going on between the bins. The Baucis barely moved. And when she did, it was to stand up and stretch out her back. The detective paused the video again.

"Now, this is where things take a turn. This is the reason we brought you in here, hoping you can shed some light on this. Can you please explain what happens here," the woman detective said and hit play again.

When the video started, the woman, back to the camera, put her hand to her face. When she moved it away, you could see her pulling something off. On camera, it looked like it could be fabric, something like a scarf, but I'd already seen what it was at another scene. I knew it was her skin, the old husk getting pulled away just like the ones we found at the other crime scenes. When she was done, she took the former identity, and put it into the same bin that the employee had put trash into. She lingered there a moment before closing the lid and then turned to the camera. I felt my stomach churn and I was worried I was going to throw up.

It was Rouge.

Her face was there, alive again, just like before. Only I knew the truth. It wasn't her. It was an imposter, a thief. The Baucis was wearing her the way someone might wear a new suit they just bought. She looked down at herself and was either admiring the new look or making sure everything was in place. Then, her head came up again and the cops paused the video, freezing the image on her face. I wanted to jump up and get away from there or I'd smash the screen. I felt the rage boiling in me. There was a growing need to hurt this monster.

"Please explain what the hell is going on here," the male detective barked and pointed to the screen. "That was not the woman who was crouching down. That is the first one, the one with the red hair that is lying there, dead, but this is also her. How the fuck is that even possible? What kind of fucking game are you people trying to pull here?"

"Did you look in the dumpster yet?" I asked, not wanting to give them any other answer. They needed to find their own way there. I just asked them that and they shook their heads.

"And what will we find in there if we do?" he asked, and crossed his arms over his chest. "That this is all some stunt for YouTube or TikTok? Is that what it all is, and you're wasting our time?"

Well, if they wanted the truth inside of looking for it themselves, that's what I would give them.

"If you go to the dumpster she was at and look inside, I'm nearly one hundred percent sure there will be something resembling a snakeskin in there. That's what it was pulling off. The woman that chased my girlfriend and then turned around and looked like her, she's no woman. It's called a Baucis. It steals people's identities. I know it sounds impossible, but it's true."

"So, you mean that thing isn't human?" the woman asked and pointed to the screen.

"No. It's something else," I told her, throwing caution to the wind.

"Bullshit. There is no such thing as what you're saying. You think something is stealing people's identities? Shucking off old skin for new? Bullshit," her partner said, and even though he sounded as though he really thought it was all made up, he didn't get up and walk away. He sat there, and that told me he wasn't convinced by his own disbelief.

"Look in the dumpster. My girlfriend, Rouge, she is this thing's seventh victim. Seventh. I don't want there to be any more. So, can you please call Detective Garcia? I'll give you his number. He's the one working the other cases."

"Garcia knows about this?" the woman asked. "Why didn't you tell us to call him in the first place?"

"I told him," I said and pointed to the male detective. "I told him to call Garcia and he would tell him everything."

"Well," the male detective said angrily. "If he tries to tell us some bullshit like you're offering, what do you think is going to change."

"If you think he's lying, Aaron, then please explain what we are looking at on the screen. And someone needs to look in the bin there and see if there is skin inside it. Maybe you can go and get someone to check," she offered to him, and he crossed his arms again.

"I'll send this guy," Aaron said defiantly, and put his hand on the uniform officer's shoulder. I could see there was a power struggle here. I wonder who had seniority.

As it turned out, she did.

"I'm not asking, Aaron. Both of you can go and I will stay here with Dillon and get some more details. We'll also call Garcia and get him down here on this. If he already has six bodies, he can take the whole case from us, as far as I'm concerned."

There was a flash across Aaron's face. At first, I thought he was going to be like a typical cop that didn't want anyone touching his cases. Sometimes, cops can be a little territorial, like a dog. But when I saw him smile and look a little more than relieved, I realized this was not something he wanted to deal with at all.

"Okay, Mary, I'll go and do whatever I can to get this dropped into someone else's lap. This whole thing will be a nightmare for us."

After that, he left the back office with the uniformed officer, leaving just me and Mary in the room. She asked if I was okay to answer a few questions, and I told her I would do the best I could. She wanted to know the background of how I had met Rouge, how long we had been dating, where we lived, what kind of work she did, and all the regular questions police will ask in a case like this. I gave her everything and was honest about it. The only thing I held off a bit on was what she had been currently doing for work, because that meant explaining what I did. Mary seemed like she wanted to be open to some of the strangeness of this case, but to tell her we were monster hunters, that might push it over the edge.

"So, now that we have all that, let's move to what happened to you tonight. You look in pretty bad shape," she said and pointed to my jeans, which were more red than blue.

"It was cats," I offered, and waited for her to be like her partner, but instead of saying anything she just nodded and waited for more. I guess it was now or never to give her some of the weird lives of Dillon and Rouge and see how she reacted. "We were working a case, trying to help Garcia find who has been killing all these people."

"So, you normally work with the police? Are you in security or are you P.I.'s?"

"I guess you can say I'm a P.I. We work independently, and sometimes, when Garcia or any other cops need it, we help out with strange cases."

Her eyebrow raised at that, and I knew she would have a hard time believing the whole truth, so I would offer only a bit of it.

"We specialize in the occult, and the unexplained," I said, and she nodded, letting me know I'd made the right choice.

"So, like the X-Files?"

"Sure."

"And cats are involved in this then?"

I shook my head. "No. Not really. We were tipped off that the suspect we were looking for, the woman you saw, was in an abandoned house close by to here."

"The one you called the Baucis?"

"Yeah. That's what it's called."

"And what does that mean? Is that the name of it, like you're Dillon, or do you mean this is some species of I-don't-even-know-what called a Baucis?" she asked, and I didn't know if I wanted to throw it all at her or not. In the past, most people who have seen the unexplainable were able to accept what I was saying as a possibility. It was a hard pill to swallow, and I knew it, but when you come face to face with shocking sights, sometimes it's nice to know that you're not losing your mind, that there really are weird things out there in the world.

"A Baucis is a species of creature that's not from this planet. How it got here, I don't know. What I do know is it drains people of their blood, life force and in the end, identity as well. It's done this seven times now, and it doesn't look like it wants to stop any time soon."

SHAUN MEEKS

She leaned back in her chair and let out a long breath. I could see the stress in her face. I'm sure she was wondering if I was out to lunch, if I was just some person who believed in conspiracies and lizard people. If I was her, I would be wondering the same thing, but she had seen the video, and soon, Aaron would come back in and tell her that he had found the skin.

"So," she said, clearly wanting to just go with it for now, "you two were following a tip about this thing. What happened?"

"We were told that it was hiding out in an abandoned house near here. We went there. I took the front; Rouge took the back. I went in and it turned out the place was full of cats—a lot of them—and they started attacking me."

"And they were actually cats? They weren't like some sort of monster or anything?" she asked, no sense of sarcasm coming from her.

"I think so. They came at me and did all this. And while I was dealing with all of them, I guess Rouge was dealing with the actual Baucis."

"And then you ended up here over an hour and a half after she died?"

I couldn't believe it had been that long between her dying and me finding her. I nodded and looked at the frozen screen. I could see her hand, grainy and flickering there as the killer was paused running from the scene. Where was I when that was happening? Had I already left the boarded-up house and was just sitting in the Jeep looking for her? Or was I still in the house fighting off an army of feline distractions, keeping me busy so I had no idea what was going on outside?

Her mention of the time that had passed made me spiral down again. I didn't feel the seat I was in. The room became darker. I didn't want to succumb to the depression and despair that was trying to pull me down. If I was talking about the case, and not really thinking about losing Rouge, it seemed easier. But the second I took a breath and started to allow the scope of what actually happened, that she was gone forever, I wanted to close my eyes and be lost with her.

And then, that made the other part of me rise, the rage.

I wanted to leave. I wanted to rush out of there and find someone to hurt, to make them pay for Rouge's death. I didn't want to waste time sitting around answering questions that wouldn't help us find the Baucis and stop it before it killed someone else.

"So, you had no idea she was here at all, or that she had run from the house?" she asked me, pulling me back to the interview.

"No. When I got away from the cats, I went outside and couldn't find her. I tried to call, and it went straight to voicemail."

"So, you drove here right after?"

I shook my head. "I stayed there and waited to see if she would come back. I didn't know what had happened to her, so I just stayed there thinking she would come back or call me once her phone charged. I didn't want to drive off only to have her wander back there with a dead phone and find me gone."

She nodded and wrote the information down. "That makes sense. But then you finally left. Why?"

"I felt like I was wasting my time. I figured she must've gone home, or would be there soon, that maybe she lost her phone, or it got damaged, so I just left."

"And came here?"

"Yeah. Gas was low and I drove here because it was the closest station to where I was. I was filling up, the guy and the girl drove in. He began to fill up while she went over to where Rouge was and found her there. That's how I ended up finding her. I wouldn't have even known if they hadn't shown up. Not right away. I…I just want to…I don't want this to be true."

Mary reached over again and put her hand on mine. I didn't look up at her, because I didn't want to see the pity there. I knew I sounded and looked as bad as I felt inside, but there wasn't just sadness in me. I worried if I looked up at her, she might also see the rage brewing, the need for revenge growing, and that was something I didn't need anyone to know about until it was done.

"Jesus Christ!" Aaron barked and burst back into the room, making me jump more than I should have.

"Dude," Mary yelled, and clutched her chest as though she was about to have a heart attack. "Do not just come into a room like that with your overly enthusiastic male energy. I nearly shit a brick."

"Do you know what I just saw?"

"Obviously not. I've been in here talking to Dillon."

"There is a full, human-sized skin in the garbage bin. I thought it was some sort of rubber suit, or latex. I was sure this was another part in an elaborate hoax, but there's hair, and fingerprints. I held this thing in my hands, and it was horrible. It ripped apart a bit as it was taking it off, but it is in there. What the actual fuck are we dealing with here?"

I tried to imagine how it would be for someone like him, a skeptic, to see something so unusual as that. To hold the shucked off skin of what appeared to be a human, while your logical side tried to argue that it couldn't be possible. Yet, there it was.

Both of them were silent and clearly they wanted an answer from me. I bit back my rage as best as I could and raised my head. Both were staring at me, waiting for me to give them something they would be able to wrap their heads around and write in a report.

I couldn't help them with either of those.

"It's like I told you. It's called a Baucis and it's not from this planet."

"Don't do this to us, man," Aaron pleaded, and the jerk he was earlier had drained out of his face and voice. I knew why, too. This was something that reeked of unclosed case. It was unsolvable and they didn't want the stain on their files. It was a career killer too, especially if they acted like Kajal had and reported it all as facts. Truth, and what some people want to admit to, are not always hand in hand. "You have to give us something better than this, or..."

He trailed off and I didn't like where that was heading.

Or what?

Or they would bury the case and pretend like nothing happened?

Or they would delete the video and book me as the one who killed her?

I didn't like either of those choices, so I gave them a third option, repeating myself again.

"Call Detective Garcia and give him the case. Like I said, he's already on the other ones."

"I already did, and he is on his way, but I still need to write something in my report."

I shrugged and gave the male detective nothing to go on that wasn't what I had already said. I decided it was a waste of time to give either of them my energy anymore. Better to just wait for Garcia to show up and go through it all with him.

"I'm sorry for your loss, Dillon. I really am," Mary said to me, and then the two of them left the room. I waited in silence for Garcia to arrive, and I was glad for it. I needed it.

🐾 · 🐾

It took a little less than fifteen minutes for Garcia to finally show up. Without a word, he walked over to me and gave me a hug. I wasn't used to that from him, but with everything that had happened, it was nice. And it broke me a little, too. I tried to hold back the tears as best I could, to be brave, but as soon as he pulled me into his chest, it was as though he was giving me permission to let it out.

I blubbered like a baby.

"I'm so sorry, Dillon," he said as I sat back down. He didn't say anything for a while, letting me collect myself a little, I guess. When the tears and sniffling slowed down, he leaned in towards me a bit. "How did this happen?"

I laid it all out for him the same way I had for Mary. I added a bit more to it, telling him about Kajal and the Maanx, and everything that led up to us getting to the house, and then what followed. He listened and looked like he was about to cry too. If he did, I would full out sob and I knew it.

"We'll get this fucking thing, Dillon," he whispered, his lip quivering.

"I know we will. I will. I owe it to Rouge."

"And what about the Maanx?"

"What about him?"

"He clearly set you both up, right? He gave you the house, told you to call him when you were going, and then the place was full of cats that were there to keep you busy. Everything you told me about him and what he is, he had to be part of that, I'd guess. The only thing to find out is whether he had been working with the Baucis all along and knew one or both of you were going to die tonight."

He was right.

Damn it.

The rat bastard Maanx set us up and Rouge paid the price. Well, I knew what my first stop would be when this was all over. There was a cat man who was about to lose all nine of his lives in one shot.

"Where is the Maanx now? Want me to come with you so you can question him?"

I shook my head. I was used to being alone. I'd been on Earth since the 1800s, and until I met Rouge, I'd never really worked with a partner. Sure, there were times I'd help someone, or they would help me, but Rouge was the first time I had someone always by my side, an actual partner who not only pulled her weight, but had saved my ass. Now, with her gone, it would go back to the way it was. I couldn't afford for anyone else to get hurt because of what I do.

I told him this and he accepted it without a fight. I told him I would get to the Maanx as soon as I could, but there needed to be a BOLO put out for the Baucis wearing Rouge's face. If anyone spotted her, Garcia needed to be called so he could call me. There was no way any of these cops would be able to do anything to stop it. If they tried, they might just end up being the next skin this monster wore.

Garcia knew I was right and agreed to do that.

"I'm not doing this for you though, Dillon," he corrected my assumption. "I'm doing this for Rouge. She was so great and didn't deserve this shit. I wish I could do more to bring this asshole down, but I'll start with this. Are you going to be able to face it if it is still looking like Rouge when you find it?"

I didn't know, but I really hoped so.

I was pulling into the driveway of our house, Rouge's grandmother's place, about forty-five minutes later. I was drained. I didn't get out of the Jeep right away and go inside. I sat there, behind the wheel, engine off, just staring out the window not knowing if I could go in there. I'm not one of those people that believe in ghosts the way they are portrayed in movies. I didn't think some partially see-through spectre would be floating through the house.

But her ghost would be in there, haunting me nonetheless.

Her scent.

Her clothes.

The memories we had in there.

That's how real hauntings worked. There wasn't some spirit trapped forever in a part of the past, bleeding over into the now. It was the things the dead left behind that tormented us, wouldn't allow us to let go of things. Inside there was a place Rouge had grown up, redecorated herself, and she'd given life to those old walls. I needed to go in, though, and do my best not to just come apart.

"Stop being like this," I told my reflection in the rear-view mirror. "Stop being so afraid to face this. The sooner you do this, the sooner you can find her killer."

I touched the door and immediately pulled my hand away. I took a deep breath and closed my eyes and pushed myself forward. I had to do this. I needed to do it now. The pup was in there and needed to eat. I couldn't let the poor darling starve.

"Okay. Let's start with that," I said, and finally got out of the car. Going into the house took a little more work.

I stood on the stairs leading to the front door. I tried to take a step forward, but my body was rejecting the idea. My subconscious knew what was waiting in there for me. It wasn't a monster, or demon, another hunter, or just a hungry dog. My failure was in there. My inability to protect her. Falling for a stupid trap. Letting her die while I fought off a bunch of cats. All of the parts of her waiting in there would be screaming at me once I stepped inside.

"And if you don't, and her dog dies, then she will come from whatever afterlife there is and kick you ass. You owe it to her to be stronger than you are showing."

I was right. I had to be someone more than I was being. I failed her in the moment she needed me, and now it was time to make up for that any way I could.

Revenge.

And feed the pup.

I finally managed to get inside the house after a little more hesitation. I froze after a step inside. I could smell the perfume she used on our last date. Floral. Roses. I remembered kissing her neck, breathing in as my lips touch her skin, pulling her close to me.

My knees weakened and I dropped to the floor. I whispered her name to the rooms and wanted her to answer back. I wanted ghosts to be real, for her to appear in front of me and call me to her arms. Instead, I heard the tip-tap of the puppy's claws clicking off the hardwood floor and saw the little one come towards me, her face sleepy, and tongue poking out of her mouth. She stopped and looked at me on all floors before she began to look around, no doubt wondering where mommy was.

"Come here, darling," I said, my voice cracking a bit. "Come on."

The pup toddled up to me and jumped up into my arms. She began licking my face like crazy, something she'd never really done before; at least not with me. That kind of affection was usually for Rouge only. Maybe she knew something was wrong, that there was something off with me coming home and her mommy not being there. I hugged her, sitting on the floor, crying that neither of us would ever see Rouge again.

"It'll be alright," I whispered to the pup. "Everything will be alright. I will make this right. I will make them all pay for this."

I slept on the couch and woke up with a pain in my neck. I couldn't bring myself to sleep in the bed we had shared. Just managing to be in the house was hard enough. I opened my eyes and saw the puppy was laying on my chest. I checked my watch and saw that it was already past noon. I wasn't surprised I had slept in so late. Depression can do that to you.

"Let's get you some breakfast," I told her, and sat the little one on the ground. We went to the kitchen together and I made her food. I didn't bother to make anything for myself. couldn't even think about eating, so I just made some coffee and hoped I would be able to keep it down, if I could even drink it at all. There were more important things on my mind than food. I wanted to go out there and get started hunting down Doc and then the Baucis. I wanted to kill each of them slowly. I knew it wouldn't bring her back, or give me any sense of true peace, but it would get the need for revenge out of my system.

My phone rang, startling me.

Reluctantly, I pulled it from my pocket and saw it was Godfrey calling. I wondered what he could want, and then thought about hanging up on him. I wasn't sure I wanted to even talk to him, or anyone, at the moment. If he was aware of what had happened to Rouge, then he would want to know how it happened, who did it, and then if I was okay. I didn't want to admit to him or anyone else how I really felt. I didn't want to cry in front of him or even on the phone with him. I wanted to wallow, to bury myself in my work, to walk down the violent roads I planned on without being bothered by anyone. I ended the call and turned my phone off.

No distractions.

It was time to work.

I made sure the pup had plenty of food and water for the day and the rest of the night. If things took longer than that, I would call up one of Rouge's friends and ask them to check in on her. I didn't know if her death had hit the news yet, but if so, it would be easy for them to understand why I might need help.

I packed two bags full of more tools than I'd need. I didn't just want to pull the soul from the Maanx, I wanted to cause it pain, to hurt it, to slowly draw the answers out of it while he screamed for me to show him mercy. He'd get none. I'd hurt him, give him a touch of death, but pull him back before he could leave me. When I saw he had suffered enough, that he was as hurt as I was, I would continue for a few hours more, just to make a point.

I loaded the Jeep, not with snacks or coffee for this, just water and Advil. Once packed, I drove back down to the rooming house near Bathurst and parked half a block away from it. I watched the door and waited.

This time, I was ready to be much more patient. No complaining about how long I was going to have to wait around for this asshole to show up.

The day was sunny, and warm. Spring was in the air, but I kept the windows rolled up and the engine off. My eyes were glued to the door. While I waited and watched, I began trying to come up with a plan on how I was going to handle him when I did see him. Would we go up to his room? Would I take him somewhere? How would I even approach him? Those small details didn't seem as important as what I would do to him when I did get my hands on him. I longed to look in his eyes as I broke him.

I looked over to the passenger seat for a second and my heart cracked a little. Seeing the empty seat brought it back to me. I would never see her sitting beside me again. She'd never be here on a stakeout with me, laughing at my bad jokes, telling her own terrible ones. It was too fresh. Too much to deal with, and I felt like I wanted to get out of the Jeep right then and there. I put my hand on the door, but where would I go? I was here for a reason, and that reason was also why the seat sat empty. I needed to stop overthinking it all and do what I came to do.

That was easier said than done.

Four hours later and I was still sitting there and there was no sign of the Maanx, the sonofabitch, Doc.

I was suddenly worried the bastard had taken my advice and skipped from the apartment. I thought that I could call him, but I was sure that if he saw my number ringing, he would go so far underground that he would never be found. Hell, he might even skip out of that body and go into something else to hide, even into a dead cat, where he would feel more at home anyway.

I decided to just leave the phone off and avoid the distraction. I would have liked it more if I had brought the puppy with me after all. Before I met Rouge, I hadn't known how nice it was to have someone to talk to, or to at least sit with and just be in there with. I had never realized how lonely it was sitting in a car alone until I had someone whose company I actually enjoyed. And now she was gone.

I missed her already. I had no idea how long this empty feeling would last, but I knew something to fill it with.

And as I thought about that, the universe provided me with what I needed.

"There you are, asshole," I whispered as Doc walked out of the rooming house.

He had an air about him, as though he was someone without a care in the world. There was nothing on his face to show he was scared, or even concerned. Was he so sure the Baucis had killed us both? Had nobody told him I was still alive and kicking? Well, I'd give him a pretty good wake-up call.

I started the Jeep and began to follow him. It was harder to do when the person you were following was on foot and you were in a vehicle. I had to let him get a block away, then drive close to him and park, only to let him get another block away. I made a choice to grab him and get him in the Jeep somehow. I didn't want to do it at his place. I wanted it somewhere that nobody would hear his cries or screams. I couldn't do it while he was on a main road like Bathurst, so I had to hope he would turn somewhere a little more private.

Better yet, he stopped and went inside a pet store, and I knew this would be my chance.

I parked right in front of the doors, just a sidewalk between it and the passenger door of my car. I went into my bag and pulled out my gloves and the coin as a backup. I got out of the car, took a deep breath, and felt my knees buckle a bit. The world felt so heavy on my shoulders. The depression was coursing through me, mixed with the adrenaline of what I was about to do in clear view of the public. I put my hand on the roof of the Jeep to catch my breath and steady myself before I slipped on my gloves and got into position.

"You got this," I whispered, and got ready to spring into action.

The door opened inward to the right, so I stood on the left and waited. I tried not to look too suspicious as I waited for Doc to finish up whatever he was doing in there. I looked up and down the street. It was a nice day and there were quite a few people out, but it wasn't as busy as Yonge Street of Queen West, even. So, I just waited and hoped there wouldn't be a surge of people passing when Doc finally came out.

I took slow, deep breaths as I waited. I fought to clear my head, to go into work mode. I didn't want to think of Rouge's face; living or dead, I couldn't allow the dark cloud to blind me. I was a machine when it came to this part of the job. I had done it so many times before, and I did it well. There would be time to mourn later, properly. For now, it was work, work, work.

The door opened and I nearly sprang too early. It wasn't Doc. It was an older lady carrying a huge bag of dog food. If I wasn't hunting, I would have offered to help her. It looked like it might weigh over twenty-five pounds.

The next time the bell chimed I waited and saw the cuff of his pants as Doc stepped out, and gathered myself for what I was about to do. I stayed against the wall, out of his sightline, and once he was fully out of the store, I stepped behind him and put my gloved hand on his bare arm.

He froze in place.

I moved in closer, my chest against his back and could feel him trying to fight it. Three cans of cat food dropped to the ground and rolled across the sidewalk and into the gutter.

"Remember me, asshole?" I whispered in his ear. "Let me jog your memory. I'm the guy you set up?"

I was boiling and had to turn down the heat a little. I couldn't do anything here. Not with so many people around. Without letting go of him, I moved him slowly towards my Jeep and put him in the passenger seat. While still holding him with one hand, I used my other one to pull the cursed coin from my pocket and pushed it against his forehead so he would stay where he was and wouldn't be able to move. After that, I shut the door and looked around the street. Nobody was even looking my way.

Perfect.

I got into the Jeep and drove off. I said nothing as we went.

I wasn't even fully sure where we were going until I got there. Years ago I had done a job down near Cherry Beach, where there were a lot of industrial buildings. There were also a lot of abandoned and empty ones, which would be perfect for this. This one had once been a security company building, owned by a guy who wanted to start something called Parapolice. He had a dog kennel area, and horse stables to go along with the cruisers and guards he hired. The place had been terrorized by a demon made of horse shit. He knew his guards wouldn't be able to help, so I was called after his wife convinced him I wasn't a hack. It took two days to rid the place of the demon, who just managed to move from one pile of shit to another, even getting into the kennels at one point. Since the company had moved to the east end of the city, the place had stayed empty, so I was sure it would be the perfect place for what I needed to do with Doc.

I parked around back of the building, out of sight from the street in case anyone drove past. I didn't want anyone to notice us while I went to work.

I took Doc by the arm and removed the coin. I held him tight and grabbed my bags. It took a lot of work leading him inside, but once we were there, I sat him on the floor, and put the coin back on his forehead. I pulled some duct tape out and taped up his ankles and put his wrists behind his back. Once he was fully secured, I removed the coin and let him be free. I wanted him to react to what I was about to do.

"Dillon…what…where…what are you doing to me?" he asked, his voice full of panic.

"Did you really think what you did would work? That the Baucis would be able to kill me?"

"I didn't do anything—"

"NO!" I yelled, my booming voice echoing in the empty building. "You're not going to lie to me. Not after all you've done to me. Do you get it? If you try to lie to me, let me warn you that things will only get worse and worse for you. If you think you know what pain is, I'll make you see you've never even been in the same room as true agony. So, keep those lies buried inside and tell me only the truth. When I ask a question, you will answer me. Tell me what I want to know, with no bullshit sprinkled in. Do you understand me?"

"I don't know what you want me to say," he said and began to cry, snot bubbling from his nose.

"You sent me to that house, set me up. It was full of your cat friends. Do you want to know how many I killed?" I asked with a smile.

"You hurt them?"

"So, you know them?" I said, and watched his head droop a little. "Why did you do it? Why did you set us up?"

"I…had to. They came to me and told me I had to help, or they would kill all my friends and then me."

"They? Who are they? Is there more than one Baucis here?"

Doc shook his and leaned back away from me. "I can't tell you. They will kill all of them. They will kill everyone I know and care about."

"They will?" I barked and smashed my fist into the bridge of his nose. I felt the bone crunch under my knuckles and blood exploded from it when I pulled my hand away. "You don't think I will kill them and you? I will start bringing them all here and killing them one by one while you sit there and watch. Is that what you want? I will hurt everything you love, just like you hurt the only person I ever loved."

His eyes flew open, blood streaming down his face. I guess there was nothing in the news yet, or he didn't have cable TV. But I could see the light go on behind his eyes. He knew what I was getting at. Doc's eyes looked around the room as if to confirm Rouge wasn't there. He opened his mouth to say something— what, I don't know—but only a choking sound escaped him.

"Who got you to set us up? Who told you to make it so we would get killed?"

"I didn't know they would—"

I hit him again because I knew he was lying. He knew what he was doing. There was no way the Maanx was that stupid. They had told him to lure me to a certain place. What did he think they were going to do to me?

"One more lie comes out of your mouth, and I place this coin on your head while I round up some of your friends," I warned him. "Just tell me what I want to know and no lies. Got it?"

"You're just going to kill me," he cried, and more blood bubbled out of his nose. He sounded congested; nose clearly shattered.

"You're right," I told him calmly. "I am going to kill you. You don't get to just walk away from the choice you made. You knew what they were going to do to me. To her. They killed her. Took her from me, and for that you are not going to see another meal. But you can die fast and alone, or slow with bodies of all your cat friends around you. I'll leave that choice to you."

"You wouldn't hurt any of them. You think of yourself as the good guy."

I shook my head.

"I might be the good guy, but I am also the person who you broke when you helped to take her away. You did that. So, get the idea out of your head that I'm going to be fair or make a deal with you. You're going to give me what I need, and then you're going to say farewell to your pathetic life."

Doc went into full sobbing mode. He must've seen it in my face or heard it in my voice. I was not joking or messing around. This was it. His final moments. He could do it alone, or with company. I really hoped he would take my threat seriously, because I really didn't want to have to leave there and try and find any of his cat friends, or just any random cat for that matter. Looking back, I think I might have been so mad I would have, but it would have been a huge pain in the ass.

I was glad I didn't have to find out.

"It was the Baucis," he whispered, and hitched his breath between tears. "She came to me with a human, and they threatened me. They told me they would hurt all my friends I had brought over and the—"

"Wait," I interrupted. "What do you mean friends you brought over."

"I...I don't want to tell you that. It doesn't matter. They threatened me and—"

"You don't get to tell me what matters and what doesn't. What the hell did you do?"

He looked at me, unblinkingly, and shook his head. He didn't want to say it, but I wasn't going to just let it slide. I went into one of the bags and pulled out a tool called a Fraazi. It is a paddle. Looks a bit like something you would play ping pong with, but there was no fun to be had with this one. A Fraazi is made up of the bones of a Fraazinti demon. They are strung together with the sinew of the same demon, and then wrapped in the leathered skin of its wings. Once that is done, it is dipped into a mix of its blood, urine, and excrement and left to bake in the three suns of the planet it is from. Once it is set, the paddle will irritate the skin to the point of boiling wherever it makes contact.

"You know what this is?" I asked, and held it inches from his face. He nodded carefully. "Tell me what the hell you did, Doc, or I start with your arms, then your chest, and then, something a little more sensitive below the belt."

"Please...don't do anything to them. They're...they aren't here to hurt anyone."

And then he laid it out.

All those cats he was bringing into the rooming house, they weren't just strays or friends he was feeding. He had been killing them, murdering them all to bring other Maanx over through a weak spot in his little rooming house apartment. I don't know how the lucky sonofabitch managed to find an apartment with a doorway to his home world. That's why he was afraid of them, why he agreed to help them try to kill me, and to kill Rouge. The cats he had brought over were part of his family.

"They said they would kill them all, bring a creature here that would devour them and let them rot in its stomach for a century. I couldn't let them hurt them."

"How would they bring a creature here?" I asked, not fully buying the whole story.

"The human. He has a porter."

"How does a human have a porter?" I asked, and didn't want it to be true. The last time I had dealt with something that had a porter, it had been a Hellion. That made sense. A human being able to find and make someone a porter was a box I did not want to open.

"I don't know, but he does. He had two other creatures with him, in their real forms, not like me, or my family."

I walked away from Doc for a moment. This wasn't going the way I had thought it would. When I imagined how things would play out, I was expecting something different. He would tell me they offered him something he couldn't refuse, and I would torture him until the sun rose.

That's not how it was playing out at all, and I didn't like it.

"What can you tell me about him? The human?" I asked when I was finally ready to try and wrap my head around it all.

"His name is Angstrom. He's taller than you or me, and very thin. He has stringy, black hair, but he is older than you as well. His face skin is yellow, gaunt, and waxy. His eyes are dark and set deep in his head, but he is human, even though he looks like a skeleton in a suit."

"And you're sure he's human?"

"I think so. I can usually smell when someone isn't, when there is something not of this world living in a body. Just like you. I can smell it, but I can't place it. I could smell it on her too, but I don't know what she was either."

The floor felt like it moved.

"What did you say?"

"The woman you were with. I could smell that she wasn't human, but I don't know what she was any more than I know what you are."

No.

That wasn't right.

Rouge was human. She wasn't like me or him, or any of the things I hunt. No. This was just another fucking game, something to mess with my head. What they hell was this Maanx getting at? Why would he say it?

"What the hell are doing? Why would you say some bullshit like that?" I barked at him and wanted to break his nose all over again. "She wasn't alien. She was normal. A human. What the fuck are you trying to pull here?"

"No...I'm not trying...I didn't mean to... It's just...just that when...when you two...I smelled something... I'm sorry. Please.

I'm trying to tell you everything. I'm sorry."

I couldn't take this. He seemed sincere in what he was saying. But there was no way to tell for sure if he was lying. I had been doing this for a long time and staring into his already broken face, the pitch in his voice made me think it all had to be true. But how? What in the name of everything I knew was going on?

"Okay," I said, taking a deep, long breath. I needed to move away from that line of the story. There was no way to prove what he was saying was true. I couldn't believe it was true. There was no way I could let any of that be. And even if it was, there was no way it changed anything that happened, or what I was about to do. "Just tell me what you know about them, the one who told you to set us up. How did they contact you? How did you contact them? Do you know where they really live? I want it all. Everything. And you're going to tell me if you want your friends left alone."

He spilled it fast, between the crying and the occasional pleading. I wanted to move away from what he had said about Rouge. I didn't like how confused it made me feel, and how I started to question if any of it could be true. I knew it couldn't be. I had been with this woman for years. We lived together, made loved, watched TV, played with the puppy. There is no way she had been living with the secret that she was not human.

I listened to Doc tell me all about how he had been approached by them weeks before I had found him. They probably had gone to others who were living here illegally and told them the same thing. They had told him if I showed up and began to ask about the Baucis, to lead me on and then set me up.

"I told them I would help, and then you showed up and I did it. I was more afraid of them than I was of you. I didn't know they would try and hurt you."

I knew that was bullshit. He had already said it, and I didn't believe it the second time any more than I'd believed it the first. Doc knew what we were walking into. He knew what a Baucis was and what it was capable of, too. I didn't bother to hit him for it, though. I would hurt him plenty in a few minutes, anyway.

"Where are they staying?" I asked, watching his face carefully so I could see if he was lying or not.

"I don't know. They just gave me a phone number to call. It's in my cell under the name Spooky. That's what they are. They're both scary. If they hadn't made me feel so afraid, I wouldn't have helped them at all."

"Even the human?"

"The human was worse than the Baucis," he admitted. "There is something in his eyes I didn't like. And he had a bad smell too, like a warning was coming off him. It's the same thing as when you can smell where a wolf or coyote sprays to keep people away."

I didn't know what that smell was, but I got the gist of it.

"Where's your phone?" I asked, and he told me it was in his front pants pocket. Not trusting that he wasn't going to try and headbutt me, I pushed the coin to his forehead, so he was frozen in place while I fished it out. There was no password on the phone, and there was the number. I thought about calling it first, but second-guessed myself and decided to just hold onto it and give the number to Garcia and see if he could find anything.

What did that leave?

I could ask him more about what he said about Rouge, but it was pointless. It was a distraction. He was saying it to keep me talking, and to keep himself alive longer, if not forever. There was nothing else to ask him. He gave me what I needed on the Baucis, and added something more with the one who has the porter, someone he said was a human. The phone number may or may not help, but there was nothing else Doc could give me to help other than his last breath.

I tucked his phone into my pocket and went to my bag. For the next hour, I did things I'm not proud of. Seeing Rouge's body had made something in me snap, something that had never been broken before. There was rage, sorrow, loss, and depression swirling around through my head and my heart. My vision was clouded, and I thought the only way to take some of the pain away would be to bleed it out of Doc, to remove parts of him piece by piece until I could find the parts of myself that were missing. I had never in my life been so cruel, so vicious. I won't write down what I did here, even if what I did was in the name of Rouge and love. I can't take back what I did, and even if I could, I can't say that I would. The choices we make are part of what makes us who we are. We learn from the good things, and the bad. But when I got ahold of the Baucis and this human, Angstrom, I doubted I would take it easy on them.

Tuesday/Wednesday/Thursday

I got home after midnight. I don't even remember the drive back. It almost felt as if I was asleep and someone else was behind the wheel. My thoughts were all over the place. I couldn't stop seeing Rouge's body, shifting into the Maanx's body and then back again. And all the while, the dead cat-man's words and accusations echoed in my mind. I hated him for saying it, and even making me think it was real for a second. The idea I'd been lied to by the woman I love — or loved — was almost as bad as knowing she was gone.

I sat in the Jeep, parked in the driveway of her house until I was sure nobody was around that might see me. I was very bloody. The last bit of the Maanx were all over my hands, face and clothes. When I looked in the rear-view mirror, I saw there were bits of skin in my hair, too. It was proof of how much self control I'd lost during my time with him. Rage and revenge blinded me. Grief had put a hand on my shoulder and told me it was okay to do it, for Rouge's sake.

Once I was sure I was in the clear, I went into the house and jumped in the shower. I kept my clothes on as the hot water washed the remains of Doc off me and them. I peeled the clothes off and let them drop to the tub floor and began to scrub my skin. I would have to wash or burn the clothes afterwards. When and if the cops found Doc's body, they would only see him as a human, not as a Maanx in a human body. His death would just look like a brutal murder, and I knew that may pose a problem for me. Luckily, I was wearing my cursed gloves when I went into the building, so there was nothing there for them to find fingerprints-wise, and I didn't leave any DNA that I was aware of. Not that the police had my DNA or fingerprints anyway, or any way to connect me with Doc.

At least, I didn't think so.

If I was wrong, well, I would have to deal with that, if and when it came up.

After the shower, I went to the living room and then fed the pup again. The little one was very happy to see me, and I was happy to see her, too. She was my connection to Rouge. The little one was hers, Rouge's little fur baby. I set the food down, a small bowl of kibble, but she didn't seem interested in it at all. She wanted to follow me around as I got dressed and then sat down on the couch. The pup jumped up, quite a height for something so small, and curled up beside me. I began to pet her and stared off into the dimly lit house, my mind drifting to places I didn't want it to go.

Instead of allowing those thoughts to intrude, I laid down and closed my eyes. The pup stepped up onto my chest and laid down, and I wished it was Rouge, coming to snuggle with me, her head on my chest. I felt myself on the urge of tears and sat up abruptly. I didn't want to do that. I nearly sent the dog flying but caught her before she could tumble off and hit the floor. I needed to get my mind off Rouge and everything else. I needed to disappear and not think about anything.

In the kitchen, I found six bottles of wine, a bottle of unopened Jack Daniels, and a nearly full bottle of gin. Rouge hadn't been much of a drinker, and nor was I, but I wondered if these would help me fall into a shadow place where my sorrow and pain wouldn't be able to find me. Figuring I was willing to give it a shot, I started drinking the first bottle of wine. By the time the last drop was out, being the lightweight I am, I was stumbling to the bedroom and passed out without even pulling back the sheets.

For most of the time I was out, there was nothing, but as the booze in me started to wear off, the pain came back in the form of nightmares. I woke up with a start and nearly screamed. I don't remember what was so terrible, but I was covered in sweat and my eyes burned from the tears. The only thing I could think to do was to drink some more and go back to sleep.

This was me for the next three days. I went to the bathroom and fed the dog. Other than that, I was lost to my depression and trying to escape facing reality. I left my phone off and didn't once think about checking to see if anyone had reached out. I didn't care. What is there to care about when you lose someone who means so much to you? I just wanted to grieve my way, and that was in a drunken stupor.

Without any food in my stomach, it made it easier for the alcohol to do its job, but on Thursday, I realized I was going to run out before the day was over. I could've gone out and bought more, but since I could barely walk a straight line to the kitchen or bathroom, driving was out of the question. Getting myself arrest for a DUI—or killed—wouldn't solve anything, and there were still those that needed to pay for what had happened.

When I drained the last sips of the foul-tasting gin, I went to sleep in a drunken state for the last time. I pulled the pup onto the bed beside me. She normally likes to sleep in her own bed, snuggled near the vent that lets off cool air in the summer and warm in the winter, but since Rouge hadn't come home with me, she'd been stuck to my side. Even as a lush, she still wanted to be near me, which was sweet.

"Don't you worry, little one," I told her, my eyes already heavy, ready for sleep. "This is the last of it. And then, we go back to work. I promise. I'll be a better person when I wake up."

I kissed her head, fought back vomit threatening to rise from all the booze, and went to sleep. I hoped there would be no dreams.

Friday

When I woke up it was late—or early, depending on how you look at it. There had been no nightmares pulling me from sleep, which was nice, but my head was pounding. Reluctantly I got up and went to the bathroom and then let the pup out in the back yard to do her business. When she got inside, I gave her a treat, poured some fresh food and water, and made a pot of coffee. I hoped the caffeine would quiet the head-pounding a bit.

Once the coffee was poured, I sat in the living room with only one lamp on, waiting for the sun to rise before turning on my phone. The pup was at my feet, acting like she wanted me to pick her up and put her on the couch, even though I knew she could do it.

"If you want up, jump up, silly," I told her, but she just sat on the floor and whined a bit. "Fine. I'll do it."

I picked her up and sat her next to me. She kept trying to get on my lap, but I didn't want to spill hot coffee on her. I asked her to wait until I was done, but she's a dog after all and not the most patient one at that. So, I allowed her onto my lap and began to pet her while I started the dreaded taste of reality.

"Did you ever notice anything strange about your mommy?" I asked the dog, and she looked up at me with her wide eyes, head cocked slightly to the side as if she was trying so hard to understand what I was saying. "Did she have strange tastes in food when I wasn't around, or ever tell you she wasn't from this planet?"

The dog made a chuffing sound and began to lick my hand. I

didn't know if that was poodle for yes or no, but whatever it was, she was no help answering all the questions I had about Rouge. I needed to think about it. There was no way it could be true. Had she ever shown signs that she wasn't who she said she was? I played back memories, fought to look at it as best I could, and there was nothing there. She was like every other human I'd ever met, only so much better. She drank water, ate food, and didn't have any strange tastes in things. She was...

Something in my head popped.

It was a small thing, but I couldn't deny it once it popped in there.

Then, a second one showed up as if to try and confirm the first.

Once, a while back, I accidently touched her with my gloves, and she froze for a second. She played it off like it was just a moment she was having, a little brain fart, but maybe it was more than that. And when we were dealing with the Doll Maker, the soul stealer grabbed Rouge by the face and looked at her, called her special and asked what was inside her, saying there was something special within Rouge too.

Was that proof of it? Did those two things make what Doc told me add up to something real? Or was I looking for something more to focus on to avoid dealing with her being gone?

I wasn't sure, but if it helped me not hyperfocus on the fact that she was gone, maybe it would be better. Time to go into detective mode.

I nudged the pup off my lap and stood up, telling her to stay on the couch. She didn't listen. She jumped off gracefully and began to follow me as I went through the house and started to look for any shred of evidence to prove she was or wasn't something more than a human. I started in the bedroom and paused in the doorway when a faint whisper of her shampoo and perfume found me and hit me in the stomach and in the heart. No. I couldn't let that stop me. I needed to not stand there and want to cry, wish that she was lying in our bed asking if I was coming to bed or just going to stand in the doorway like a dork.

She wasn't there.

She never would be.

But maybe the answers to who she really was could be found somewhere here.

I got to it. I took out a stack of old photo albums. I managed to find some of her purses that had items in them, including her wallet, and brought them too. I found boxes in the basement full of papers, photos, and clothes she'd kept from her past. There were birthday parties at a Playland McDonalds. Graduations. Visits to Walt Disney World. Partying at some bar. Photos of her with her grandmother, and her puppy. The photo albums were a glimpse into who she was and what she had been. There were no photos of her performing days though, but if I really wanted to see them, I'm sure I could go online and Google those.

When I was done skimming through the photo albums, I went to her wallet next. Inside was everything you'd expect to find from a normal person living a normal life: credit cards, bank cards, receipts of *Tim Hortons*, her health card, SIN card, and driver's license. There was also a library card for the City of Toronto that looked to have expired long ago. Was there anything there at all? Something that would tell me what I was looking for was or wasn't true? Rouge looked like someone who just had a normal life. No; *had* one. She was gone now. And I was alone without her.

The pup whined from the floor while I sat on the bed with everything open in front of me.

"I'm sorry," I whispered and leaned down to pick her up. I sat her down and she sniffed the items there. She pawed one of the photos of Rouge and looked at me. "No, little one. She's gone. I'm so sorry."

I picked her up in my arms and hugged her. She started to lick my cheek and that's when I realized I'd been crying at some point. I let her do it. Just hugged her and let her kiss away the tears I was shedding for her mom. I was about to lay down, to just sleep among the memories of her I had, but as I was about to, I saw something that gave me pause.

Sitting the pup down on the bed, I reached over and grabbed the driver's license. It all seemed right, with the exception of one thing. Her eye colour. It said her eye colour was blue, but it wasn't, not since I had known her.

I grabbed a random photo from the album and looked at it closely. Her eyes were blue in it. I took one from when she was younger, and then older. They were all blue.

"That's impossible," I whispered, and pulled my own phone out. There were pictures of her on it, selfies of us. I opened one, then another, and ended on a third. From the time I met her, until the last time I had seen her, her eyes had never been blue. They were hazel. She had hazel eyes. I had spent so many days looking into them, the bits of brown, spatters of yellow mixed into the green. Those were the eyes I knew, the ones I dreamed of. "What the fuck is going on here?"

I looked from my phone to the photo. Everything about her was the same, aside from a slight age difference, but her eyes were wrong. Did that mean something? I went to the bathroom and there was no sign of her using coloured contacts. I didn't think it meant that she was not human, but it might. I didn't like the uncertainty about it.

I went back to the room and looked around as though there was something that would just yell the truth at me. I wanted a banner posted to call it out to me and give me peace of mind with who Rouge was. I knew her, or thought I had, but what if she had been lying to me? What if all of this was something different than I thought it was? Would it change how I felt about her, or whether I would still try and hunt down the ones who killed her?

I didn't even know anymore.

"Who was she, really?" I asked the pup still sitting on the bed among the old memories. "Was she who I thought she was? Or was I lied to and she was like me, a creature from somewhere else?"

The poodle gave me no answer and I laughed. What was I doing asking a dog for an answer in the first place? How desperate was I to think this little beast could tell me anything? There was nobody who could tell me what I needed to know, aside from the Baucis. It would know. When it drained her, it would have found something in her other than a human soul.

The pup began to chuff again, probably wanting to be let down from the bed, but I was too busy trying to work things out. I wanted to add one thing to the next to the next and make sense out of the nonsense my life was becoming. She got louder and louder, nearly sounding like an old man coughing than a dog having a fit. I tried to keep ignoring it, but she was determined to get my attention.

"What is it?" I asked the pup, as if it was going to be able to answer. Instead of words, she began hopping around on the bed and made little grunting sounds. I guessed she wanted down and wouldn't quieten until I did.

After putting her on the ground though, she kept going nuts. She pawed at my calves and hopped around on her hind legs. This was ridiculous. She had just gone outside not that long ago, had finished her food and water. There was no reason for this. I put her back on the bed and told her to calm down. I was patting her head and telling her everything was alright, when rustling grabbed my attention, and I looked at the papers sitting on the dresser.

"What the hell was that?" I asked, and then the noise changed.

"D-d-d-dill!"

What the hell?

I stopped thinking and moving. My brain was clearly not working right. I was hearing things. Still, I looked around the room, trying to figure out what it was. It had sounded like my name, but the voice was hoarse and sounded muffled. It was exactly what people would imagine a ghost to sound like and it sent a chill down my spine, and yet, I wanted to ask who was there. I felt like I was some terrified character in a teen horror movie, but I was more worried that I would feel like I was snapping more than I already felt. I slowly backed out of the room, figuring it was better to just get away from everything overwhelming me, when the pup barked. I guess she sensed it, too.

"I won't leave you here," I said and scooped her up off the bed when she barked again and made a weird noise.

"D-d-d-ill-on," the dog coughed out at me, and I stumbled backwards.

"What the fuck?" I didn't know what else to say, and kind of dropped or maybe threw the dog back onto the bed. "Please tell me you're not talking to me, that you didn't just say my name."

The dog chuffed several times, like it was clearing its throat. It barked again, chuffed some more, and then everything spiralled down even further into Wonderland.

"Dill, it's me," the dog said, and even though there was a hint of the pup's barking sound in those words, there was something else there I knew.

"Rouge?"

"Yeah. I-I-I'm having troub-bark-le talking through-ough-ough her," the dog said, and it was official: I was out of my head with it all. The stress, the violence; something in me had clearly snapped. "Say-ay-ay something, D-d-d-dill."

"No. No. This isn't real so I won't say anything. None of this is," I told the talking dog. "I don't even think I'm here right now. Am I? Or when I fainted did I hit my head and now I'm in a hospital tripping balls? Is this from all the damn booze in my guts?"

"You're he-he-here. This is so frus-frus-frustrating!" the dog said, and barked and coughed several times. "I think that got it."

"Got what?"

"I'm not used to being in a d-d-d-dog. Sorry. This is a first for me."

It was a first for me too. It's not every day you start to talk to a dog that sounds like your dead girlfriend.

"You can't really be you," I said and slowly walked back over towards the bed where she was sitting looking like the toy poodle I knew.

"I'm sorry about all of this. It wasn't supposed to be like this, and I hate that you're having to find out this way. I did want to tell you, but I didn't know how."

"Tell me what? That you're not human?"

"Maybe you should sit down so we can talk," the puppy/Rouge said, and used her little dog paw to awkwardly pat a spot on the bed next to her. "You can pick me up and sit me on your lap like earlier if that's easier."

I laughed. Nothing about this was easier. In somewhere around eighty hours or so I'd found out my girlfriend was dead, that I'd been set up, that there was a human out there who had a porter and was working with a killer to try and kill me, that my girlfriend hadn't been human at all, and now, that she was inside her toy poodle wanting to have a heart-to-heart with me. That was a lot to take in already. Nothing could make any of this easier, and it sounded like it was about to get worse.

"I don't know if I'm ready to hear this," I admitted, and refused to sit on the bed. "What do I even call you now? Is the pup even in there anymore?"

"Of course she is. I would never hurt her."

"So, you're both in there. At the same time. And if you leave, will she die?"

"No. She'll be fine. I don't plan on staying in here for long enough to do any long-term damage to her. I wouldn't do that. I'm not a monster."

"Jesus!" I said, because it was starting to add up. I did this for a living, so there were certain things I knew that others might not catch on to. "But you actually are a monster. You clearly aren't human, that much I know. There's apparently a whole hell of a lot I don't know, but I figured that one out. Can you at least tell me how long you were in the real Rouge's body?"

"Three months before we met."

"Three months? And was it you all along talking to me, or was it her, unaware that you were even there? Were you letting her be herself while you slowly ate who she was?"

"Oh! So, you know then?" the pup asked and gave me her sad, puppy dog eyes. I noticed they were hazel now too. This kept getting worse.

"That you're a Shadow Person?" I asked, putting it out there in the world and making it real. "It all adds up, doesn't it? Now I know why you came up to Innisfil to 'help me' on that case. Were the other ones up there your friends? Were you part of that whole plot? Was the plan for you to help them kill me?"

"Please, Dillon. Let's sit together and talk. I can explain it all."

"Just tell me. Were you part of that plan with the Hellion and the other Shadow People to kill me?"

She said nothing, but her head drooped quite a bit.

"I'll take that as a yes."

"At first I was, but that was before we met. When I met you, I felt something right away. I knew you were not the bad guy in this, that we were. I wanted to be near you, to help you, and I did. I saved your life. I know it doesn't make a whole lot of sense, but the moment we met, I knew there was something between us. You made me feel alive. But by then, everything was already in motion. All I could do was make sure you didn't get hurt."

"But you came there knowing what I was facing all along and didn't even give me a heads-up. You never mentioned the Hellion or the other Shadow People."

"How could I? I didn't know what you would do to me if you found out the truth. When I betrayed them all, it doomed me. I could never go back. And I didn't want to. I only wanted to be with you, even though I knew I wouldn't ever be able to tell you who I really was."

"So, you thought building a relationship on a lie was the way to go. Better to lie to me than to be honest and hope for the best?"

"I was drawn to you. I wanted to be near you, to see if there was more than just this electric attraction. And I knew you were a hunter, so what was I supposed to do? I knew your reputation, but when I met you, there was something so innocent and kind in you. I had never met anyone like you before."

I was getting angrier than I would have thought. The truth was, I had felt the same way about her when we met, too. I fell in love with her faster than most people would think was possible, or maybe even healthy. But I felt like there was a real connection there. Sparks flew between us, and it felt so real.

So, to know that it was all built on a lie, that the Rouge I was looking at was not the Rouge that lived in that body, it pissed me off. What else might she have lied about? Was she a she? Was the Shadow Person living in her a woman, a man, something else entirely? There wasn't a lot known about them, so for all I knew they were sexless beings that could shift into whatever form fit their needs. Of course, I knew they could enter a body and become them as well, but what were they when they were just themselves?

"Please, Dillon, know that I never really lied to you about anything," the pup said in a version of Rouge's voice. It was small and pathetic sounding, and even as mad as I was, I could feel those pleading words plucking at my heart. "I was wrong, but I want to make this work. I love you so much. I don't want to lose you, and I didn't want you to lose me, either."

"But I did lose you. I looked at you dead between those dumpsters. It killed me."

"That was just a shell. It's not who I really am."

"And who are you really? I don't even know," I told her, looking at this talking pup sitting on a bed I had shared with the thing inside her.

"I'm the one you fell in love with, the one you kissed and told you loved. I'm still me."

"In a dog's body," I pointed out.

"So what," she said, and huffed. "Does that change how you feel about me? Does it matter if I look like a dog, or a man, or the woman you first met? Those are just facades. Don't be so human with the way you see things in such set terms of man or woman. You know what the universe is really like. You know that better than anyone. How many faces have you had over the years?"

"That's not the same. I told you I was a Treemore when we first met. You knew everything there was to know about me."

"I know, Dill, but I'm still the one you fell in love with, even in this body. No matter what body I'm in, if I'm a man or a woman, or even a dog, nothing about me has really changed as far as who you fell in love with. The outside is just the dressing, the façade."

I turned away from her and walked across the room to the dresser. I didn't want to look at her. I was so mad at Rouge, or whatever her or his or its name was. I wanted to leave there and be done with it all, but then what? Would I still want revenge on the Baucis for what it did? Was I still upset and hurt over it killing Rouge, even though what lived inside Rouge was sitting before me in her dog?

"What happened to the woman who was in that body? The

real Rouge, the one in all those pictures around you?" I asked, but looked at the door I was considering walking through.

Silence.

"Answer me, or I'm walking out of here."

"You know what happened to her. She was here with me for about four weeks. We shared the body. When we first met there was a small part of her still in here, but it was little more than a tingle here and there. At first, we had shared her body and her consciousness. I was always in control, but in the time she was still here, I came to know her and instead of just devouring her, I incorporated her into me. Now, she's still in me. I still have her memories, her hopes, her dreams. I can close my eyes and see her first kiss, the time she drank too much red wine at a friend's housewarming party, and how she felt the first time she got on stage. I will always carry her with me, but you never met her. It was always me."

"And the same thing will happen to your pup?"

"Not if I get out of here fast enough. I won't spend too long in here, because I love her like a mother loves her child. She's my baby, and always will be."

"Then why did you go into her in the first place?" I asked, and finally turned around again to look at her. "You didn't even know if you could, did you? You didn't know if going inside her would be too much and your soul might tear her to shreds and kill her. But you did it anyway, right? Why?"

"For you. I need to see you, to be near you. I didn't want to show up as some other woman or man and try to explain all this to you. You would have thought I was lying, or crazy or...I don't even know. But I did it for you, Dillon."

"For me," I whispered and shook my head. I couldn't believe her when she said that. If she wanted to do something for me, why not tell me who she really was, or let me know she was not gone before I brutally tortured and murdered Doc? Would I have even killed him the way I had if I had known the truth? I looked at the pup, staring up at me from the bed, surrounded by the memories of a woman I didn't truly know, and I knew there was no way I could be there at that moment. I didn't even want to be in the house or near her. I needed some space and time to allow all this to set in, and then I would make up my mind about what to do next. "I think you should leave the pup now. I think you should release it, and then I can take her over to one of your friends' houses for a while."

"And where will I go?"

"I don't know, and for the moment, I don't care. You can stay here, because I can't. I need some space to think where I'm not surrounded by memories of you and us."

"Dillon, please. Let's just—"

"I can't. Not yet. This is all just…so much for me right now. I lost you. I saw you dead and it ripped me apart. I've done things now that I can't undo. In here," I said, and pointed to my heart and then my head, "I'm a mess. You need to give me time to think and be alone."

"And what about the Baucis?" she asked, sounding on the verge of tears.

"That will have to wait. Everything will have to wait."

We spoke little more after that. I left the bedroom and waited for her to separate from the dog. I didn't want to see that. After a few minutes, the pup came bouncing out of the bedroom and ran up to me. I looked up to the doorway it had come from and there was a dark silhouette looming there, but then, it was gone.

I wasn't sure if it was harder seeing her dead in the alley, or going through all that with her, and then seeing her in her true form. Nothing was easy these days.

"Time to get you somewhere safe," I told the pup, Rouge— whatever she really was—and picked the dog up. I walked out of the house and got into the Jeep and I drove around for a long time. When the sun came up, I would start to call around and find someone to take the pup. And then, it would be time for me to figure out what came next.

On the drive I tried not to look over at the dog, or what was once the dog. I didn't want to think about what was going on, what had happened and what it all meant. I fought against the way I was feeling about the lying and the deceit all this time we had been together. Everything we had done and shared was built on a lie. She was someone who had set me up, nearly got me killed, and never once had she told me anything about who she truly was. I didn't have time to think about it all, to let the anger or sense of betrayal set their claws into me. No matter if it had been Rouge or not, I needed to find the bastard who was doing this before it could switch bodies again.

After dropping off the dog at Susan's house, I thought about where I should go. I could try and check into a motel, but wasn't in the mood for bedbugs, or bugs of any kind. The next idea was going to Godfrey's, but I'm sure there were things I didn't know about his lifestyle, so the thought of couch surfing at his shop did nothing for me. Who knew what weird shit he got into when nobody was around to see it?

There was also Garcia, but he had a family, and I didn't want him to have to explain who I was and why I needed to sleep on their couch or in their guest room. Garcia seemed like someone who would actually have a dedicated guest room.

My next choice would be Kajal. We had only started talking again recently, but I hoped that he would be cool with the idea of me staying there short-term. I would do my best to convince him it would be, and even offer him money or anything I could. I gave up my apartment a while back to move in to Rouge's house, and I didn't want to sleep in the Jeep even for a night.

I crossed my fingers and headed to his shop.

My head was still a mess, and no matter how much I tried to shake it, I couldn't let it go or stop thinking about it. I could still see Rouge's body in my head, something that nearly broke my heart, only to find out the woman I was dating, that I had loved, wasn't who I thought she was. She was dead, but she wasn't at the same time. Was I supposed to be happy? Was I supposed to be mad? To feel betrayed by her? I felt so much, but didn't know if any of it was right, or which one I should be more accepting of. I wanted to talk to someone about this, but the one person I would turn to with something like this was the person who was at the center of my misery.

I pulled over three shops away from Kajal's shop and put the car in park. I took a deep breath, not sure how Kajal would take my request to stay at his place. We had only reconnected and I wasn't sure he was fully over how our relationship had soured. I hoped it was fixed at least a little bit, that giving him a way to find Aamir had softened his feelings towards me. If it had worked, there was hope that he might be open to helping me out.

Fingers crossed.

The store was still closed. There was mail sticking out of the slot in the door, more than there was the last time I was there. I stopped and wondered if everything was okay. I hoped that all this meant was Kajal and Aamir had found a way to separate from one another, and they were just busy catching up. That was the hope. If they were somewhere else, catching up on years lost, leaving the shop unattended, that would be fine. I didn't want to think of the alternative.

But the alternative crept into my head. With everything else going the way it had, there's no surprise that I was stuck thinking the worst. I tried knocking on the door again and when there was no answer I pulled out my phone and dialed his number. It rang over and over again. I could hear it from outside and couldn't detect any movement. I hung up before the voicemail came on and tried again.

Nothing.

I didn't like it.

I tried the doorknob and was surprised to find it was unlocked. I knew right away this wasn't a good thing, but there was no going back now. I needed to make sure everything was alright. It could have been just another thing piled onto the mountain of bullshit I was already facing, but I had to make sure he was okay.

He wasn't.

The store was dark, but I could see a light from the back room. I nearly tripped over a pile of books, but when I got to the back room, I nearly fell over Kajal. He was lying less than a foot away from the back room door. He was face down, a dark puddle under him, his neck twisted to the right in a bizarre angle. I knelt and looked at his face; his eyes were gone, his mouth open, and

I saw a few insects looking for something to eat. That means he couldn't have been dead long, but the real question was, who had done this.

I stood up and looked around the room. I didn't want to touch too much because eventually the police would come and I didn't want to make them think I had anything to do with this. I would call Garcia when I was done here, have him deal with the evidence if there was any, so if I did contaminate anything, he could rule me out.

The room was mainly books, a desk, and a chair. So many books. I didn't know if anything was out of place. I hadn't paid that much attention to where everything was the last time we were here. I looked on his desk to see if there were some papers he had out, something left behind that might give me a hint, and when there was nothing to see, I went back over to his body.

I wanted to move him, to flip him over and see if he had something under him, or in his hands. I would've also liked to see the wound, to maybe see what had done the damage to kill him, but I knew if I did that I would leave evidence I wouldn't be able to cover up unless I burnt the place to the ground, and that seemed a little extreme.

"You're too late," a small voice said from the far right corner of the room. I jumped a little at it, but couldn't see who had said it. I squinted into the darkness, and then saw movement, a thing as small as the voice that had spoken. "Why didn't you come sooner?"

"Who are you?" I asked, even though if I had thought before I spoke, I would've been able to put two and two together.

"I managed to get out since we met last time. Not that it helped my father, Kajal."

"Aamir?" I said, and a small stuffed bear waddled out of the darkness. Even though the bear had no facial muscles, it was clearly sad.

"Where were you, Dillon? You weren't here when he needed you."

"I had no idea this had happened," I said, and watched as him walk over to me.

"You had no problem being here when I was just trying to live my life with Kajal, but when he actually needed you, you were nowhere to be found. Did you send her here to do this?"

"Send who?"

"The woman who came here and killed him. He seemed to know her, so did you send her?"

I looked down at Kajal's body again. Was it possible? Did the Baucis in Rouge's body actually do this? I could feel my hands ball up into fists as my rage against the bastard grew in me.

"The woman who came here and killed him. Redhaired woman, acted like she was his friend and then she stuck a knife in his stomach and killed him."

Fuck!

"Did she do anything else, say anything, take anything?"

Aamir said nothing. He just stood in the middle of the floor, his plastic eyes looking down at his dead friend, or family, or whatever he thought Kajal was to him. I thought that maybe I should just get out of there. I wasn't sure there was anything to be gleaned from what happened here. The Baucis clearly had some sort of access to the memories of the victims they killed, and if that was true, then it knew Kajal had been trying to help us out and probably came out here to make it so he couldn't help me out anymore.

"She only told him to keep his nose out of the affairs of others before stabbing him. Then she took a piece of paper my father had been writing on. Why did she have to kill him, take him away from me just when we found each other again?"

I felt for the little guy. I knew I had made a mistake all those years ago, and then got Kajal involved in all of this. I have to admit, I was feeling a little guilty about it all. I did want to know what it was he had been writing down that she had stolen, but there was no way to know unless I could find her.

"It was from that book there," Aamir said, and pointed to one sitting on the corner of the desk.

I walked over to the desk and lifted up the leather-bound book with the name *Symbiotic Beings* burnt into the cover and spine. I went to open it, when I heard a sound coming from the front of the store.

"What was that?" Aamir asked, and I turned towards the front door.

"I don't know, but I think you should hide, and I should get out of here. Where is the back exit?"

"It's there," Aamir said, and pointed one of his stubby arms towards a dark hallway.

"Get somewhere out of the way or come with me. Up to you."

"I don't want to leave him. I'm staying here."

"Suit yourself," I told him, walking rapidly towards the hallway and the back door. I didn't know if it was Rouge come back to look at her handiwork or not, but I didn't have anything on me to fight a Baucis. I'd left the S'Borouth iron in the Jeep. I didn't have any wishes to become the next victim of the damn creature, so it was time to get out of there.

With the book in hand, I all but ran to the door and pushed out into what I expected would be an alleyway. I wasn't sure if it was or not, because as soon as I stepped out, I was blinded by a bright light in my face. I raised my hand to block it, and tried to see what the source was.

"Drop the book and get down on the ground!"

Shit.

I didn't need to be a rocket scientist to know what all of this was about. It was the cops. This was going to be messy. It would be even messier if I didn't do as I was told. I let the book fall from my hand and dropped to my knees and interlocked my fingers and let it happen. Two uniformed officers came towards me from the area of the blinding light and placed handcuffs on me. As soon as the cuffs were locked in place and I was made to stand up, the door I had just come out opened, and two familiar faces appeared.

Mary and Aaron, the two detectives who had questioned me about Rouge came out, giving me the once-over. Aaron, no surprise, had a smirk on his face. Why them?

"Look at this. Another dead body, and who was there before we were?" Aaron said and grabbed hold of my arm. "You have quite the knack for being around dead people, don't you? I can't wait to see what bullshit you try to tell us to get out of this one."

I tried to explain things, opened my mouth ready to offer something that would make sense, but they didn't want to hear it. I was told to shut my mouth and then was roughly put in the back seat of the police cruiser. There was a lot to take in with all of this, and I decided instead of trying to argue or fight them, I would take the time to roll things over in my head.

First thing I knew was that the Baucis had the ability to know what the victims did, which meant it knew everything we already did before Rouge was killed, or at least her body was stolen. Or should I say when the Shadow Person's stolen body was stolen? I didn't even want to get into that maze of thought, because in the end it didn't matter. What did matter is that everyone who had been made aware of the details, mainly myself, Godfrey and Garcia, were probably on the creature's radar.

And by me getting arrested, I was off the board now. I wondered if the Baucis had been watching Kajal's shop after killing him and had been the one to call the police. It made sense. How else had the cops shown up for this just as I arrived? I walked right into a damn trap.

Then, there was the book. I didn't know what Kajal had found in there and had written down, but clearly it was important enough for the Baucis to steal the paper with the notes on it. If it was just how to kill the thing, I already had that down, with the tools to do the job. If it was something else, I couldn't imagine why I would give a rat's ass about it since the only thing I planned to do when I found it was to send it on a one-way trip to oblivion. Once I did that, I would then try to figure out the whole mess with Rouge, or whatever her real name was.

First, I had to be done with all of this garbage, which I knew couldn't take that long. I mean, once they ran prints, checked for time of death and so forth, they would know I had nothing to do with it. Unless they didn't care about the evidence at all and they simply wanted to close the case, I would be fine. Luckily I would have Garcia on my side to help me out through this.

Well, as long as the Baucis didn't go after him, too.

Shit.

The drive didn't take long to get to the station, and when we arrived, I was pushed forwarded and dropped off in a brightly lit room. In the movies and TV shows, interrogation rooms are always so dark and moody, but in reality, they are brightly lit with horrible fluorescent lighting, and have grey and beige walls the same texture as ceilings in an elementary school. They kept the cuffs on me when they shoved me into a room furnished only with a two metal chairs on either side of a metal desk. I knew the drill. It was time to sit and wait.

There was no mirror here like in the movies, either. Nobody on the other side watching me to see if I would sleep like someone guilty, or jitter and freak out like someone innocent. They were more advanced than that. Each corner was fixed with a camera, and there was no doubt a microphone in them to make sure they captured everything before, during, and after the questions started. I had to give them what they wanted, I had to give them the movements of an innocent man so they would already be questioning what they thought they knew.

I started with bouncing my leg nervously, followed by shifting in my chair every thirty to forty seconds. Two minutes of that and I started to look around the room nervously before I started to sniffle as though I was about to cry. I hoped they were watching it all, seeing I wasn't relaxed or napping and think maybe I wasn't the bad guy here, because I wasn't. I needed them to at least hear me out and look at the evidence before they got too comfortable. This could go on for anywhere from thirty minutes to two hours before they came in to speak to me, so I had to pace myself and not actually let it all overwhelm me to the point where I actually became tired, and therefore looked guilty.

Only they didn't keep me waiting.

That had me worried.

The two detectives came into the room with a file folder and slammed the door shut behind them. Mary stood off in the corner, while Aaron slapped the folder down on the desk and sat across from me. I looked at Mary, but she wouldn't even make eye contact. Aaron, on the other hand, wouldn't take his eyes off me and was smirking still. Was there something I didn't know about? Was this a bigger setup than the Baucis just calling the cops to get me caught while I was at Kajal's shop?

"You've been a busy boy since we last talked, haven't you, Dillon?" Aaron asked, and opened the file. "Very busy, I see."

I couldn't see what he was looking at because he had angled the folder up towards himself.

"If by busy you mean stayed inside for the last three or four days feeling lost and depressed, then yes. I was busy grieving over the woman I loved."

Aaron nodded but didn't take his eyes off the folder. "So, you've spent some time in a mental hospital, haven't you?"

And here we go.

"I did, but it was a misunderstanding."

"Really? You attacked some kids, and then a cop. You were having delusions and had to be put on some serious anti-psychotics. According to the records I have, the doctor was putting in to have you fully committed before you were signed out for release by Detective Garcia. Is that right?"

I didn't know what to say to that. Garcia had helped me out of that jam, but admitting it threw him under the bus. But they already had to know the answer to it. If they actually had the hospital records, they knew exactly what had gone down.

"Things are a bit hazy about that," I offered. "They put me on medication that had me blanking out a lot."

"Do you still blank out a lot?" he asked, fishing for a line to hang me with. I said nothing. I knew this guy wasn't going to listen to me because he already had his mind made up. All I had to hope was that he wouldn't be able to string enough ideas together to actually make anyone else believe him. "No comment? Don't want to say anything, that's fine. I have some things to say to you and the way I see it. Here you are, a guy with some previous mental health issues, violent, blackouts, delusions—"

"Delusions?" I asked, wondering if he meant seeing people's faces melt.

"Well, you think you're a monster hunter, that there are aliens and demons on this planet— which is, without a doubt, delusional. The shrink we talked to also thinks it leads into the fact that you might have a form of schizophrenia. Do you disagree?"

"I disagree."

"You can. That's your right. But if you'll let me finish… Mental health issues, delusions, a car full of strange things that may or not be weapons, involved in a YouTube prank, and recently you were involved somewhat in the murder of three people."

He paused, and I took in a sharp breath. When I did, he went from a smirk to a full smile. "Three?" I asked, and tried not to stammer.

"Oh, you didn't think anyone would be able to put two and two together?" he asked, and rifled through the file he had he pulled out three photos and laid them between us. I tried not to react as I looked down at them and saw the horrible things I had done to Doc. The piece of shit had deserved it, but still, I didn't like that I had lost so much control and had brutalized him the way I had. "Does this look familiar, Dillon?"

I shook my head and tried to swallow, but my throat felt dry, like I was being strangled.

"Well, we received some information that you were seen with him on more than one occasion and had been seen leaving the scene where his body was found. Are you going to tell us you don't know who this is?"

"How the hell am I supposed to answer that? Look at these photos. It barely looks like a person at all, and you want me to tell you if I have or haven't seen him or her before?" I blurted out, hoping it sounded convincing.

"His name was Donald Dennison, but people called him 'Doc'. Did you know him?"

I paused and acted like I was trying to think about it. "I don't know anyone named Dennis, but there was a guy named Doc that I met with about the case I was helping Garcia with. He wasn't much help, but I had nothing to do with whatever happened to him."

"So, what you're saying is that there are three bodies on our hands, all people you know or have had recent dealings with? We have three dead, and the only common denominator is you, and yet you know nothing about it?"

"I know about one of them," I told him, biting back the anger that had begun to boil in me. "I told you who—or should I say *what*—killed my girlfriend. You watched the video. You heard from Garcia, but you still want to act as though these are normal murders and I had something to do with any of them? Let me ask you this: how long had Kajal been dead for?"

"I'm not going to divulge that," he told me.

"You don't have to. I know it didn't just happen, because of the colour and state of the blood. I was there to see my old friend, and clearly the person who killed him was watching the store and called you. Doesn't that make more sense than whatever you think?"

Aaron leaned back in his chair and then looked back at his partner. Mary shook her head at him and then he turned back to me.

"We're not buying any of it, Dillon. I don't know what the game is you're trying to pull, or what you're trying to do, but we know you're hiding something and there's enough evidence to link you to at least these three deaths, that any jury will convict you on it. So, why waste our time with dragging this out and just explain your side of the story? We can help get you a deal with the crown attorney if you just come clean with us."

I shook my head. "I have no idea what you're expecting me to tell you. I didn't have anything to do with these deaths, but if you don't let me help out, they're going to keep happening."

"See, Mary? Like I said, he has delusions of grandeur. So, Dillon, you think that you're the only one that can solve these cases. Our years of schooling and police work are nothing compared to you. Dillon the Monster Dick. The only one who can save the day."

A knock at the door kept me from telling him to go and fuck himself. I watched as Mary walked over and when she opened the door, she stepped aside and let in a tall, thin, creepy-looking man in an expensive-looking suit. His skin was yellowish and almost looked waxy. I would've thought he was ill, but he walked into the room with the confident stride of a younger man.

"Alright, detectives, I think we're done here," he said in a low tone. "Dillon, say nothing else."

"I'm sorry," Aaron said, not moving from his seat. "And who

the hell are you?"

"I'm his lawyer, and he's done talking. I'm assuming you aren't filing any charges at this time, correct?" he asked, and crossed his arms. "No? I thought not. Did you even read him his rights? Dillon, did they read you your rights?"

I shook my head and said no. To be honest, I hadn't even thought about that. Everything happened so fast, I didn't even remember that they hadn't read me my rights.

"Well then, I think we're done here. If you two want to speak to my client again, call me, not him. Let's go, Dillon," the lawyer said, and held his long hand out with overly long nails towards me. I stood up and walked out of the room with him. Before I did, I stopped and turned to the two detectives, who already looked deflated.

"You both know I had nothing to do with any of this. Try looking for the actual killer and stop wasting your time looking at me because there's nothing here. The killer is out there."

"Let's go, Dillon."

We walked away from the interrogation room and headed to the front desk so I could collect my belongings. They handed me everything in a bag, but the only thing in it was my keys and my wallet with some cash in it. I asked the guy behind the desk where the rest of my things were.

"The detectives said it's all evidence. You're not getting it back any time soon."

I opened my mouth to say something, but the lawyer, who I had never met, stopped me with a hand to my chest. "I have this, Dillon. Excuse me, Sergeant, but as you see, my client here has been released with no charges. And no charges mean that nothing on his person can be held as so-called evidence. I think you should either call your higher-ups, or return his items posthaste to avoid any media coverage of violations to his rights. You know how the media loves to hear stories like this about police misconduct and mistreatment of citizens. So, should we just avoid all that and give my client back his items? Does that sound good to you?"

The officer's brow furrowed, and he let out a grunt before he produced a second bag and handed it to me. I looked inside and saw the book and some of my tools, including my dagger, gloves, and the S'Borouth iron. With my belongings in hand, we headed out to the parking lot. I said nothing to him until we were out of earshot of the building full of cops. I had no idea who this lawyer was, or how he knew to come and save the day, but I was hoping it was Garcia who had sent him. Even if he did look like a mortician from a horror movie.

"Thanks for that, Mr..." I said, and trailed off since I didn't know his name.

"The name is Angstrom, Dillon. And it was no problem at all. My pleasure."

Angstrom.

You've got to be kidding me!

I could feel the blood rushing to my face as I balled up my fists. This had to be some kind of joke, or a coincidence. There's no way it could be the same one Doc had told me about, but how common of a name was that? It wasn't one you heard every day.

"You really have caused a lot of problems for us, Dillon," he said as we walked, confirming he was who I thought he was. "So, it was high time we met. The rest of the members believe you should just be dealt with; killed, if you will, but I think we can work something out to avoid any more bloodshed. Murder is so easy and so final. Better to make an arrangement that works for everyone, and then we have the start of a potential relationship, even a friendship of sorts."

"So, you're the same Angstrom that set me and Rouge up, and you're talking about a friendship?" I asked through gritted teeth, wanting to smash him in the face as hard as I could, even though there were police that could see us.

"I assure you, Dillon, none of that was my idea. The plan was to bring you to the house, yes. That's true. After that, I was supposed to be called so I could attend to make an offer. As it turns out, not everyone was on the same page with the idea. I'm very sorry for that and what happened because of the detour from the plan. In the interim, I did hear word that your friend, Rouge I believe, was not quite whom she claimed to be. But those facts not withstanding, I want to sincerely apologize for how things happened. It is not my intention to cause any problems."

"But you did cause problems, a lot of them, in fact," I said through gritted teeth, trying my very best to push down my rage. "I have a good mind to kill you here and now."

"Oh, you know you can't do that," he laughed, as though he didn't have a worry in the world. It wouldn't be hard for me to just pull out my dagger and jam it into the empty space where his heart should be. "Killing a human is against the rules of the Collective. Kill me and you get in trouble. But I'm sure you already know that, so let's not make threats we never intend to see through."

"It would be worth it."

"It might be, but then you'd never be able to easily find the Baucis. It is a clever one, and it will continue to cause pain and spread mayhem across the city. With that being said, I'm here to make you an offer."

"I'm not interested in anything you want to offer me after all this."

"Don't be hasty, Dillon. This will be good for you and yes, before you ask, it will also give us something we want, too. If you agree to the deal, we can not only tell you where the Baucis is, we can all but hand it over to you. And not only would we provide the location and a hint with how to kill it, but we will make sure all evidence the police have on you will disappear."

"What evidence? There can't be anything against me," I objected, trying to sound sure of myself, but I was starting to worry. I wasn't in the best headspace when I went after Doc.

"You sure about that, Dillon? Are you sure those cats that scratched you up didn't have skin and blood and DNA that could then be planted at crime scenes for the police to find? Maybe after we saw what you did to that poor Maanx, someone showed up and left something there to tie you to it, in case you hadn't done that yourself."

"You motherfucker!"

"Keep your voice down, Dillon. We don't want people to over-hear us, do we? No, of course not."

"What do you want?"

"I want to help you out. We're offering an olive branch for you. We're going to give you the Baucis and destroy the evidence against you. With those two things, everything is back to normal and you're in the clear all around."

"And then what do I owe you? I know there's got to be a catch here somewhere."

He smiled and when he did, it made my skin crawl. Even in the low light I could see the crooked yellowness of his teeth, creeping out of his overly large mouth.

"Yes, we would like something. And it's not much. All we want you to do is not fight the future. When the Collective falls, and trust me, they will, do not fight against what will happen. The plans we have are inevitable. Anything you do to stop it is like throwing a cup of water on a raging forest fire. It's simply useless."

"And up until the time that happens?"

"You do what you have to, but when they fall, you can just step aside and let nature take its course."

"And if I don't do that? If I just deal with this all on my own, and then deal with you all on my own?"

"You won't be able to stop it when it happens, Dillon. The Collective is a broken system and it's set to fall. I am going to be the one here who helps it come to fruition. You can either sit on the sidelines and let it be or fall with the rest of them. I've learned a lot about you since I was brought into the fold, and I know you do not lack in the knowledge department. You're a rule breaker. You see the truth where others simply tow the line. The Collective likes to invent rules for everyone to follow with no reason why, and you've already pushed back against it so many times. This is no different. There is no stopping the flow of progress. You can't stop a train with your bare hands. So, if you know this, be a futurist like us, and join in or step aside. Do not stand in the way with a dying system."

I didn't like it. I hated him and wanted to cut the stupid, smug look right from his face. This man, this tall, skinny, ugly bastard was the reason everything around me was falling apart.

If he hadn't stuck his hand into my life, I would be happy still. I would be living a lie, but at least I would be happy and ignorant.

"What choice do I have?" I asked, even though I was still thinking of ways I could find a loophole to screw him over. It's not as though he was being totally honest with me, so why should I make a gentleman's agreement with a human monster?

"It's yes or no. Freedom or jail. It's up to you."

"Where can I find the Baucis?"

Saturday

It was just after midnight when I left Angstrom. He dropped me off at the Jeep at the police impound. The glove compartment hung open, and my empty bag was sitting in the front passenger seat. I put all the stuff the cops had taken from me back where it belonged. Before driving out, I opened the book and began to leaf through the pages to see if there was anything that popped out. It was full of strange names of beings I'd never heard of before, many of them from Earth, which surprised me. I was halfway through looking at the pages when my phone rang. I sat the book down and pulled my phone out and saw it was Godfrey calling. At this time of night, I was sure it must be important.

"Everything good?" I asked as soon as I answered.

"Where are you, Dillon?"

"At the police impound. Are you okay? You sound a little stressed out."

"Rouge was just here. She was trying to get into the shop, nearly smashed my window out to get to me."

"Where is she now?" I asked, and started up the car.

"She's thankfully gone. I pulled out a weapon and it scared her enough to leave, but I think she might come back. I'm guessing this is the Baucis and not a ghost of her?"

"It wasn't a ghost, it was the damn thing that killed Rouge. But it looks like…"

Shit, it looked like the Baucis wasn't wasting time taking out anyone who'd been with me and who might know about it. If it went after Godfrey and failed, it might have already tried to go after Garcia, or was going there next.

"I think you're safe for now, but you might want to throw up some curses and protections around the shop to keep the thing out of there."

"What if it doesn't work? What if it's coming back before I can do anything or while I'm sleeping? I don't feel like dying at the moment."

"I don't think you'll have anything to worry about, but you know how to protect yourself. Others might not be able to. It already got to Kajal, who had no idea what to do. Now I'm a little worried it might be going after Garcia next."

"Shit. Go find out."

I hung up and started to dial Garcia's number while I drove out of the lot and headed towards his house. Angstrom told me he would call me with a time and date of when and where to find the Baucis, but if I could kill it before then, all the better.

Garcia didn't answer on the first try, so I called again. When he answered on the third ring, he didn't sound happy.

"Do you know what fucking time it is, Dillon?" he barked, but kept his voice low, no doubt so he didn't wake up his wife or kid.

"I do, but this is important."

"I kind of don't care. I was suspended today pending an investigation, all thanks to you, so I don't really give a rat's ass about what you might want to say," he managed to yell and whisper at the same time.

"I'll find some way to make it all up to you later, but it will have to wait. We have a situation here. You might not be safe. You or your family."

There was silence from him on the other end, but I could hear his feet shuffling; more than likely he was leaving the bedroom to go somewhere better to talk. I hated having to bring this to him, but if the Baucis showed up and hurt him or his family and I didn't do everything I could to stop it, it would eat me alive.

"What the fuck are you talking about, Dillon? How is my family in danger? What did you do?"

"It's the Baucis. When it killed Rouge, it didn't just take her form. It also took her memory, and it knows you are aware of it and what it can do. She…it…already killed Kajal and it just tried to attack Godfrey. I'm on my way to you now."

"Save yourself some time, Dillon. I'm not even at home. When I was suspended, we decided to go stay at my mom's place. Seeing as I didn't have to go to work and my son is out of school, I thought it would be a good idea."

"Well, that's a relief. How long can you stay there?"

"As long as I don't have a job to go back to, I don't see the need to rush back" he said, and I could hear the relief in his voice already. "How long until you put an end to this bullshit?"

"I'm working on it. Trust me, nobody wants to end this more than I do," I told him, and waffled about how I had met with Angstrom. "Did you get in a lot of shit at work?"

"Well, I'm suspended, what do you think?"

"I think the detectives that pulled me in tonight and tried to rip my ass open are out to get us both."

"Wait," he said, and I could hear the anger in his voice. "You were brought in? For what?"

"Three murders."

"Three? Who?"

"My friend Kajal, Rouge, and the asshole who set us up and got Rouge killed."

"You didn't have anything to do with those, did you?" he asked, nearly whispering as though someone was listening. "No, you know what? I don't want to know."

"Well, I didn't have anything to do with it," I lied easily. "You should know I wouldn't do that. Especially Rouge, who I loved, and Kajal, who was a good friend." I told him what had happened with Kajal, from the time I arrived, until I was released from custody. I didn't bother to tell him anything about Rouge. It was a mix of embarrassment at the wool being pulled over my eyes for so long, and just the sheer insanity of it all. "I need to stop this Baucis and then put all this bullshit behind me."

"How did you even get out so fast if they're looking at you for three murders? We usually like to let suspects stew a little while."

"A lawyer showed up and told them to charge me or let me go."

"So, your lawyer got you out? I didn't even know you had one."

"I don't. I'd go into more detail, but it's a bit of a long story that doesn't fully make sense even to me."

"Well, you woke me up, you might as well tell me. I'm sure it's fascinating."

I took a deep breath and told him everything I knew about Angstrom. I went through it all, starting with the conversation with Doc, and how he was connected to everything, but left out the part of what I did to the Maanx. He was surprised that I hadn't hurt or beaten him to death after finding out he'd been involved in Rouge's death, and I teetered on what I should say to him next. When it first popped into my head, I was sure I was going to keep this part of it from him, but then, would I be any better than Rouge? She'd lied to me, kept a major part of her story to herself, so if I wanted to keep things honest with Garcia, I knew I had to tell him.

"About that," I started, wondering how he would take it. Best to just let it out and hope for the best. "The Baucis killed Rouge, but she might not actually be dead. She might be in her dog."

"I'm sorry, what the fuck are you talking about?"

"It's complicated, but it turns out the Rouge we knew wasn't the woman we thought she was. As it turns out, she was something called a Shadow Person. So, when the Baucis killed her, the thing inside Rouge's body left the body and went into her dog."

"I need to sit down," he groaned, and let out a long breath. "You know, there's times I wish I'd never meet you. This is one of them. See, if we'd never met, I wouldn't have to be sitting here in my mom's living room, suspended from work, listening to you tell me that a woman I knew, and thought was dead, is now living in a dog. Do you know how weird that sounds?"

"How do you think I feel? Anyway, I'm going to deal with all of this—the Baucis, Angstrom, and the issue with Rouge—but until then, stay where you are and if you see Rouge, the woman, not the dog, take your family and run, and call me as soon as you can."

"I will, but if I get called back into work, I have to go," he told me. "But thanks for the heads-up anyway, and don't get yourself killed, okay?"

"I'll do my best."

I hung up and called Godfrey back and told him I was heading to his shop. Fifteen minutes later, I was in his store and telling him the same thing I'd just finished telling Garcia. The look on his face went through a winding trail of emotion. Anger. Confusion. Sadness. Shock.

"All of this is too crazy," Godfrey said and took a sip of tea he'd made for himself. "I don't think anyone else I've ever met in my entire, long life has had more strange and bad luck than you have, Dillon. Never have I ever met someone who lives such a truly insane life. Even though it sounds like madness, I believe everything you just told me. There is a part of me that doesn't want to, but I know it is. So, what are you going to do about it?"

"I'm going to find and kill the Baucis."

"No, not that. I'm talking about Rouge. What are you going to do about her?"

That was the question, wasn't it? It was what I had been avoiding the most. What was I going to do about Rouge? She had lied to me, been involved in a plot to kill me at first, but then again, I loved her, and she had saved me more times than anyone else. Did that excuse the lies? Did it make all the deceiving just go away? I really didn't know.

"It's getting to you, isn't it?" he asked, and then gave me a slap on the back before laughing. "You love her. I mean you really love her, but you're torn because she didn't come clean with you right away. I get it."

"I'm glad you do, because I don't get it, or even want to think about it."

"Look, everyone lies. Every day we lie to people about how we feel, what we're thinking, and keep bits of ourselves hidden. Look at you. You walk around looking like some normal human, but inside you there's something else. You don't tell a lot of people about it, but does that make you a liar, or just someone who knows people would react strange if they knew, or worse, hate you for it? They might even consider you a pariah and curse your very name for not fitting into the idea of who you should be because of how you look."

"But I told her who I was early on. I never lied about who and what I was."

"Of course you did, but that doesn't mean that she has to be just like you, does it? That's a rhetorical question, and the answer is no, she doesn't. You built her up to be something she wasn't. You don't like that she lied, but what was she supposed to say to you? If she was honest early on, would you have fallen in love with her, or would you have monster-hunted her ass back to where she came from? I didn't tell you what she was either, so does that make me a bad guy in your book?"

"Wait! You knew she was a Shadow Person too?"

"You know what my true form is, Dillon. You've seen my snout. I can smell something non-human from a mile away. So, yes, I knew what she was. I always assumed you knew too, being the astute hunter you are and all."

"This is great. First her, and now you! Has anyone been honest with me?"

He shook his head and then laughed. "You are such a drama queen, Dillon. I didn't think you were so blind with love that you didn't see it. I mean, you're one of the few hunters that's dealt with Shadow People and lived to tell about it. And besides, how is it my place to tell you something like that if she didn't. But let's be honest, she lied for a good reason if she liked and cared about you. What you need to get over is that she kept something like that from you out of fear of losing someone important to her. I also really don't see what the problem is at the end of the day. You do love her, right?"

I said nothing. I did love her. No matter who she really was before we met, I loved who she was when we were together. She was funny, smart, sweet, and thoughtful. What was there not to love? And yet, I felt betrayed by the lying. She wasn't the woman I thought she was. It wasn't that she had a past she was keeping from me, she had actually lied to me about who she was, and wasn't even from this world. How was I supposed to just move on from that?

"I saw you two together," Godfrey continued when I didn't answer him. "I know how you felt about her. I saw the way you looked at her, laughed at her jokes, even when they weren't that funny. And I saw how you looked when she was taken away from you. You were a wrecked man. And that's because you loved her, and you still do. Now, you need to find out how to get her into a body that isn't a dog, because that would not be cool."

"No, it wouldn't. I just don't know how I could do anything to get her old body back."

"What about getting the Baucis out of the body it's in and giving that to Rouge? I mean, if it looks like her anyway, it could work, right?"

I shrugged. I had no idea if it would. As a concept, it sounded like it would, but the reason a Baucis needs more victims is due to the fact it devours the life force of the people it absorbs. That's how they differ from a Shadow Person. One of them only absorbs the soul, but the body stays intact, while the other sucks all the juice out of it and steals the identity. As time goes on after taking a form, it slowly eats away at the life it took, making the body age and start to wither until it drinks the very life essence from its victim. I didn't know how slow or fast it would happen, but if it was fast enough, I wouldn't be there in time to stop the current Rouge form from wrinkling up like a raisin and the Baucis needing to find a new life to take. If it did that before I found it, not only would I not be able to recover Rouge's form, but it would make things even trickier, not knowing who I was looking for. Especially with Garcia off the case, I had nobody to keep me in the loop of the current victims.

More ways to complicate my life.

"Oh wait," I said, and moved towards the door. "I have something out in the car."

I ran out to the Jeep and grabbed the book I took from Kajal's and brought it to Godfrey. He took it from me and inspected it, opened it and leafed through the pages just as I had.

"What's this?"

"A book I took from Kajal's before I was arrested. His friend, Aamir, told me he'd been reading this for me, to find out about the Baucis, and had made some notes. Those notes were stolen when he was killed. I was hoping you could go through it and see what you can find."

"Why don't you?"

"You're so much better at this kind of thing," I told him, not wanting to admit that reading these kinds of books was the most boring thing I could possibly imagine. "But seriously, it would be a huge help if you could, while I try and track it down."

"I can help, but you should really learn to do this kind of work yourself. What are you going to do if one day I'm not here to help you?"

"Pray that day never comes," I offered.

"Too bad, Dillon. We all die eventually or get our prison sentence cut short for good behavior."

"You have to be good for that to happen," I laughed.

"You're right. So, what am I looking for here anyway?"

"How would I know? I'm guessing anything about a Baucis would be obvious, but hey, even if you see something about getting a creature similar to a Baucis out of a body without destroying the body the way a S'Borouth iron does would be great."

"If it's here, I'll find it. But does this mean you're thinking of giving Rouge another chance?"

"We'll see."

I went to a hotel room in the downtown area that wasn't too sketchy and decided I would try my best to get some sleep before I turned into a zombie. I was utterly exhausted. All I had to do was hope my brain would quieten down enough to allow me to fall asleep.

As it turned out, that wasn't a problem.

As soon as I slipped into bed, I fell into an uncomfortable, dream-heavy sleep. It was full of monsters, Rouge, and things chasing me. It felt as though I'd woken up twice every single hour, even though I didn't see the sunrise, and when I picked my phone up off the side table, I saw it was already past noon. I shouldn't have been surprised it was so late, since it was nearly five in the morning when I checked into the less-than-stellar hotel. I should have slept longer, but my head wouldn't shut off.

It didn't make it better when I looked at my phone and saw there were two missed calls. One was from an unknown number, something I could ignore, but the other was from Godfrey. No voicemail from either. I called Godfrey back after I showered, brushed my teeth with a towel since I hadn't brought any toiletries, and put on my clothes. At first it didn't seem like he was going to answer, and I worried. What if the Baucis had gone back to the shop after I left, found a way to get in, passing all the curses and spells he had hopefully put up, and killed him. That would have fit in with the way of the world these days. A little icing on a shit cake.

Luckily, he answered on the last ring before it would typically go to voicemail.

"I found something. And it's good news, I think."

I rushed back to his shop after he told me everything. According to the book Kajal had been reading, there were two ways to deal with a Baucis. The first way was the one I already knew about: take some S'Borouth iron and pierce the skin of the body. That would kill it outright, but it would also destroy the body it was in as well. That would be fine, but it begged the question about where Rouge was supposed to go.

That was where the second part came in.

"Here it is," Godfrey said after I got to his shop. He held out a small, triangular off-white object that looked a lot like a shark's tooth. I took it and looked it over.

"So, what is this exactly?"

"A tooth of an Aygooni."

"And what am I supposed to do with it? Do I stab her with it, throw it at her and hope for the best?"

"No," Godfrey said shaking his head and looking disappointed in me for saying that. "You press it to the victim's forehead, and that'll eject the Baucis from the body. You're lucky I happen to have a few of them."

"Why do you? You didn't even know that much about a Baucis

when I first brought this all to you."

"Turns out these don't just work against a Baucis, but they also work as a fertility charm in certain circles."

"I don't want to get the thing pregnant. I want to get it out of the body it's in."

"You won't get it pregnant, Dillon. It doesn't work like that. But according to that book, it should work for your purposes. I mean, hopefully it does, and the body keeps looking like Rouge after the fact, right?"

"What do you mean?" I asked, and turned the tooth over in my hand to study it. "Why wouldn't it still look like Rouge?"

"Well, the Baucis didn't come here in its own form. The Doll Maker brought it over, right?" he asked, and I nodded. "Well, that means it was given someone's body originally, and then it started to eat people and take their forms, which means when you evict it from the body, it might revert back to the original body it started in."

"Might? What are the percentages here? Fifty percent? Eighty?"

"There's nothing in here that says anything about that, but what can you do? It'll either work or it won't."

I nodded and put the tooth in my pocket. "I guess you're right. One way or another I get it out or kill it. But does it say what happens when I eject it from the body it's in? Is it just going to try and get into me? Or someone close by?"

"There is something about that. Hold on."

Godfrey walked over and grabbed the hefty book. He flipped through and I watched as he moved his lips while he read. I tried not to chuckle at that. Rouge used to do the same thing. It was one of those cute things she did. Same as when she used to play with her hair and curl it around her finger while she watched TV or a movie. I slumped a little. I really missed her. I wanted to be angry about the lies, but I would do anything to have her back the way she was, to just erase everything that had happened since we first started to work this case. I hoped this would work.

"Here it is," Godfrey said and handed me the book so I could read it myself.

I took it and skimmed through the words quickly. The gist of it was that once the Baucis was out of the body, it would try to find a new body, unless you could use a brass container that had been dipped in oils from a Dhark. That seemed like something I didn't have; nor had I any idea what it was.

"What's oil from a Dhark?" I asked.

"Don't worry, Dillon. I have you covered," he said, and handed me a small, black velvet bag. I peeked inside and saw exactly what I thought it would be but was not expecting the smell of it. It was not good. Like dirty feet and spoiled milk. "Yeah. Try not to stick your face in there. A Dhark is not something that is familiar with bathing. But it'll get the job done."

"I hope so. I want to get rid of this bastard and try to get everything back to some semblance of normal."

"There is no normal in our line of work," Godfrey said, and I couldn't agree with him more. Still, I miss the days when things used to be so much easier.

My phone rang as I handed Godfrey the book back. It was an unknown number again. Normally, I would never answer an unknown number because they were usually spam. I didn't need someone telling me they could clean my ducts, or telling me they had overcharged my credit card for something and needed my details so they could organise a refund. Since there weren't usually two in the same day, I thought I would see who it was.

It was Angstrom.

"I have some news for you, Dillon," he told me after some niceties.

"I hope it's about where to find the sonofabitch."

"I have found out where the Baucis is hiding out. I will tell you this, but I want to make sure our deal is still on. I give you this, you kill it, and then you stay out of our business."

"The deal was I wouldn't bother you once the Collective has fallen. But until then, the gloves are off still," I said, and saw Godfrey raise an eyebrow. I made a motion for him to hold on, that I would explain it.

"Yes. That was the deal. Once the Collective falls, you step back and let the chips land where they may."

"That's the deal, and if you don't fuck me over, I'll stick by it.

Now, where can I find it?"

A fter I hung up on Angstrom, I explained it all to Godfrey. He wasn't very keen on the idea of me going along with the lawyer plan. He thought it was a bad idea to turn my back on the whole monster hunting thing so Angstrom and those interests he was representing could do as they wished. I wasn't all that fond of it either and really considered whether I should live up to my end of the bargain or double cross them as payback. Godfrey was even more confused as to why the man was still breathing at all. I tried my best to tell him why I agreed to it, but in all honesty, I wasn't even totally sure why I was doing it. If Rouge was still around and this asshole had come to offer some other monster up on a silver platter, I would have handed him his own ass. I wouldn't have killed him because he was human, but I would've loved to make his life a living hell.

Rouge wasn't around though, and this was my road to revenge. We sometimes lie with evil when seeking vengeance.

I told Godfrey not to worry. I had things in the works, even though nothing was solid yet. There were ideas floating through my head of how to handle the Baucis, Angstrom, and whatever other creatures were behind him. I also was still trying to figure out what I was going to do about Rouge, which was the thing that caused me the most confusion. I knew that some of what Godfrey had said was true, and if I really did love her, it shouldn't matter what had happened. I should be happy that she was still alive, not completely gone forever. If it was as easy as just saying "you're forgiven," then I would just say that and get over it. Nothing in life is that simple, and every time I considered letting it go and moving on with her once she was out of the dog, the betrayal I felt began to tingle in the back of my head and made me spiral downward.

I needed some time.

Maybe killing the Baucis, or at least getting it out of the body it was in that looked like Rouge, would be just the thing I needed. If I did manage to get it out of Rouge's body and was able to get her back inside it, that would be a whole other can of worms I'd have to deal with when that time came. For now, I needed laser vision forward on the task at hand.

I left Godfrey and was on the road. I took long, deep breaths as I drove at the speed limit, despite wanting to get to the end of all of this as fast as the Jeep would take me. I had to head to Etobicoke to hopefully wrap this whole case up. To be honest, it's not my favorite part of the city. But beggars can't be choosers.

When I'd been on the phone with Angstrom, he'd explained that the Baucis was hiding out in some abandoned mall near Kipling subway station. He then corrected himself and told me it was only sort of abandoned. I wasn't sure how a mall could be *sort of abandoned*, but I guessed I would find out soon enough.

The mall was called Honeydale and was on Dundas Street West near another street called East Mall. These streets in Etobicoke— Royal York, East Mall, West Mall, Martin Grove... What were they trying to go for with them? They couldn't just do a normal street name, something based on someone's last name? Did they run out of horrible people through history to name these places? No more Dundas or McKenzie's or Ryerson's?

If I thought the names of the street in Etobicoke were bad, the condition of the so-called mall was even worse. I wouldn't have even been able to find the place if it wasn't for the fact I was using the GPS on my phone to get there. From the outside, it looked like no more than the shell of a building. It had all the vibes of the kind of place Jake from Bright Sun Films on YouTube would have made an episode about in his *Abandoned* series, it was that bad. From the outside, it didn't even look like there was a way to get in. I could see plywood up on many of the windows and some of the mall doors. If I didn't know better, I would've said it had been locked up and forgotten. There were ghosts of former signs on the front façade. There were nearly invisible outlines announcing Radio Shack, Wal Mart and Golden Griddle. I couldn't see a single hint on the outside showing what was open in there, if anything at all. Still, I parked in the all-but-empty lot and grabbed my bag with the S'Borouth iron, the tooth, my gloves, and dagger, and then headed to one of two sets of plywood-covered doors. Maybe the place wasn't sort of abandoned as Angstrom had suggested and was actually locked and sealed. If it was, I might have to break into the place in broad daylight. At least there were next to no other people going by, and most of the cars parked in the lot were covered in layers of dust and looked as forgotten as Honeydale.

I pulled on the door and surprise washed over me when I found the entrance was actually unlocked and saw there were a few people already inside. Wonders will never cease.

The mall was even more of a disaster on the inside. There were three stores open inside: a rent-to-own place, a variety store, and a grocery store. Despite those doors being open and the fact that I could see employees in them, they were as near to being a ghost town as they could get without being boarded up too. There were ten rental spaces, once stores, that were closed. None of them had signs up, the lights inside were shut off, and they were empty of people and any sort of furnishing or equipment. I could tell which one used to be a huge department store, a Wal Mart. Over the huge glass doors was the dirty outline of its name, but it was clearly long abandoned. This mall was a mess. It was a perfect place to hide out if you were a monster who was stealing bodies, I guessed. How many people even bothered to come in for the three open stores at all? I even doubted any of these places had alarms.

I walked around brown-tiled floors that screamed out 1970s as I tried to figure out which one of the closed-up stores was the old Radio Shack. That's where Angstrom said the Baucis was hiding. There was no dirt outline of the names left on any of the signs to tell me which one it could be. I wondered if Radio Shack had been one of the first ones to pack up. Maybe if there was a security guard around, or even an information booth, I would ask, but there was nothing and nobody.

Great.

I went from empty shop to empty shop and peered inside. All of them were dark and void of anything other than dust. I started to try the doors, but they were all locked. I wanted to see if there was anything inside like food containers -obviously not a Radio

Shack- or electric cables or a sign that said maybe "Transistors half price this week" to give me a little hint whether I was at the right place. But each and every one of them looked like the previous.

Dark.

Dusty.

Desolate.

I was starting to feel like I had been sent on a wild goose chase. It wouldn't have shocked me that Angstrom, a lawyer, had lied to me. But as I started to retrace my steps and relook into some of the old shops, I saw the reflection of someone behind me.

Shit.

It felt like an ambush.

I slowly turned around, expecting to see Rouge's face, but instead, it was the pains-in-my-ass, Toronto's finest detectives. Mary and Aaron. What now?

"Fancy meeting you here," Aaron said, and looked as smug as ever. Behind him, Mary stood looking stern, like a disapproving parent, her arms crossed. Aaron had his hand on his hip as though he was getting ready to pull out his gun and shoot me if I made a wrong move. "What are you doing in this utter shit hole?"

I looked around and acted as if I was confused by what he was saying. "What do you mean? This place is my favorite mall. They have everything a guy could ask for. A lady too," I said, looking directly at Mary, whose face didn't change at all.

"Mind if we see what's in your bag, Dillon?" Aaron asked, pointing to the canvas bag in my hand.

"Why do you want to see this old thing?"

"Because we're cops, and we're asking to see what's in the bag."

"And if you give me a good reason, I'll actually consider it, but unless you have a warrant, or you're arresting me...and hey, didn't my lawyer tell you to speak to him if you need to see me?"

"I don't need to call your lawyer if I think that I'm following up on a crime, or a possible crime in progress."

I laughed and looked around the deserted mall. "What crime in progress? What exactly am I doing? Loitering in a dump? Standing too long in a cemetery? Look, this is starting to feel like harassment, so if you don't actually have cause to stop me, I would suggest you leave me alone, or I'm calling my lawyer."

"Okay, how does *prowling* sound to you," Aaron said, not skipping a beat and clearly not worried about my lawyer. "We were here, in the mall—what's left of it—and saw you peering into the closed stores. I think you have tools to do a break-in. Now, if you want to show us what's in your bag and prove that there's nothing illegal in there, you'll be free to go. So, come on. Pass me the bag."

"I don't think I'm going to do that," I said, not wanting to deal with him right now or try and explain the things that were in there. I didn't have time for them.

"Okay, asshole. I'm done with your shit. Your lawyer's not here, and I'm not asking to see what's in the bag. I'm giving you a goddamn order. Hand it over, or I'll just place you under arrest here and now."

"You have no cause, detective. So go ahead and…"

The words died on my lips and the bag slipped from my hand. It wasn't even because Aaron had started to pull the gun out of his holster, clearly intending to arrest or shoot me. It slipped from my hand because something I spotted behind him had drained me of all my strength; a ghost in a ghost town.

"Rouge?"

The words left my lips even though I knew it wasn't her at all. It was an irrational thought that I couldn't control. Obviously, it wasn't really Rouge, it was the Baucis. The detectives didn't know that, though. I can only imagine the shock they must've been in when they turned around and saw her standing there. Well, not a perfect version of her. Something was slightly off, but I didn't know what it was right away.

"What the fuck!" Aaron yelled when he saw her. "How the hell is it poss—"

He never got to finish that thought because before he could the Baucis that looked like Rouge sprang forward and punch her fist through Aaron's chest. Blood sprayed out when her hand burst through the back, and I jumped so that it didn't get on me.

"Get on the ground!" Mary said, acting faster than I might've.

She already had her gun free and was raising it to aim and maybe fire at the Baucis. The problem with that was, I was on the other side of the fake Rouge, which made me feel like I need to get the hell out of there.

Mary never got her shot off, though.

The Baucis ripped it's arm free from Aaron, letting the body drop to the ground, and lunged at Mary. I watched as the Rouge-thing swiped at Mary's gun hand and knocked the weapon to the ground. Mary gasped and then, in the blink of an eye, the Baucis tossed the detective across the mall as though she weighed nothing. Mary slammed into a wall, and I could hear her head hit with a forceful sound that made me worry that she might be as dead as her partner.

I may have underestimated how strong this thing was.

There was no time to worry about that, though. I needed to act faster than either of the detectives had, and grab the tooth or the iron, whatever came out first, but then I realized my hands were empty.

My bag!

I tried to keep my eyes fully on the Baucis, but knew I needed to get it. The monster was still looking at the cop, so I had time. At least I thought I did. But as my hand was a few inches away, the Rouge-thing turned towards me.

"Dillon!" she…it…the imposter said and charged at me. It was so strange hearing her real voice again, but knowing it wasn't her. I made one last attempt to get a weapon, but it was so fast. Before I could even brace myself, it had me. "Did you miss me, Dillon? Do you wish we could still be in bed together, making love?"

With more force than I could have expected, I was shoved backwards and slammed into the glass I'd been peering into when the detectives showed up. I tried to fight back as I felt the wind knocked out of me, but it seemed useless. This one was strong as anything I'd ever faced before.

"Want one last kiss before I kill you, Dill?" the Baucis said and leaned in close to me. That's when I was able to really see what was wrong with this version of Rouge. Up close like that, our faces inches away from one another, I could see the wrinkles spreading out all over her face. They were like surface cracks, creeping across the skin I once knew. It was as though she had aged forty years since the real Rouge died. No doubt it was because the Baucis was devouring Rouge's lifeforce and needed a new fix. It needed a new outfit.

And here we were at the mall, and I was the perfect size for the Baucis, apparently.

Well, not today, Satan!

I slammed my forehead into the Baucis' face as hard as I could. I could feel the nose break and blood pour onto my face. The Baucis stumbled backwards, and I went to grab my bag. I might have ruined the thing's nose, but if I could get the Tooth of Aygooni out and use it, I could get Rouge her body back before any more damage was done. And there are plenty of plastic surgeons that could fix that mashed nose.

The Baucis cried out and the iron grip it had me in loosened ever so slightly. I used that moment to reach down and try to get the bag up and the tooth out. My hand had just grazed the handle, hope of something good just inches away when I felt the creature's grip was back. This time I was lifted into the air. I was up nearly a foot off the ground before I was slammed to the tile floor. Light exploded behind my eyes, and it felt as though I would never be able to suck air back into my crushed lungs. It hurt so bad.

I really hated this thing.

"You can try something like that again if you want, Dillon. I don't care about her nose, hunter. It means nothing to me because when I'm done eating you, it'll get fixed. Everything wrong gets repaired once I've had my meal. Now, I guess we're done with the all the foreplay. I think we should get to know each other more intimately."

I fought back again, but I couldn't get the Baucis off me. I was pinned to the ground and was starting to think this was going to be the end of me. After all of the time on this planet, it was going to end like this; drained of my life in a ghost town of a mall. What a way to go.

The Baucis pushed the fingers of its right hand to my chest

and though we hadn't known exactly how the Baucis drained the previous victims, I was about to get a front row seat to it. I wouldn't be able to pass that information on to anyone, but at least I would know.

"This was a fun body to be in, but yours will be my prized possession, Dill. I can't wait to see all the things you've done and know everything you know so we can bring the Collective down once and for all," the Baucis said and gave a huge smile. "And don't worry, this is going to hurt quite a bit."

The Baucis laughed and the hand pressing on me felt like fire. I was sure it was melting into my skin and going through me. I didn't want to look down, but I had to see it, to see if it was inside of me. The Rouge-thing's hand just sat on my chest, but had turned black and throbbed. I could feel the pulse of it and knew that was it drinking me. The Baucis' hand was acting like a straw sucking me up into it. That was when the pain came. It was a lot like being burned and stabbed at the same time. Agony exploded all over my skin and I couldn't do a thing other than let out a terrible scream. I knew if I didn't do something, the pain would only get worse, until it didn't, and that would mean I was dead.

It was now or never.

With everything I had in me I tried one last time to break free. I went to raise my arms and punch or tear at the thing's face, but they didn't move. I tried to buck it off me, but I only laid there screaming. I was paralyzed on the tiles. It was over. I was done.

"One way or another, I'll make sure you burn for this," I growled in between cries of torture.

"You're not the first person to think you could get back at me," the Baucis laughed, but her laugh was cut short, and I felt the pressure release from me a bit. The pain was moving back, and I could feel my arms and legs again.

I used that moment to struggle again and push away from the imposter version of Rouge. I scuttled backwards and heard her screaming and saw her flailing on the ground, the S'Borouth iron jammed in her back. She was trying to get it, reach for it and pull it out, but it was too late, the weapon was already working. I just hadn't known how fast or bad it would be.

Flames exploded from her skin. Her mouth opened and more came from there before her eyes burst and ran, liquefied, down her face. She withered on the ground, burning up from head to toe, making the place smell like barbeque and burnt hair. It was horrible. I'd never wanted to see someone burn up like that, and I was also watching the last chance to have Rouge back in her body again.

But who had done it?

"Can I help you up?"

I looked to the right, away from the burning monster, and saw a chubby security guard with a moustache that looked like it would be more at home on a fifteen-year-old, holding his hand out to me. Had he done it? Had he killed the Baucis? How the fuck had that happened?

I felt so weak, but slowly reached out and took his hand. He pulled and I groaned and did my best to stand up. My body felt like it was covered in open nerves. I managed to stand and then winced as I felt blood trickling down my chest. I touched the area and came back with bloody fingers. It felt bad, but at least I was still alive, not like the two detectives. Aaron was dead for sure, and Mary still hadn't moved. It didn't look good for her.

"Are you okay?" the guard asked me when I was fully up.

"I think so. He's not, for sure," I said, motioning to Aaron. "I'm not sure about her," I said and pointed to Mary.

"She's breathing, but she's badly hurt."

"We need to call someone for her," I said, and fished my phone out of my pocket. "Thank you, though. Not how I wanted this to turn out, but thanks anyway."

"No problem," the guard said, and stepped in close to me. "Not the first time I had to save you, but I did tell you that I wanted to kill the Baucis, didn't I?"

"What?" I gasped and looked at the guard.

"I think you heard me just fine, Dill."

"Rouge?"

He didn't answer, instead he kissed me hard on the lips and pressed his body against me while the flames of the thing that had looked like Rouge petered out in the background.